MW00476783

THE MEASURE OF MAN

BY ANDREW ROBERTSON

The Measure of Man

Trilogy Christian Publishers A Wholly Owned Subsidary of Trinity Broadcasting Network

2442 Michelle Drive Tustin, CA 92780

Copyright © 2021 by Andrew Robertson

All scripture quotations are taken from the Holy Bible, New International Version®, NIV®. Copyright © 1973, 1978, 1984, 2011 by Biblica, Inc.TM Used by permission of Zondervan. All rights reserved worldwide. www.zondervan.com. The "NIV" and "New International Version" are trademarks registered in the United States Patent and Trademark Office by Biblica, Inc.TM

No part of this book may be reproduced, stored in a retrieval system, or transmitted by any means without written permission from the author. All rights reserved. Printed in the USA.

Rights Department, 2442 Michelle Drive, Tustin, CA 92780.

Trilogy Christian Publishing/TBN and colophon are trademarks of Trinity Broadcasting Network.

For information about special discounts for bulk purchases, please contact Trilogy Christian Publishing.

Trilogy Disclaimer: The views and content expressed in this book are those of the author and may not necessarily reflect the views and doctrine of Trilogy Christian Publishing or the Trinity Broadcasting Network.

Manufactured in the United States of America

10 9 8 7 6 5 4 3 2 1

Library of Congress Cataloging-in-Publication Data is available.

ISBN: 978-1-68556-133-8

E-ISBN: 978-1-68556-134-5

To my family,
who always encouraged
me to keep writing.
Thank you!

CONTENTS

CHAPTER 1

"Oh no! They're kissing! They're kissing! They're kissing!" Jill screamed.

Kyle whipped around just in time to see a five-year-old cross his skis and plow into the snow. Kyle rolled his eyes. Jill had always been overly dramatic when giving lessons. Kyle turned back toward the chair lift. Jill had skied to her student and was still talking, this time in her normal voice.

"When you make the pizza wedge, you can't have the skis kiss. If you do, you'll get off balance and fall down. Let's try to go down the bunny hill one more time; then, we can go into the lodge and have hot chocolate!"

"Yay!" the kid agreed. Kyle smiled to himself. *So that's how Jill became the favorite ski instructor! I've always wondered.*

Jill was Kyle's favorite too, though for different reasons. They had met a couple of years ago while they were both instructors at the Killington resort. They connected instantly and spent every moment possible together. When it was time to leave, they realized that they both lived in Boston and attended the same university. That was almost two years ago. They had been dating for nearly that entire time.

Whenever they revisited Killington, Jill chose to ski; Kyle had always preferred snowboarding.

He had just finished his last snowboarding lesson for the day, beating Jill yet again. Kyle's students today were starting to get good. After a few more hours of practice, they could be going down any of the black diamond trails on the mountain. Kyle would look for his students, although he knew he might not see the fruition of his work.

Kyle boarded the lift toward the highest peak of the mountain.

He would return to college at the end of the week. This was the home stretch of Christmas break. Fortunately, he only had one more semester before graduation, and then he was free to do whatever he wanted—at least for a couple of months. He had heard from the previous ROTC cadets that graduates usually had several months of leave before they received their orders and needed to report at their assigned bases.

Kyle had already compiled a list of possible activities for the summer—backpacking across Europe, hiking the Appalachian Trail, vacationing at Cancun, sightseeing in Hawaii, snowboarding in the Rockies… Kyle really wanted to go snowboarding in *real* mountains. New England was nice and had plenty of slopes, but—Colorado, Idaho, Montana—those states had more than New England's mere hills.

I could go for spring break while there's still plenty of snow, Kyle reasoned with himself. *That way, I can take Jill to someplace tropical after graduation. She* has *been lobbying for either Hawaii or Cancun.*

Kyle glided off the lift at the mountain summit. *The air is so clear up here!* Kyle thought. He could see for miles in every direction. This was certainly the highest mountain in sight; each of the surrounding mountains seemed like small hills compared to the one he was on! *I definitely need to go snowboarding out West.* Kyle decided. *I'll still need to work out the logistics of traveling for spring break, but Jill will most likely have her wish for the summer.*

Kyle strapped his other foot onto the snowboard and looked down the mountain. This was one of the hardest trails in New England and one of Kyle's favorites. *Time to beat my record,* Kyle thought. He leaned forward and began his descent.

Kyle raced across the snow, weaving past amateurs. Whenever he had the chance, he aimed straight down the slopes. Kyle almost beat his record. If his students had not been obstacles in his path, he probably would have. At the least, he had trained his students well.

Kyle returned to the top of the mountain. This time, he took the path through the terrain park with the most ramps and rails. Technically, Kyle was supposed to use a snowboard specifically made for stunts. That did not deter Kyle. He was careful. He knew his limits and the limits of his equipment. Plus, he had not yet been caught. Kyle accepted every challenge and even caught twenty feet of air on the last ramp. He did not crash once. Kyle felt exhilarated! *This is the life!*

Next, Kyle challenged himself with the moguls. Here, he flattened several of the bumps with his body before leaving himself sprawled at the bottom of the hill. Kyle lay on the ground staring at the darkening sky. He had crashed fewer times on the moguls than he had any other time, including yesterday. *At least that's one "personal best" for today,* Kyle assured himself.

Kyle heard a pair of skis glide closer to him. He did not move. Jill appeared in his line of sight and stood over him.

"How was the hot chocolate?" Kyle asked, still flat on his back.

Jill shrugged and removed her skis. "It was okay. It would have been better if you were the one across the table from me." She knelt beside Kyle's head and leaned over him.

"How'd the moguls go?"

Kyle still did not move. "Come closer, and I'll show you."

She leaned forward, and they kissed for a few seconds. Kyle chuckled to himself as he stood. Now that Jill's lesson was finished, Kyle had the rest of the day free to snowboard with his girlfriend and nothing to distract them. Kyle glanced at Jill. She was busy with her skis and did not notice. He had forgotten how beautiful she was! *This is the life!*

Kyle and Jill chose and rode to one of the mountain peaks together. When they reached the summit, they would choose the trail and follow each other down the mountain.

When they grew bored of that arrangement, they would invent games for the slopes. One of the mountain slope games that Kyle enjoyed was seeing how close he could cross in front of Jill without either of them crashing. He would always wait until Jill least expected him to cut in front of her. Jill never appreciated the game, especially when Kyle would openly award himself bonus points for riding over the tips of her skis. In retaliation, Jill would try to stick her poles between Kyle's legs when he passed. Usually, Kyle's game and, more often, Jill's adaptation of it would result in at least one of them losing their balance and careening into the snow, followed by an infinite number of laughs. Eventually, they would make a truce to suspend the game for the remainder of the day and descend the mountain like everyone else.

Kyle and Jill rode the lift to the top of the mountain countless more times. Hours passed. With fewer people on the trails, Kyle tried racing down the mountain again. This time, he beat his record.

On the last lift run of the night, Kyle spoke about the summer plans.

"I've done some thinking. It looks like you've got your wish. We can go to either Cancun or Hawaii this summer."

"Yes!" Jill screamed. She lunged at Kyle and hugged him and kissed him repeatedly. The chairlift rocked violently in the fray. Kyle smiled. He loved pleasing Jill. "Let's go to Cancun!" Jill decided. "My passport's in order!"

"Oh…" Kyle began in mock disappointment. "That's

right…you do need a passport to get to Cancun. I don't know if the Air Force will let me go out of the country…"

"Liar!" Jill shouted, painlessly slapping his coat. "You told me at the beginning of Christmas break that you *could* go!" They reached the peak of the mountain and glided off the lift. Kyle reached the start of the slope first and turned to face Jill.

"A liar? That's a very serious accusation," he said, grinning. "Tell you what: if you beat me down the mountain, we can go to Cancun; if I beat you, then I get to choose where to go." He did not wait for her to respond. "Ready—set—go!" he shouted, already gaining momentum. Of course, it was not fair, but he needed to tease her somehow.

Kyle was the first to the foot of the mountain. Jill never stood a chance. An indignant Jill slashed snow at him as she stopped, mere feet from where Kyle stood.

"I guess I get to choose where we go!" Kyle said, grinning.

"Have you already made up your mind?" Jill asked. She inched toward him on her skis.

Kyle considered. "I guess I could be persuaded."

Jill leaned forward as if she were going to kiss him and whispered, "Then follow me."

The lifts had stopped. Slowly, the lights surrounding the lodge blinked off. The trails fell into darkness. No one other than Kyle and Jill was walking on the mountain. There were no other sounds in the area. Sleep had come to Killington.

The couple headed to their cabin for the night.

****

Kyle's father, James Baker, had always told Kyle that "The measure of a man flows from his mind, spirit, soul, and body. Without these, a man is nothing." Kyle had done all that he could to embody the "Four Qualities of Man," as he called them. Whenever he had the chance, Kyle would evaluate each of the four qualities and determine how he could improve himself. Kyle had spent years shaping, molding, and honing himself into a man that fully embodied and developed his mind, spirit, soul, and body. Kyle took great pride in his achievement, and his father could not have been more pleased.

Kyle considered the four categories and how he measured as he finished his morning shower.

Mind: Kyle was brilliant. He was triple majoring in finance, business management, and accounting. He had a 3.9 GPA for the last seven semesters. He had made the dean's list all seven times. Graduate schools had, for a long time, been contacting him with temping degrees and research opportunities. Several professors had said that he was the brightest student that they had taught in years.

Spirit: He had great willpower. When he set his mind to a task, Kyle completed the work rapidly and efficiently. He was disciplined and managed his time well. He prioritized his school, work, and other duties, but he was never too busy to socialize with his friends or hit the clubs on the weekend.

Soul: He was dauntless and determined. When Kyle believed in his cause, he refused to shrink from a fight—

verbal or physical. He was selected as the university's "wing king" for that year. His newfound power and authority brought him into many conflicts, even with the ROTC cadre on campus, but he was respected by everyone, including the cadre, nonetheless.

Body: He was in excellent shape. ROTC and the swim team made sure of that. He had even placed in the top half of the contestants for the "Little Arnold" weightlifting competition at his university. Kyle wiped the fog from the mirror and examined the grainy reflection of his chiseled body. Each muscle was clearly defined. All the women at college worshipped him. The dirty blonde hair and the grey eyes helped. He looked pretty hot.

Kyle measured well against the "Four Qualities of Man."

There was some overlap among the categories, obviously. But no aspect of his being was forgotten. As far as Kyle could determine, his mind covered the rational aspects of his being: his thoughts and reason. Kyle's spirit encompassed his emotions, willpower, and feelings. For a long time, he had difficulty distinguishing his soul from the other parts of his being, but he had come to realize that his soul held his beliefs and his decisions to live his beliefs and change them from mere concepts into a lifestyle. His body covered not only his physical desires but also his plans to improve his body through exercise and restraint.

Kyle argued to himself that he and Jill had satisfied all four categories last night, especially the "body." Kyle's father would have agreed. He had relayed that same assessment to

Kyle when Kyle was twelve years old. The advice was true, and Kyle strove to follow his father's advice as often as he could.

Kyle was living the life!

****

Kyle and Jill ate a quick breakfast before attacking the slopes again. Neither of them had lessons that day. So they spent every descent together. Kyle and Jill both tried to improve their personal records; although they did well, neither were doing exceptionally enough to improve their score.

Jill was tired and sore from skiing the last few days and especially from the previous night. Kyle hardly felt the impact from crashing or performing the stunts on his snowboard. Over years of training, he had developed and maintained a vast reservoir of stamina and strength. Kyle was pleased with his endurance; he had done well developing his body. Even still, he, too, was tired from spending the previous night with Jill.

Around two o'clock, Kyle and Jill stopped at the ski lodge for lunch. When they had almost finished, Kyle signaled the waiter and began to break the bad news.

"This has been fun, Jill. I'm glad that we were able to spend some time together, despite having to work."

"It's not over yet!" Jill contested. "We have, like, a whole day left."

Kyle shook his head. "I'm afraid this is it for me. I'm

going to have to head back home now." The prompt waiter appeared. Kyle gave him a credit card without looking at the bill. The waiter disappeared again.

"What? You're not tired already, are you?" Jill teased.

"No," Kyle answered with mock exasperation. He became earnest again. "But I have to get back to Boston and pack."

"Classes don't start until Wednesday. Come on. Let's just take one more ride down the mountain." Jill knew that if she could get Kyle on the mountain one more time, he would stay on the slopes for the next few hours. Kyle had recognized that shortfall in himself—that weakness—and learned to control that aspect of his being.

"I know what you're doing, and it's not going to happen," he smiled. "I have some 'wing king' stuff that I need to take care of before the semester starts."

"I'm starting to think you don't like my company," Jill teased.

"Hey! I just bought you lunch—"

At that moment, the waiter returned.

"I'm sorry, sir. But your card was declined—I tried it twice," he added before Kyle could object.

"'Bought me lunch,' huh..." Jill said as she gave her card to the waiter. He disappeared again.

"Just the same, if I didn't like your company, I wouldn't have spent last night with you. We should do it more often."

"That was fun, wasn't it," Jill agreed. "Let's do it again tonight. I'll come over at eleven."

Kyle shook his head. "Not at my place. My father doesn't like it when anything goes on in the house without him knowing about it, and I'm not going to tell *him* what we're up to. I'll come to your place."

"My parents are religious, remember. They'll flip out."

Kyle vaguely remembered that aspect of Jill's parents. Her parents had found religion about a year ago. Then, it was like someone had flipped a switch. All of a sudden, everything Jill did was not just wrong but evil. Jill said that she felt uncomfortable at home and tried to avoid her parents at every opportunity. Kyle remembered that he had scoffed at her descriptions. She had never complained about her parents before then and usually got along with them well. Kyle knew both of her parents. They were nice people. Before the change, they were sociable and courteous to Kyle when he arrived and let Kyle and Jill do what they wanted. Unfortunately, the first time Kyle visited them after their change, Kyle was lectured on what he could and could not do with their daughter, which included spending the night with her. Since then, Kyle and Jill never did anything at her parents' place. They always had to go "out."

The waiter returned with the check.

"That's right. I forgot about your parents," Kyle said. "You didn't get a dorm room this semester, did you?"

"No, I decided to follow your lead again for this year. Commuting does save money."

Kyle nodded in agreement. "Then I guess we'll have to wait until I figure out what's wrong with my credit card.

Unless you want to pay for a hotel room."

"I might already have to pay for the one this weekend!" They both laughed.

"Thanks for lunch," Kyle said.

"You owe me big," Jill replied.

"It will be repaid when I can afford a hotel room."

CHAPTER 2

Kyle drove the three hours from Vermont back to Boston. As soon as Kyle pulled onto his street, he sensed that something was wrong. He could see lights from police vehicles flashing further down the road. *That's strange,* he thought. *I hope there's nothing wrong with the neighbors.* Kyle inched closer to his home. Kyle felt his heartbeat quicken. Four police cars and a van were parked along the road and on the snowy yard around *his parents'* house. Kyle did not remember hearing his phone during the drive. *If something bad happened, my parents would have texted or called, right? There must be some misunderstanding!*

A police officer had just finished unrolling a ribbon of yellow police tape across the mouth of the driveway. Kyle stopped on the road.

"What's going on? Is everything all right?" Kyle shouted out his window.

The officer waved him down the road. "Nothing to see here, sir. Please move along."

"But I *live* here! What's going on?" Kyle shouted again.

Kyle noticed the officer tense and casually rest a hand on his holstered weapon. "What's your name, son?" the officer asked.

"Kyle. Kyle Baker." He noticed the officer relax but leave his hand at his side.

Before Kyle could add anything more, the officer said, "I think you'd better come inside."

Kyle pulled off the road and exited the vehicle. Only then did the officer fully relax his arm. As far as Kyle could tell, the officer had watched him since Kyle had initiated the conversation. Kyle ducked under the police tape and briskly followed the officer up the front steps. He could hear hysterical sobbing coming from inside the house. Kyle swore silently. *Oh no! What happened? What's going on?!*

The officer opened the door; Kyle rushed past. "Mom! Dad! Are you okay?" he called.

The house was swarming with police! The police forensics team was dusting the entire house for fingerprints. Lights flashed from multiple cameras, capturing every square inch of each room. People were talking and shouting above each other. But the loudest noise was the sobbing coming from the living room.

Kyle rushed into the living room, followed closely by the police officer from the driveway. His mother was collapsed in a chair, her face buried in her hands. A second police officer sat across from her.

"Mom, are you all right? What's going on?"

With great effort, his mother looked at him. She was still

crying.

The second police officer, now standing, responded instead, "What is your relationship to James Baker?"

"He's my father... Why? What's going on?"

"So you're the son, Kyle—no other siblings," the officer assumed. "Have you heard from your father today?"

"What—no! Mom, what's going on?" His mother was still sobbing. She could not respond.

The police officer continued, "When was the last time you heard from him?"

"It was two or three days ago before I left!"

"'Left' where?" the second police officer interjected.

"To Killington! I teach snowboarding lessons there! Now, what is going on!?"

"He's gone!" Kyle's mother blasted through her tears.

"Gone! He's dead? Where is he?" Kyle's panic increased.

"Not dead, vanished," the first officer clarified.

Now Kyle was confused. He vaguely recalled that neither of the cars were in the driveway when he pulled up to the house. "What? What happened?" He searched the police officers' faces. They remained silent. Kyle's mother was recovering.

"He's gone, and he took everything!" That was all she said before she was again overtaken by emotion.

Kyle nearly snapped at his mother! She needed to get control of herself! "What do you mean 'he took everything'?" Kyle asked. She was unable to respond. "Mom!" Kyle fumed. His outburst only caused the sobbing to grow louder.

Kyle began to resent her.

Kyle looked to the officers for elaboration. The first officer glanced at the second to confirm his actions, flipped through his notepad, and began, "According to your mother, the cars are missing; the lockbox is empty; the deed to the house is gone; all the bank accounts were emptied and closed…" The officer was still talking, but Kyle did not hear. *What does all this mean?*

The second officer broke into Kyle's thoughts. "The banks confirmed that the accounts were closed by your father. No one has seen or heard from him since."

Kyle's head was spinning. *They're lying! My father couldn't have done that. He wouldn't have done that!*

"No! It must have been someone else!" Kyle shouted aloud.

The second police officer responded. His tone was not gentle. "Son—"

"Don't call me that!" Kyle snapped.

The officer had not stopped talking. "No one else could have done this. It was your father."

The first officer interrupted to preempt a shouting match, "Kyle, did anyone else other than you and your parents have keys to the cars?"

The answer was no, and Kyle said so. He was going to contend that the thieves could have hotwired the vehicles, but he was interrupted before he could say more.

"Did anyone else know the combination to the lockbox?"

Kyle's answer was no, but someone could have cracked

the lockbox. Kyle responded and was interrupted before he could continue.

"Would anyone else have had access to the bank accounts?"

Again, the answer was no. Kyle did not have a chance to think of a retort or even respond before the officer continued.

"What about your accounts?"

Even though the officer waited for a response, Kyle could give none. An expression of horror froze on his face as he realized the truth. The waiter said that his card had been rejected. The police waited while Kyle viewed his online bank statements. They were all showing a balance of zero. The pieces started to fall into place. His father was a cosigner on all his accounts. Kyle opened his wallet. His cards were still there. Kyle certainly had not emptied his accounts. His father was the only one who could have done this. His father *had* done this. *Why?*

Life blurred around him. The officers tried to ask more questions, but Kyle could not hear them. Everywhere around him, the CSI teams flashed cameras and dusted for prints. Though he could not hear, Kyle listened for the CSI conclusions that he had expected since the revelation:

There was no sign of forced entry.

There were no other prints anywhere in the house.

Everything of value had been taken.

Kyle's father had done this.

Through his stupor, Kyle could only concentrate on one sound: the sound of his mother's wailing.

****

Kyle returned from the university financial aid office. He had just finished talking to them about his newfound need for financial aid. The college and his ROTC representative had taken pity on him for his unique circumstances.

Kyle had already reached the highest tier of scholarships available from the university, and that still left a significant cost that Kyle needed to fund. The university recognized Kyle's exemplary grades across the previous semesters and offered to expand his scholarship, provided that he work as an—unpaid—teacher's assistant during the semester.

The military had been more tricky. Kyle did not currently qualify for any ROTC scholarships and would not qualify without completely changing his field of study. Switching his majors during his last semester of college was the last thing that Kyle wanted to do. Fortunately, the ROTC cadre knew that Kyle had "demonstrated great potential and would be an exceptional asset to the Air Force"; the cadre was more than willing to risk his career to secure Kyle a scholarship. In their research, they eventually found an existing precedent to provide Kyle a scholarship, as long as he served an additional two years in the military.

Kyle jumped at the offers and signed any papers they pushed his way.

He raced home. He was going back to college after all. No thanks to his father.

The police had determined with absolute certainty that Kyle's father had indeed stolen their assets. Kyle and his mother had watched and rewatched video footage from the banks and confirmed, numerous times, that the man closing the accounts was James Baker: their father and husband. The police immediately issued an APB for him and the stolen vehicles. Over the last twenty-four hours, nothing was found.

Kyle's mother was miserable. She had completely fallen apart, inside and out. She would not eat and could not sleep. She had hardly stopped crying since Kyle had first seen her with the police. Kyle resented her for it. She was demonstrating power in neither mind, spirit, soul, nor body. How his father had married her, Kyle never knew. Though Kyle hated his father, his father was the epitome of the "Four Qualities of Man." He was a brilliant, shrewd, fearless, powerful, charismatic, and exceptional man. Kyle aspired to be like that.

And he was well on the road to accomplish that goal. After the initial shock, Kyle rebounded. He calmly assessed his current situation and his next steps forward. He willed himself to succeed at his plan and was determined to do so. Regardless of the pain and suffering involved, he would remain strong. He would overcome this trial. Kyle would use his father's advice to overcome his father's actions. It would be better revenge than spitting in his father's face. Kyle steeled his being. He could overcome anything! He was resolute.

Kyle arrived home to tell his mother the good news about his college finances. He found his mother sitting in a chair with an empty pill bottle in her hand. She was dead.

Kyle resented her all the more.

****

Kyle was determined not to let his father's treachery or his mother's death derail his current plans. He would finish his degrees and commission as a second lieutenant in the Air Force at the end of the semester—at whatever cost.

But his father seemed one step ahead.

Kyle had just finished the arrangements for his mother's funeral. Jill had offered him a ride to the funeral parlor for Kyle's errand and for support. Kyle appreciated both.

As they returned to Kyle's house, Kyle noticed, for the second time in recent days, a strange sight parked on the front lawn. This time, it was not police vehicles; it was demolition equipment. Kyle swore. *What devilry is my father doing now?* Jill parked on the side of the road, in front of the neighbor's house.

"Call the police," Kyle ordered as he jumped out of the vehicle. Members of the demolition crew were milling around the property. "What's going on here?" Kyle barked at a small group standing near a machine.

The crew looked at each other like Kyle belonged in an asylum. One of them said, "We're going to tear this house down," as if it were the most obvious conclusion in the world.

"I live here!" Kyle snarled.

The tone of the conversation immediately changed. "You live here?" the original construction worker asked.

"Not anymore," a second guy quipped. The rest of the crew, with the exception of the first worker, laughed.

Kyle's already thin patience was ready to snap. "Who's in charge here?"

"That would be me," the second guy spoke again. He did not move from his position, leaning against the backhoe.

"Call off the project, pack up your gear, and go home," Kyle ordered.

"You don't have any authority here, son," the man growled. Kyle stiffened. *Why is everyone calling me that?*

"The police are on their way," Kyle asserted. His house was close to the local precinct. He would hear the sirens any minute. "I suggest you get moving."

"I don't take orders from you." The burly construction worker stood from the machine and faced Kyle squarely. He was bigger than Kyle. Kyle did not back down. He had fought bigger and won. He could do it again if needed; he hoped it would not come to that, though.

"The police are on their way," Kyle repeated.

The man in charge glanced at each of his coworkers. "We don't have any problem with that. All our paperwork's in order."

"But this is *my* house!"

"Look!" the man in charge shouted at Kyle. "I don't know who you think you are! But the person who *actually* owns this house wants to tear it down and build a seven-bedroom, six-bathroom palace on the lot."

Kyle could hear the police sirens now. "Let's let the

police straighten this out."

When the police arrived, Kyle argued his case, highlighting throughout his speech that "it's my house."

The demolition crew, in their rebuttal, claimed that the real owner had hired them to destroy the existing house and prepare the grounds for construction in the coming spring.

"Do you have a copy of the deed from the new owner?" the police officer asked.

"Of course."

"I'd like to see it."

The construction worker called his office and was sent an electronic copy of the deed. The police viewed the image and showed it to Kyle. Kyle cursed aloud. The deed to the house was transferred to a new owner on the same day that Kyle's father left. *Was selling the house one of the first things that Dad did when he left? Or did he leave that day because he had sold the house?* Kyle swore again. He did not have the resources to hire a lawyer. Even if he did, no lawyer would be able to challenge the house deed and have a judge rule in their favor.

"All my stuff's in there," Kyle gasped, both enraged and deflated at his discovery. He proceeded to recount what his father had done. "Can I grab a few things?"

The officer turned to the crew. "Can you give him a few hours?"

The head of the demolition team considered for a moment. "Let me make a call."

Kyle did not wait. He headed for the front door with Jill

by his side.

****

Kyle was packed within an hour. He had found two large suitcases in the attic and knew that he had to limit himself to only slightly more than that. He had no idea where he would be staying that night. He might have to sleep in his car.

Couch, mattress, dresser, nightstand, bookshelf, microwave, toaster, lamp, table, chairs, books, magazines, games, most of his clothes—everything that Kyle could not fit in either of his suitcases and especially, his car had to be left behind. Jill supported him as he made every decision.

In the end, Kyle packed his military uniform, some civilian clothes, and supplies for college. Everything else Kyle left to be destroyed with the house. Nothing left held any value; Kyle was not sentimental, and his father had already stripped the house of valuables.

****

Jill unhesitantly offered for Kyle to stay with her at her parent's place. Jill's parents attempted to make room for Kyle. Their guest room was on the upper level of the house… adjacent to Jill's room, and that was not something that Jill's parents would allow, especially with Jill commuting to college from home. Instead, they offered a couch in the den on the main level. Initially, Kyle was more than willing to agree to any of their rules and secure a place to stay; but after considering the offer, Kyle resolved not to accept the makeshift bed on principle; Kyle and Jill were, after all, both adults.

Jill, on the other hand, exploded. She was adamant that Kyle should not agree to any such treatment and that he stay in the guest bedroom like any other guest. After a heated argument between Jill and her parents, without progress, Jill offered the solution that they rent an apartment for Kyle for the semester. The expense automatically disqualified that option. Jill's parents also insinuated that they did not want Kyle and Jill living or sleeping together, whether in the apartment or elsewhere, which unleashed another round of arguments.

Kyle knew that he could not afford an apartment near Boston on his own. His only real asset was his car, and if he sold it, he still would not have enough to rent an apartment close enough to Boston to live without a vehicle. And that was without even considering costs for food and utilities.

Kyle called his school. There were no empty beds in any of the dorms. They added Kyle to a waiting list in case any became available. Kyle pressed further and asked if they could reduce the costs for the rooms. The answer was no. Kyle relayed his experiences over the last few days and asked again. This time he was put on hold before they informed him that the college was unable to expand his scholarship *and* supplement the costs of room and board. Kyle remembered his father saying that Kyle could save money by commuting; all that saved money was now stolen by his father. Kyle unleashed a silent oath and gestured toward the ceiling as if his father were looking down on him. Kyle asked that his name be removed from the waiting list and hung up the phone.

Kyle consulted his other friends at college and anyone he remotely knew. No one had a place for him to stay. One of Kyle's friends from ROTC finally offered him a couch and only asked that Kyle pay for his own food and half the utilities. Kyle accepted the offer without even asking where the apartment was. Within the hour, Kyle's friend rescinded the offer; the guy's girlfriend had decided to live with him. Kyle's friend said that his apartment was too small for the three of them, but Kyle understood that they did not want him around when they had each other. Kyle resigned himself to his friend's decision. He was not angry; Kyle would have done the same if their situations were reversed.

Kyle tried to find another job. There was no other way he could afford an apartment or a dorm room. Kyle examined every single job that he could find on the Internet. He made nearly one hundred phone calls. None of the jobs worked with his existing schedule for his classes and TA job. He needed to sleep and study sometime.

In the meantime, Kyle slept in his vehicle. That lasted for two nights. The first night was brutally cold. The second night, a police officer woke him and informed him that he was parked illegally. Kyle drove somewhere to finish sleeping and drove back to campus for his classes. His car was almost out of gas.

Kyle knew that something in his situation had to yield.

Kyle needed food and shelter. And, if his car was his shelter, he needed gas too. Kyle had no money for food or gas. He needed a job. But every job he saw either conflicted with his existing work and class schedule or prevented him from getting any sleep. Kyle knew that he probably needed to choose between starvation and quitting school. He was not ready to do either just yet.

When he attempted to get a loan, the person at the bank almost laughed at him. Kyle tried to reason that he would have a steady job as an Air Force officer. All he received was a condescending smile and a wave toward the door.

That truly was the last chance for Kyle. He only had one option left.

CHAPTER 3

Kyle's only remaining living relative was his grandmother: his mother's mother. She lived in Florida; Kyle's mother had grown up in the same house. After his mother's funeral, Kyle pawned his car for a mere fraction of its meager worth, bought a plane ticket (mostly with his grandmother's money), and moved down to live with her. Kyle had no choice. He could no longer live in Boston—not without a loan or a free couch. When Kyle said he was moving to Florida, ROTC almost dropped his scholarship but again agreed to honor their revised agreement at a college down south. The university refunded as much of the tuition as they could, which, due to the classes having already started, was not much. Between the two of them and an additional part-time job that worked with his new class schedule, Kyle scraped together enough money to pay for his final semester at a college in Florida.

****

After his father's treachery, Kyle was unable to focus

on any of his duties or tasks for his transition. Kyle lacked the determination to redirect his attention and to fight for his scholarships. For the first time in his life, Kyle was afraid of the future and its uncertainty. The worry disrupted his sleep and caused his body to fatigue. Kyle was falling apart.

His father—every time Kyle thought of him, he raised his finger to the sky and cursed him—his father had said that Kyle "wasn't going to succeed in life without pushing forward." So Kyle shoved the old life behind him and moved ahead. Nothing pleased him better than to shut his father out of his life.

Kyle did not stop there. He shut out his mother, her suicide, and his friends from Boston. That decision hardly mattered; no one bothered to stay in contact.

Jill was the only remnant of Boston that remained in Kyle's life. Jill called and texted almost nonstop since Kyle's father left. When Kyle moved, they continued to talk, but they both knew that their relationship had ended. Their conversations became shorter and less frequent. They continued texting each other, but after a while, those conversations dwindled. Halfway through the semester, Kyle and Jill stopped calling and texting altogether. Neither one was solely to blame. Both had trouble with the long-distance relationship, and Kyle had his own demons.

One "demon" that Kyle did not expect was his grandmother, Joan. She was quite difficult for Kyle to ignore, especially in her little old house. In reality, she was a sweet woman, but she set strict rules that she expected Kyle to obey: no swearing, no smoking, no drinking. Kyle was only fine with the second rule.

Kyle could not count the times he had broken her rules since she had first recited them.

The first time Kyle broke "the swearing rule," he had been working on homework early in the semester when something reminded him of his life in Boston and how his father had forced him to leave that life behind. Without thinking, Kyle shouted a curse at his father and produced an obscene gesture.

"There will be no swearing in this house!" Joan had called from the other room, hardly missing a beat.

"Why not?" Kyle retorted, swearing again. "He deserves it!"

"Do *not* swear in the house!" Joan ordered, stepping into the same room with Kyle. "Your father may deserve a lot of things, but so do each of us. And if you don't stop swearing, you'll end up sleeping on the front porch!"

Kyle knew she could not force him out of the house on her own, and she had no one to assist her. But to be safe, Kyle resolved not to swear out loud in her presence again.

Joan left the room to resume her interrupted work. When her back was turned, Kyle gave her the same gesture and silently mouthed the same expletive.

The next weekend, Kyle broke another rule. He attended a party hosted by one of his new college friends. Kyle had a great time! For a little while, he forgot about the pain of the previous weeks. A couple of drinks helped with that.

Kyle returned to his grandmother's house early the next morning. The noise of closing the door behind him roused his grandmother. She had fallen asleep in the living room armchair.

"Where were you? I've been worried sick!" Joan exclaimed.

"I was at a party. Don't worry about it." Kyle brushed off the comment.

"I do worry! And you can't just—" Joan sniffed the air. "Is that alcohol?"

"It *is* legal," Kyle quipped.

Despite the hour, Joan began a long soliloquy about the "evils of alcohol" and "respect for one's elders." Kyle could feel the hangover starting. He began to walk away.

"You get back here!" Joan screamed, interrupting herself. She had followed Kyle and resumed her speech with increased vigor and volume. Kyle closed his eyes to ward away the headache and provided noises of supposed agreement when appropriate. Joan ended her speech with, "If I catch you drinking again, you'll spend the night on the front porch!" Only when Kyle finally grunted in acknowledgment of the consequences did Joan dismiss him for bed.

The next day, when he returned home from work, Kyle noticed a deadbolt on his grandmother's front door. He was certain it had not been there when he had left that morning. Kyle silently cursed his grandmother and resolved to cover the smell on his breath when he drank in the future.

Those three rules were only the first that Kyle had to

follow.

Sometimes, Joan would add a rule, usually because of something Kyle had done. To celebrate the end of ROTC field training at the end of their Sophomore year, Kyle and his ROTC friends from Boston had decided to each get a tribal tattoo on their shoulders. When his grandmother first saw the tattoo, she made a fourth rule: no tattoos in the house. She made Kyle go upstairs to his room and change, even though he was already late for class. Every day, Kyle packed a sleeveless shirt in his backpack and changed after he arrived on campus.

Not all the rules were "thou shalt nots," as Kyle called them. Their first Sunday together, Joan created her first "thou shalt" rule: go to church.

Church was a new experience for Kyle, and he hated every minute of it. Half the songs were written before the American Revolution, and the other half were emotional and repetitive. Then, everyone had to shake hands with everyone else in the congregation. And, of course, since he was a new face, everyone swarmed straight at him. He was "rescued" from that by the pastor droning on for almost an hour about the ancient peoples and kingdoms of the Middle East. Based on the sermon, little had changed over the last few millennia.

The service was finished, but his grandmother wanted to reintroduce him to many of the people he had met during the greeting time. The only highlight from church was meeting Claire. She was gorgeous. Seeing her again might be worth the pain of coming to church. Maybe next week, he could ask for her number.

Joan hardly needed to force Kyle to the Sunday evening service. However, he was disappointed when Claire did not attend. Kyle resolved not to go to any more services than necessary to see Claire. He was already permitted to forego the Wednesday night services, to his grandmother's chagrin, due to his part-time job. Kyle would need to use homework as an excuse to get out of the Sunday evening service. With his job, he might not even have to lie. Classes had already started before Kyle enrolled, and he had a lot of work ahead to catch up.

****

Kyle's job certainly kept him occupied. Finneman's Market was a "mom and pop" grocery store downtown. It was originally run by the current owner's parents and was eventually passed onto him. He was an ex-marine and did not know the first thing about running a business. So when a college student with finance, business management, and accounting knowledge asked for work, he hired Kyle on the spot. The financial records for the last five or six years were in complete disarray. Kyle wondered how the owner had paid the correct taxes; Kyle hoped that they would never be audited.

Kyle started work at six, after his classes. When he was not assisting the owner with general principles of store management, Kyle was restocking the shelves or working the cash registers with the other employees. When the store closed at ten, Kyle would sift through the financials in the back office. On most nights, he would be at the store until after midnight. Kyle's boss did not stay at the store a minute past ten. He entrusted Kyle with a store key—a new milestone for Finneman's Market—and threatened innumerable punishments if Kyle ever misused it or forgot to lock the store. The schedule and conditions were far from ideal, but Kyle was relieved that his boss would be leaving him alone. Kyle planned to do a lot of studying in those two hours.

The store was on a main road in what had steadily transformed into a bad part of the city, and the alley behind the store led to a district that was even worse. Kyle was not afraid, and even if he were, he would never admit it. He was strong enough to take care of himself, and he knew when to mind his own business. One night, when he was taking out the trash after closing, he saw a drug deal. Kyle did not bother them, and they finished their business in peace.

****

The new semester renewed Kyle's possibilities. Given his unique situation and the registrar's office showing him mercy, all his classes had transferred. His only duty was to take a few general education classes and a couple of major-specific classes required by the school. Other than that, Kyle was set to graduate in the spring. Now, Kyle just needed to pass all his classes. He was determined to make it work.

****

Having barely enough money to pay for his classes, Kyle did not have the luxury of a college meal plan. When classes started, he found a secluded table at the far end of the campus commons area and ate his lunch, scrounged from his grandmother's kitchen.

Kyle soon realized that about a dozen students had decided to meet and have lunch only twenty feet to his right. They arrived slowly, either one at a time or in pairs. When they arrived, they would draw the additionally required tables and chairs together and sit with the others in a large circle. The group talked, laughed, and ate together. Kyle watched.

After a while, Kyle became aware that someone was standing directly in front of him. It was Claire.

"Hi. You can join us if you want," she said.

Kyle leaped from his seat. "Hey! You're Claire from church!" he stammered.

"Yep! And you're Kyle...right?" Kyle nodded. *She remembered my name; that's good!* Kyle thought. "Okay. Well, we're going to eat lunch and pray if you want to join us."

Kyle inwardly groaned. *Not more church stuff!* But he was not about to say no. "Sure!" he said. They started walking. "Do you meet here every day?"

"We try to. Some of us have class, and we can't make it *every* day. But there usually are a few people here. People come when they can. Fortunately, I was able to move my classes around this semester; so, I'll be here every day." That was exactly what Kyle wanted to hear. Claire addressed the group. "Hi, guys. This is Kyle. He is going to be joining us today." Everyone smiled and greeted Kyle warmly. They went around the circle and introduced themselves. Kyle only caught a few of their names; he was concentrating on sitting next to Claire. But Kyle did manage to remember that he was sitting next to Josh, a Hispanic guy with large diamond earrings and a heavy silver necklace. Kyle remembered seeing him and a few others from the group with Claire at his grandmother's church.

The group continued to talk for a few minutes before starting to pray. People shared prayer requests for stress, diligence, and health, and others offered to pray for the requests. As Kyle listened, he knew that his being was superior to that of anyone else in the circle; he did not need any prayer, especially for stuff so trifling. Everyone except Kyle closed their eyes and bowed their heads for the prayer. Kyle was bored.

As soon as the prayer was over, Kyle asked Claire what she was studying. She was a senior marketing major. Kyle pressed. They shared a couple of classes together, including one later that day. Kyle asked her to save him a seat.

****

"Do you want to get coffee?" Kyle asked after his class with Claire had ended. He did not have a cent to spare, but Claire was worth it, and he was not going to let her slip away.

"What—you mean now?" Claire said.

"Now...or later is fine," Kyle corrected.

"Like a date…?" Claire clarified.

"Yeah. Sure," Kyle responded. That answer seemed to upset Claire.

"I have class."

Kyle pressed his luck. "Okay. How about later?"

"I don't know," Claire said in a way that meant "I do know, and I'm not telling you."

"Okay. I'll see you in class tomorrow…and at lunch."

Claire nodded and walked out of the classroom. Kyle would need to get more creative to catch her.

CHAPTER 4

The next four months passed. Kyle continued to get excellent grades and astound his professors. His part-time job sapped most of his time, but Kyle managed to make the dean's list again. He graduated with high honors.

Kyle worked well at his job and received great praise from his boss. Kyle's boss was frustrating most of the time. He did not explain himself well, and he almost expected his employees to read his mind. There were some days, especially at the beginning of his employment, when Kyle would climb into his grandmother's car, close the door behind him, and scream to vent his frustration. But Kyle persisted. Within a week, he had learned the peculiarities of how his boss acted and the particulars of how his boss expected his employees to do their jobs. When Kyle realized that and acted upon it, he received compliments and a raise—two commendations his boss never gave.

The ROTC cadre at the university, a full colonel, was impressed with Kyle's fearless and persistent drive to complete his duties. He pulled Kyle aside and admitted that

Kyle was more hardworking, diligent, and disciplined than any other airmen he had known during his entire Air Force career. The respect and admiration deepened when Kyle beat the colonel and the rest of the cadets by thirty push-ups in their fitness contest. That was the first time an ROTC cadet had beaten that colonel in the contest.

Even Joan was proud of Kyle's accomplishments. Though, that was the silver lining of their living situation. As long as Joan did not find out that Kyle violated several of her rules each day, they remained amiable to each other. Of course, they had their share of disagreements. Every so often, Joan or Kyle would complain about the other's use of the single car or about the hassle of chauffeuring the other person somewhere and picking them up again. Overall, though, the arrangement was adequate for Kyle; after all, it was only for a few months, and he had no other choice.

Kyle continued to pursue Claire. He asked several more times about getting coffee or dinner, and she continued to refuse. He cornered her one day and asked her why she would not go out with him. She seemed conflicted about what to say and said that she was "just not ready." Kyle could tell that there was more, but he left it alone. Kyle got her number the next day under the pretense of starting a "study group." Though, the study "group" was never more than the two of them unless Claire brought someone else. Usually, Claire brought Josh. He was studying electrical engineering. Initially, Kyle was annoyed with the additional "study" partner, but he soon realized that Claire and Josh were no more than friends. Knowing that he would not receive any competition from Josh, Kyle slightly lowered his walls. Josh and Kyle, too, became friends, eventually.

If he were back in Boston, Kyle would never have become friends with either Claire or Josh. First, they spent too much time studying. Kyle would finish with his homework, and they would still be working. He would move on to his homework due next week and complete that, but they would still be working. Then time would come for him to leave for his job at Finneman's Market, and Josh and Claire would still not be finished. Kyle resolved not to study an instant longer than his grades required. Second, everything Josh and Claire did revolved around their church. Claire played volleyball—at her church. Josh helped with the youth group—at his church. Both occasionally volunteered with the soup kitchen—with their church. All this was in addition to all their existing Bible studies and prayer meetings. They also never went to any of the parties that Kyle attended. That automatically meant that Kyle would not share any mutual friends with Claire and Josh. Finally, Kyle did all he could with his full schedule to stay in shape, whether at the school fitness center or on his own. Claire and Josh had not been to the school gym since they finished their required physical education class. Still, the two did not look bad, especially Claire. Despite his complaints, Claire and Josh were the friends that Kyle needed. Kyle just did not know it.

Kyle's other friends were a lot less wholesome, and Kyle had no shortage of friends. Between ROTC and his classes,

Kyle was one of the most popular men in his class. He was invited to all the parties and gatherings and attended all that his job and homework would allow. Somehow, he found the time to attend.

Kyle was careful. He followed the letter of the law. He never attended a party with illegal activity. He was over twenty-one, but he never drank anything close to his DUI threshold. If there were drugs, he ignored the activity and left soon after the discovery. Kyle was so close to graduating as a second lieutenant! He would not provide the college or ROTC any reason to cancel his scholarships.

Kyle learned to relax and enjoy himself again. All of the women wanted a piece of him, and he offered himself without protest. Claire was different, and that bothered him. He would shrug off his feelings, but thoughts of her would always return.

****

After months of uncertainty, Kyle finally received his diploma. Claire and Josh graduated alongside him. His grandmother watched from the audience. Kyle's life was starting to feel normal again. He had been commissioned into the Air Force a few days earlier. During the ceremony, the cadre, once again, praised Second Lieutenant Kyle Baker above all others and highlighted his "limitless potential to help the Air Force fly, fight, and win—anytime, anywhere!" Kyle would receive his orders and relocate to his base assignment sometime within the next two or three months.

The colonel speculated that Kyle, given his background, would probably be assigned to one of the acquisition bases. Kyle just hoped that he would not be assigned to Hanscom.

****

Two weeks after graduation, Kyle received a phone call from the FBI.

"We just spoke to the police up in Massachusetts," the female agent said. "Their records indicated that you and your mother had two vehicles stolen, correct?"

"Yes, that's correct."

"We have found both vehicles."

"Did you find my father?" Kyle asked, hopeful.

"No" was the quick response. Kyle was disappointed. "And unfortunately, the cars are unusable."

"What do you mean?"

"Our agents caught someone trying to sell the chassis."

"The chassis?!"

"Yes. Everything else had already been sold, including the engines. We are looking for them now, but they were probably already sold on the black market." Kyle raised his finger to the sky and cursed his father.

"And the person who sold them—it wasn't my father?" Kyle repeated.

"No. It was a low-level grunt in The New World, a well-known gang in Minneapolis—"

"Minneapolis!"

"We are still chasing down his story, but it doesn't look

like he knows anything. We will let you know if we find anything else."

The call was over. Kyle hung up the phone. He shouted curses at his father. He was alone in the backroom of the store. He did not care if the customers in the storefront heard him. He loathed his father. His father had sold everything that he had stolen to a gang. The valuables were long gone; there was no chance of getting any of them back now. Kyle vowed that if he ever saw his father again, he would kill him.

****

At the end of the semester, Kyle expanded his work shift; the new shift was long enough for Kyle to earn some extra, much-needed cash and short enough for him to party in the evenings. The store manager needed all the help he could get and, after some badgering, allowed Kyle to work the long hours. Kyle was relieved; he could use the money.

Kyle continued to live with his grandmother after graduation. Whenever Kyle returned home from work, Joan would always be sitting in her armchair, reading her Bible. Kyle tried to avoid speaking to her. He would manufacture enough noise to let his grandmother know that he had returned; then, he would march upstairs to his room. If he had a party or other plans later in the evening, he would sneak out the bedroom window, scurry across the porch roof, jump to a nearby tree, and climb to the ground. Kyle carefully concealed all his violations of Joan's rules. His grandmother never caught him, but Kyle loathed being at her and the deadbolt's mercy.

Kyle's base assignment could not come fast enough. Every morning, Kyle snatched the mail from the mailbox and sifted for the letter. Every morning, Kyle was disappointed. He knew that the letter might not come for another month at the earliest. But Kyle was not going to take any chances; he wanted to be ready to move as soon as the Air Force had room for him. In the meantime, Kyle would have to endure.

The biggest source of contention between Kyle and his grandmother, other than Kyle's demands for Joan to change her "draconian rules," was Kyle's use of her car. Kyle exhaustively searched for an alternative vehicle within his expanded means. After a couple of weeks, Kyle had scraped together enough funds to buy a used motorcycle. It was a beautiful red sport bike. He had found it, by chance, for sale on the side of the road. As soon as he saw it, he knew that he could not have found a better replacement for his grandmother's car. He paid cash on the spot.

His grandmother urged against his decision and voiced her worry about him "riding around on that infernal machine." Kyle had almost sworn at her several times before successfully communicating that he would no longer have to borrow her car or have her chauffeur him to and from work. That pleased his grandmother, but she absolutely insisted that Kyle purchase all sorts of protective gear. Kyle was unwilling to spend any more money than absolutely necessary and asked Joan if she was willing to cover the cost, which became a new argument. They finally compromised on Kyle purchasing a full-face helmet and wearing it whenever he rode.

So Kyle drove his motorcycle through Jacksonville, wearing shorts, a sleeveless shirt, and a black motorcycle helmet. The lack of protective gear hardly mattered. Kyle was extra careful whenever he rode; he did not yet have his motorcycle license.

****

The prayer group continued to meet during the summer. Since most of the prayer warriors were unable to meet with each other every day during lunch, the group chose to meet in one of the public library meeting rooms on Wednesday nights. Kyle's grandmother agreed to him missing the Wednesday night service only because he was attending a prayer meeting.

The new excuse suited Kyle perfectly.

During each night at the prayer group, Kyle tried to ignore the prayer requests, and tonight was no exception. Whenever he did hear the requests, he would be reminded that he really was superior to everyone else in the room.

Do these people actually believe that a big genie in the sky cares about their issues? If a god actually does exist and he actually does care about me, then he would not have allowed my father to leave me destitute or allow my mom to kill herself. I, and I alone, am the one who helped myself through the past few months and restored my life after being derailed. I don't need god, especially one that does not exist, and neither does anyone else.

To reward himself for sitting through the prayer meetings and to prolong his time with Claire, Kyle organized for the prayer group to go to a restaurant for "fellowship" after praying. The initial response had been overwhelmingly positive, and nearly half the attendees joined him at the selected restaurant every week. Claire came almost every night, but she never seemed to arrive early enough to sit next to Kyle. That did not bother him too much. They were always close enough to talk.

Kyle's mind snapped back to the prayer group. David, one of the consistent attendees to both the prayer group and the dinner, was sharing a request. Despite his best effort, Kyle listened every now and again. There were only so many times that he could count the ceiling tiles discreetly. David was still talking. "…a sharp increase in gang-related activity in recent months. Just pray that they don't cause more violence and that no more drugs come into the city." David drew a shaky deep breath before continuing. "As some of you know, I got mixed up with The New World a few years ago—"

Kyle sat bolt upright, his full attention back on the prayer requests. "What! The New World!" Kyle unintentionally shouted.

David hung his head in embarrassment and answered gravely. "A few years ago, I got mixed up in that gang. I did some horrible things—things I'm not proud of…"

Kyle was barely listening. *The New World!* Kyle thought.

That was the same gang the FBI said had tried to sell the cars! Could this be the same gang from Minnesota?

"I struggled too," Josh said. He had put his arm around David and glared at Kyle. "I did drugs for years. The New World was the supplier. I chose that life, and The New World kept me there."

"The New World..." Kyle repeated aloud. As soon as he spoke, he became aware that, with the exception of David, everyone else in the group was staring at him. Kyle recovered. "I didn't realize that The New World was this far south," he said haltingly. No one believed him. After an endless silence, someone else voiced a prayer request, and the prayer meeting resumed as best as it could.

Kyle did not need to try to redirect his attention away from the prayer requests for the remainder of the meeting. Someone else would have to lead everyone to the restaurant tonight. Kyle had research to do. He needed to learn more about The New World! Kyle had not bothered looking into The New World after the FBI had called him; he had thought it was just a local gang. Kyle was furious at himself for the oversight! He should have exhaustively researched every connection to his father!

Kyle seriously considered walking out of the prayer meeting. The research was too important, and he could not afford to waste any more time. Kyle eventually decided against it; he did not want to draw any more attention to himself.

As soon as the prayer had finished, Kyle discreetly

exited the room. He had hardly reached the first bookcase when he heard "Kyle!" called sharply from the prayer room. Claire was storming after him. "What is your problem!" she demanded, too loudly for a library.

Kyle knew exactly what Claire meant. "I didn't know!"

Claire did not stop talking. "David was really vulnerable back there!"

"I didn't know!" Kyle repeated.

"You need to apologize to him right now!" Claire demanded.

"What!" Kyle exclaimed in a hushed shout. *How sensitive is this guy?* Kyle thought. Then he said, "It was an honest mistake! I was just surprised. That's all!"

"Then it should be really easy to explain yourself to David and apologize to him!" Claire argued.

"I already explained myself!" Kyle retorted. "Someone just told me about The New World. They said the gang was up in Minnesota. I didn't realize they were in Florida too."

"You can tell that to David when you apologize to him," Claire pressed.

"Sure," Kyle shrugged off her comment; he was not getting anywhere with Claire otherwise. "I have to get home. I'll talk to him later." Kyle resumed his pace to the door. Claire trailed behind him. Neither said anything, but Kyle pretended to think. He waited an appropriate amount of time before continuing. "Is The New World really active in the city?" he asked.

Claire sighed. She was obviously unconvinced that Kyle

had told her the whole truth. "Yes, the gang's been in the city for years. And as you just heard, they sell a lot of drugs," Claire jabbed. Barely audible, she added, "Among other things," and shuddered.

Kyle did not notice. "Does The New World buy anything? I mean, could you sell stuff to them—?" He was going to finish with "like cars," but Claire cut him off. She was furious, but her eyes were wide with fear.

"Whatever business you have with The New World is not going to end well! I will not be a part of this!" They had stopped outside, in front of the steps of the library. With that said, Claire stormed toward her car, in the opposite direction of Kyle's motorcycle. Kyle grabbed her arm and spun her around. Now Kyle was furious.

"I don't have any business with them! Someone sold something of my family's to them back in Boston!"

Joan, not Kyle, had told Claire the general story of what had happened in Boston. Claire sympathized with Kyle, seeing the bigger picture.

"Sorry," she said. "I didn't know."

Kyle released her. "Can you sell anything to The New World?" he repeated.

"Anything that they want, they take. Why not kill the person who's selling it and then just take it? I don't think anyone sells to them." Kyle thought for a moment; Claire did have a point. Claire was still speaking, "The New World has been on a crime wave! They've killed over ninety people in the last four months! That's three times more than last year! All this has been on the news."

Kyle did not have time to watch the news.

Kyle pondered what he had just heard. *If my father had tried to sell my belongings to The New World, they probably would have just killed him like Claire said. Maybe my father really is dead after all. In that case, I owe The New World my thanks. Unless...*

"Do they have a supplier?" Kyle asked aloud.

"I guess. They have to get everything from somewhere."

Kyle mused. *That makes more sense. For my father to sell my belongings to The New World, he had to have been a supplier. If that's the case, my father not only would still be alive but also would be working for The New World!*

Kyle was about to shout curses at his father when he remembered who was standing next to him. "So the only people who can sell stuff to them are suppliers?" he asked Claire.

"I don't know...maybe someone—I don't know. I don't know! Kyle, you're starting to scare me."

Kyle ignored her complaint. "Why haven't the police done anything?"

"The police don't know anything! They haven't even been able to take one of the gang members to court in years, let alone put any of them in prison."

"They can set a sting! Watch where they sell and—"

"The police can't find them! They're too unpredictable! Anyone who has tried to go undercover has been killed before they even got close! This has *also* been all over the news."

"I—!" Kyle bit his tongue. He would keep his thoughts to himself, for now. Kyle released a legitimate exasperated sigh. "Thanks, Claire. I'm just…frustrated, that's all." The statement was only half true.

The real half was convincing enough. For the first time in their friendship, Claire thought it necessary to hug Kyle. Kyle did not enjoy the moment as much as he would have under any other circumstance.

He had work to do.

CHAPTER 5

As soon as Kyle returned to his grandmother's house that evening, he began researching The New World. Little was definitively known about the organization. Every source Kyle read did not have more than a few lines of real information. Kyle documented everything. A phrase here, a couple of sentences there—it all began to form a bigger picture.

The New World was responsible for dozens of murders and allegedly responsible for hundreds more. And that was just in Jacksonville. More research confirmed that The New World was active in every major city in the United States. Interpol was even tracking activity by The New World in several European countries, and rumor claimed that The New World was expanding into the Far East as well.

The New World had built an extensive international network for smuggling drugs, weapons, and slaves across borders. They were experts at laundering money and allegedly printed bills difficult for even the Department of the Treasury to detect. The New World made any stolen goods disappear, with estimates that authorities reclaimed a mere one-half of one percent of the yearly total; Kyle could testify that the figure was accurate.

The police and FBI had minimal success with arresting any members of The New World. The organization was unbelievably paranoid, never using the same location or contact with any predictability. When the authorities did manage to catch a member, an army of unscrupulous lawyers, paid by an unknown source, would appear, defend, and vindicate the accused. Scores of police officers and federal agents had died trying to infiltrate The New World; none lasted more than a few days before disappearing without a trace.

The detachment of The New World in Jacksonville had steadily grown in size and activity since the beginning of the year. The overdoses in the city tripled; the homicides skyrocketed. No one had an explanation.

Kyle looked from his computer. The sun was streaming into his room.

****

During the next few days, Kyle fanatically researched The New World. Every spare moment, at work and at home, he would search for any new information and add it to his growing document.

One morning, Joan tried talking to Kyle while he was still compiling his research. She had expected Kyle to listen intently and respond at appropriate intervals. After several attempts to multitask and a rebuke from his grandmother,

Kyle had enough and snapped harshly in response.

"Hmph," Joan began. "You remind me of your father when he lived down here."

Kyle's first instinct was to swear at Joan for comparing him to his father. But before the curses formed, Kyle asked a different question, "My father lived down here?"

"Oh yes. He used to live down here. That's how he met your mom."

Kyle never remembered either of his parents saying that they met in Florida. He figured that they had met up in Boston, and Kyle said so to his grandmother.

"Oh no, I distinctly remember your mom dating your father. He was a ruffian and never went to church a day in his life." Kyle knew that his grandmother probably only called his father a "ruffian" because he did not attend church. He had seen pictures from when his parents were dating, and "regular joe" seemed a more apt description. Still, the conversation was proving to have some value.

"I never approved of the match," Joan continued. "Your mom had always set her heart on living in Boston, and when she found a job and was going to move there, I had hoped that would be the end of it. But your father found someone to hire him up in Boston and followed her up there."

"Where did he live?" Kyle asked. "Down here in Jacksonville, I mean. Was he in the area?"

"I don't remember... I think he lived in the city somewhere. He kept that to himself. I don't think your grandfather or I ever knew."

Convenient of him not to mention that, Kyle thought to himself. "What about friends or relatives?" Kyle asked, already suspecting the answer.

"I believe he said his family was in Oregon, though he never said when or why he moved here; I always thought that was strange. I remember, after your parents moved to Boston, your mom told us that his parents had just died in a car crash. He had to fly out there and settle their estate for a few weeks."

Convenient, Kyle thought again. All this was consistent with the stories that his parents had told him. Kyle had tried several times over the years to find the car crash online, but Oregon was a big state, and his father had been vague on the details. "Yeah. I remember them saying that to me. Mom couldn't fly out with him after it happened—some work thing." His grandmother nodded. *That was also very convenient,* Kyle thought. "What about other family?" he asked aloud.

"He never mentioned any. I don't even remember meeting any of his friends."

Kyle mused. *Maybe my father was not from Oregon after all. Maybe he had lived in Jacksonville his whole life. Maybe he did not have a family, and the car crash was just a convenient way to tie that loose end. Maybe he did have friends; maybe they were not reputable. Maybe my father was a part of The New World. Maybe he still is. Would that be such a logical jump?*

Perhaps Kyle needed to research his father.

****

Kyle's foray into his father's past proved brief. The name was too common for a search on the Internet, as Kyle soon discovered. Even limiting the search to Jacksonville and Boston revealed only a couple of articles about the robbery.

So Kyle turned to the federal government. The FBI had already provided Kyle and his mom everything they wanted to know and more about James Baker. None of it had seemed out of the ordinary.

Kyle needed to take a different approach. In order to prove that this father was not working with The New World, Kyle would need to look at all the reports of bodies that had been attributed to that organization. If his father was among the deceased, case closed. He had been killed by The New World, and there was nothing more that Kyle could do to avenge himself.

Kyle called the FBI. He said he thought that his father might be dead and wanted to look at "John Doe" murders. The agency was immediately suspicious and wanted to know what exactly had led Kyle to believe that his father was now dead. Kyle gave a quick answer that he wanted to make sure that his father was not dead before having the FBI waste any more time looking for him. The FBI assured Kyle that they believed that his father was still alive but hesitantly conceded to let Kyle, with another agent present, review pictures of any open cases.

Kyle spent days looking at files and pictures, but none matched his father. He could not prove that his father had been killed. Either his father was still alive and, therefore, working for The New World, or his father was dead, and the FBI had not yet found his body. *Am I ready to choose one option over the other?* Kyle considered.

Kyle's mind had already decided. His mind recognized that Kyle was trying to prove a negative by looking at the FBI's list of the deceased. Since Kyle could not prove that James Baker was dead, his mind chose to assume that his father was still alive.

Kyle's spirit had also made its decision. His spirit had grown restless with waiting indefinitely for the FBI to find conclusive proof that his father was alive. Kyle was willing to assume that his father was not yet dead and, therefore, still within his reach. Kyle was set on revenge.

His soul agreed. Kyle's soul believed there was nothing worse than waiting endlessly for information that may never come. Kyle's pages of research confirmed that was often the case. Kyle was determined to act and was not afraid of the consequences.

Kyle's body, too, was tired of waiting. He needed to act. Kyle was ready to meet his father face-to-face and exact vengeance for what he had done. No better way to flush his father out of hiding than to start causing a mess. If Kyle was wrong, The New World deserved it. Plus, he could endure the fallout; he was strong enough.

There was no minority report. Kyle would assume that his father was alive and was working for The New World. That decided Kyle's actions.

Kyle was already forming a plan. He knew what he was going to do.

CHAPTER 6

During the last few months, Kyle had seen drug dealers behind Finneman's Market many times between the hours of ten and midnight. True to Kyle's research, the alley was never used with any predictability, and when it was used, the same dealers never appeared twice in a row. Kyle had noticed a large increase in the frequency of the meetings during the second half of the semester. But like the first time Kyle saw them, he did nothing. The drug runners probably figured that they were safe in the alley behind the grocery store.

Kyle had not seen a deal for weeks. Now would be the perfect time for them to reuse the alley. And then, Kyle could spring his trap.

With his boss' lack of business knowledge, Kyle was able to convince him that something was wrong with their bookkeeping. Kyle offered to stay late after the store closed to correct the ledger. His boss, of his own free will, said that he could not give Kyle time and a half pay for the additional hours. That was more than Kyle had expected, and Kyle, short on money and scruples, agreed without hesitation.

Kyle discretely kept watch every night, his cell phone out of sight, below the back window.

Kyle waited less than a week before he saw another exchange. Two vehicles, without headlights, drove noiselessly into the alley. That was what the dealers always did. As soon as Kyle saw the cars, he dialed 911.

"There is a drug deal going down right now, behind Finneman's Market," Kyle said as quickly and as clearly as he could.

"Okay, sir. How many perpetrators are there?"

Kyle tried to be discreet looking out the window. There were only two, as usual; he recognized both of the men from a couple of previous deals. "I think it's just the buyer and the seller, two males, one Caucasian and one Hispanic."

"Okay, sir. I am dispatching police vehicles to your location now."

"Please hurry!" Kyle said. He glanced out the window. The deal was ending.

"There is a police cruiser in your area. They will be there in three minutes."

"That's too long," Kyle muttered. He spoke to the operator, "Tell them to hurry!" The operator said something in reply, but Kyle had already set his phone on the desk and did not hear.

I need to act fast. I need to stop the dealers from leaving. But which one is from The New World? Kyle glanced out the window. *If I don't do something now, they will both be gone, and when the police arrive, the dealers will never return to the alley again!*

Kyle's eyes caught the large black safe in the back of the office. Kyle spun the combination as fast as he could. *I can buy some time, but I'll need to buy some drugs to do it.* He stared at the money. *How much will I even need?* Kyle grabbed a stack of bills and slammed the safe shut. He hurried to the door and glanced out the window. The dealers were headed to their cars now!

Kyle opened the backdoor into the alley and poked his head out.

"Hey!" he whispered, loud enough for them to hear. In an instant, both men had spun around and trained their weapons at Kyle. He glanced from one to the other, unsure of where to look. Kyle steeled himself and continued.

"Uh…is there any left to buy?" Kyle gingerly opened the door wider and slowly raised his hand to produce the wad of bills. The guns lowered slightly, but they were still aimed at him. "I don't want a lot," Kyle continued. "Just some for the weekend—my girlfriend too," Kyle added hastily, trying to think of what else to say. The Latino glanced at the Caucasian and motioned with his head. The Caucasian holstered his weapon; the Latino raised his gun again.

"What'll you have?" the Caucasian asked.

"Um…" Kyle started to sweat. He had not planned this far. "Cocaine," Kyle finally said.

The Caucasian rattled several more questions about dosage. Kyle just answered in the affirmative. *Where are the police?* Kyle thought. He shelled out the money. *If the police don't catch these guys, I'll have to reimburse the store.*

The Caucasian noticed Kyle's uncertainty and his stack of money. "This your first time?"

"Yeah," Kyle noticed the dealer was looking at the bills. "I just took these from the store safe. I'll pay it back later." As soon as he had spoken, Kyle mentally berated himself, *Come on, Kyle! Why did you say that?*

The dealer did not react. "See you around," the dealer said, handing Kyle several packets filled with white powder.

At that moment, a siren pierced the night, and blue lights flashed behind the Hispanic man. Both dealers swore. The Hispanic man holstered his gun, dove into the shadows, and slipped down a side alley. The Caucasian man had already started running, his car left behind. Kyle was not going to let him get away. Kyle ran after him. Kyle closed the distance before he reached the end of the alley and pounced on the seller. Kyle narrowly managed to grab the dealer's waist, and the two tumbled to the ground. Before they had stopped rolling, a second police vehicle had arrived at their end of the alley. Two officers jumped out of the car, their weapons aimed at the couple on the ground.

"Put your hands where I can see them!" one of the officers roared.

The Caucasian obeyed; he rolled onto his stomach and put his hands on his head. As he did so, he sneered at Kyle. Kyle ignored the look and stood up.

Aside from a few scrapes on my arms and legs, that went fairly well, Kyle decided.

"I said 'Put your hands where I can see them!'" the officer screamed again. Kyle looked in the officers' direction. Both guns were aimed at him.

Oh no! Kyle thought. *They think that I'm a part of the drug deal! I'm innocent! I can explain! I was distracting the dealers until you and the other police arrived!* Then, Kyle realized that, in one of his fists, he was still clenching four small packets of white powder. Kyle reluctantly obeyed the officer's orders. He fell to his knees and put both hands on his head. He watched as one officer cuffed the Caucasian. The other arrived to handcuff Kyle; Kyle complied. He let the packets fall from his hand. Kyle and the Caucasian dealer were shoved into the back of the patrol car while the officers cordoned the area.

As soon as the police had left, the two Caucasians looked at each other. The other said to Kyle, "You're a dead man."

****

Six hours later, Kyle collected his belongings from the police station. He had explained his story. He told the officers where his cell phone was and the combination for the grocery store safe. The 911 operator had corroborated his story and verified his voice. His story checked out. The police let him go...

Only to hold him hostage for his statement. For another hour, the police sat him in front of a camera and re-asked him the same questions he had answered to exonerate himself. When he had finished, the police cleared him and genuinely allowed him to leave.

Kyle produced his voucher, and an officer returned his items.

"One white smartphone, cracked screen, black case; one black wallet, contents various; one silver watch, analog; $1300, cash, various bills; and that should be it."

"When do I get the rest of the money?" Kyle asked. "The money I used to stall the dealers and buy the cocaine?"

"That's in evidence. You can't take that. It has your fingerprints and the dealer's fingerprints all over it."

Kyle swore. "So what am I supposed to do, pay back the cash register with my own money?"

The officer shrugged. "I don't make the rules. Stop by tomorrow and ask then. Maybe the analysis will be done, and you'll get it back. Don't count on it, though."

The money aside, Kyle was ecstatic. *If I can't hurt my father directly, I can at least hurt the people who are working with him,* Kyle concluded.

Kyle's grandmother was waiting outside the police station. She had been waiting since Kyle's one phone call several hours before. She was cranky and tired from the early wake-up and from having to come get him, but she was mostly indignant that "my grandson has been arrested." Once Kyle explained the situation, Joan changed her mind. She praised Kyle for "getting the hoodlums off the street."

****

Before heading to work, Kyle attempted to rescue his

boss' money. The police were still holding it, and the sergeant that Kyle asked was brief with his responses. Yes, they would hold it until the trial. No, they did not know when the trial was. Of course, Kyle would know when they were done with the money; he would be testifying at the trial. That was the end of it. Kyle hoped his boss would understand.

Kyle's boss was less understanding than any of the police officers with whom Kyle had spoken over the last twelve hours. He pounced as soon as Kyle opened the front door to the grocery store.

"Kyle! The police were bothering me all night! They've roped off the entire block! They're *still* in the office and the alley taking photographs! I've been here since 2 a.m., answering all sorts of questions! They were particularly interested in *you*! *And* they said that *you* were at the bottom of all this!"

Kyle swore silently. He was done talking to difficult people today, and he needed a few more hours of sleep than he had snatched after being released from the holding cell. "Jack," he began shortly. "There was a drug deal last night, and I stopped it!"

"Shhh!" Kyle's boss whispered harshly. "Not out here! It's not good for business." He led Kyle to the backroom, and Kyle began again.

"I saw a drug deal in the alley out back. I stopped them until the police arrived."

"You stopped it?" Kyle's boss asked, incredulous.

"Yes. The police have been trying to get these guys for

months, and I stopped them—with your help," Kyle added. He had a story to spin.

"With my help?" the ex-marine said, skepticism increased.

"Yeah…I stalled them, but I baited them with some money from the store safe. It worked long enough for the police to arrive and catch them red-handed. Without you and your money, they'd still be on the street. When I'm interviewed, I'll say that you supplied the money for our drug bust." The boss' eyes illuminated with pride. He believed everything so far. A few lies would make the truth easier to handle. Kyle continued. "The police need to keep the money as evidence until they finish the analysis, but it should be ready in a day or two," Kyle lied. The gleam left his boss' eyes, but his boss still believed the lies. Kyle wondered if he should have mentioned that part to his boss; after all, his boss had never checked the financials since he had hired Kyle. Kyle pressed his luck. "I didn't get back from the police station until a couple of hours ago. Can I take time off today?"

Kyle had pushed his luck too far. "All day?" his boss asked. "How much money did you use to stall them?"

"Just a few dollars for a couple of fixes," Kyle lied again. His boss would never know the truth.

"I'll have to take that out of your pay…but you'll mention that my money helped catch these guys?"

"Oh, of course."

"Then, I guess you can take the day off. But you need to come in tomorrow—no excuses!"

That was more than agreeable to Kyle. He fled the scene to his grandmother's house and grabbed a few more hours of sleep.

Later that afternoon, reporters and camera crews from several of the local news stations descended on the house. Kyle conveniently forgot to mention that the money he used in the bust belonged to his boss.

****

With the ordeal of last night behind him, the reporters satisfied, and a few more hours of sleep, Kyle decided that it was time to celebrate.

Kyle announced to Joan that he was going to his room for the rest of the night. As soon as he closed his door, Kyle slipped out the window, jumped to the ground, shifted his motorcycle into neutral, wheeled it beyond the range of his grandmother's hearing, and rode his motorcycle to the nearest bar.

Hardly anyone was there. Not many people drank on Tuesday nights, including Kyle's college friends. Kyle had called everyone he knew in college, except anyone in the prayer group. Unfortunately, no one could make it for the last-minute, late-night drink. Still, all Kyle's friends congratulated him on the drug bust, which was almost as good as them being with him to celebrate.

Kyle did not mind drinking alone. He hopped onto a barstool and ordered. There was one other person at the far end of the bar. Everyone else was sitting at the tables.

Kyle basked in his superiority. When his drink arrived, he toasted his father silently with a few choice phrases. The eleven o'clock news played on the screen above the bar. The first story was the early morning arrests following The New World drug bust. The news anchor praised Kyle for his involvement and played a short clip of his interview from earlier that day.

"Is that you?" the bartender asked, glancing from the screen to Kyle. Kyle nodded. "Well, good work. It's about time The New World got what was coming to them," he continued. "The first round's on me." Kyle thanked him.

A few minutes later, the waitress brought Kyle another drink. "You're the guy that helped with the drug bust, right?"

"Yeah."

"The people at that table bought you a drink." Kyle looked over his shoulder. Two young men and a woman were sitting at a table. One of the men nodded. Kyle nodded back. The guy seemed vaguely familiar.

Kyle's spirit and soul soared. *There's nothing better than being thanked for getting revenge on my father!* Kyle sighed to himself.

The waitress left and was soon replaced by the familiar-looking guy. "I just wanted to say thank you. We've been trying to catch someone in The New World for years."

Kyle remembered where he had seen him before. "Oh, yes. You were at the crime scene last night. You arrested me."

"Yep, that was me. I'm surprised you remembered. I'm Nick, by the way."

"Kyle." They shook hands. "Were you able to catch that other guy that was there? The other dealer?"

"Unfortunately, no. My partner," Nick motioned over to the woman at his table, "and I were focused on you and the other guy. The other squad car wasn't able to chase him down. But since he left his car there, we should be able to find out who he was."

"Great! Do you think you have a case against the one we caught?" Kyle continued.

"I don't see why not. He was caught at the scene of the crime. You have an eyewitness account. His fingerprints are all over everything. Should be a quick case."

"Great!"

"Hey, are you alone tonight?" Nick asked. "Why don't you come over and join us?" Kyle heartily concurred. The three police officers and Kyle talked and laughed for the next two hours and celebrated Kyle with many drinks. Kyle was usually good at holding his alcohol, but he was feeling tired and dizzy tonight. He probably should have ordered something to eat; he had hardly eaten all day. He probably should have caught more sleep too. At 1:00 a.m., Kyle left. The last thing he remembered was starting his motorcycle.

CHAPTER 7

Kyle woke up. He felt awful. His head was pounding. His hands and feet were numb. *At least I arrived at my grandma's house all right. I don't even remember driving here.* Kyle kept his eyes sealed shut. *I sure hope I haven't slept through my alarm. Jack gave me a hard enough time about taking yesterday off work, even after getting arrested. He wouldn't like me being late for today's shift.*

Kyle opened his eyes...or at least tried to open his eyes. He could not open them. Something was keeping them closed. Kyle tried to move his hands. They had been tied to a cold metal bar behind his back. He tried to shout an expletive. Something was clamped over his mouth too. For the first time, Kyle realized that he was hanging upside down. His ankles were tied to something. Kyle tried to right himself. The little slack his arms permitted caused him to hit a wall of metal. He uttered a muffled curse. Kyle felt the wall with his head. The same metal surrounded him on three—no, four—sides, along with some other piping. He could not feel if this box had a bottom.

Kyle tried to free his hands. His fingers were numb and useless, but it seemed like someone had used a large zip tie to bind his hands to the metal pole. Kyle tried different methods of breaking the ties, but they stubbornly refused to snap apart. The zip ties were starting to cut into his wrists. He stopped moving. *Who did this to me? How am I going to get out of this?*

Suddenly water started pouring into the small metal enclosure. Kyle released a startled cry. He could feel the water now, not just hear it. The top of his head was already wet. The box did have the bottom. He was in a sink!

Kyle thrashed wildly, trying to escape the rising water. The metal walls would not let him escape, and neither would his bonds. Kyle continued to writhe until he was exhausted. He let his head fall back into the water. The water was up to his forehead!

Kyle panicked!

Kyle's mind needed to find a way to get out of this! He needed to free his hands! He needed to keep his nose above the water! But Kyle's mind could not think of a solution in the face of the consequences if he failed.

His spirit needed to focus on finding a solution! The water was still rising! He did not have much time left! But Kyle's spirit could not concentrate on freeing himself!

Kyle's soul was afraid of what would happen if he could not free himself, and that fear was steadily growing! If he could not free his hands, he did not have a chance of escaping! He would die! And he would no longer be able to get revenge on his father!

Kyle's body was exhausted! His strength was gone! The skin on his wrists was raw! Kyle could not free his hands! He hardly had the strength to push himself out of the water!

"You made a big mistake, Kyle!" Kyle jumped at the voice. Someone was standing directly in front of him. Kyle uttered a curse. The phrase was muffled by the gag, but the captor did not appreciate the noise. The water flow increased. "You are going to pay for the little stunt you pulled yesterday." The water had reached Kyle's eyes. "You don't cross The New World and walk away unscathed."

Kyle could feel the water creeping up his nose. His captor was not going to shut off the water! Kyle struggled in vain to free himself. The water was covering his nose. He tried to breathe out of his mouth; the gag was too tight. Kyle arched out of the water as far as he could and took his last breath.

Kyle tried to calm himself as much as he could. He needed to free himself before he ran out of air. He tried releasing the zip ties again. He tried lifting his head further out of the sink. He tried breathing out of his mouth again. *I need to breathe!*

No! Kyle resolved. *I am not going to breathe!*

After three minutes of holding his breath and trying everything he could think to free himself, Kyle lost the battle. He released his air and breathed in the water. Cold water rushed into his sinuses and filled his lungs. He tried to exhale the water, but only more water rushed into his lungs. Kyle could not breathe! He was drowning, with only his nose underwater! Kyle panicked. He inhaled more water. He tried one last futile attempt to free his hands. His mind started to go blank. So this was what drowning felt like.

Kyle's hands suddenly fell loose. His bonds had been cut! He was free! This was his chance! Kyle banged his head against the side of the sink, but with his hands free, he pulled himself above the water. He clawed at the duct tape surrounding his head and mouth. He was still upside down. The water from his lungs rushed out his mouth. For the next several minutes, Kyle coughed up the water and vomited. Breathing air had never felt so good!

Kyle removed the duct tape covering his eyes. The room was completely dark. Kyle could barely distinguish the shapes of decaying machines around him. He was in an abandoned warehouse. Whoever had held him captive was long gone.

Kyle tried to free his legs. They were bound to the same pipe with the zip ties. Kyle reached toward his ankles. He was in good shape, but he was not limber enough to reach them. He tried bending his knees, but the pole prevented him. Kyle tried stretching again, straining himself. He reached the ties and tried to release them. He held himself there for almost a minute before needing to give his stomach muscles a break.

Kyle let himself hang. He started to feel cold; the skin on his arms looked ashen; he could feel his heart beating furiously; Kyle felt weak; he threw up again. Kyle knew he was going into shock. With nothing to do, the events of the night were starting to catch up with him. Kyle cried. He suppressed the sound at first but stopped. He let the sobs rack his body. Kyle wept. *I almost died!*

With that, Kyle realized that his being was screaming at him.

Kyle's mind argued that the price for revenge on his father was too high. He did not even know for certain that his father was still alive or that he was part of The New World. That had all been conjecture. And Kyle's mind had voted to take the risk. Now, it voted to stop until it had determined more concrete evidence.

As much as Kyle's spirit desired to follow the task to the end, it recognized the dangers of continuing. Hurting The New World could come at the cost of his life without really accomplishing his goal. Kyle needed revenge on his father; The New World was not his first concern.

Kyle did not want to die! His soul was now more afraid of death than it had ever been. His soul was determined to exact revenge on James Baker, but Kyle could not do that if he was dead. His soul voted to no longer fight against The New World and focus on his father.

Kyle's body was weak from being nearly drowned, and it did not want to experience drowning again. The New World was too large and powerful for Kyle to fight on his own. If Kyle continued to fight The New World, his body would pay the ultimate price. Kyle's body pleaded for Kyle to forget The New World.

Kyle's whole being was in agreement: he would no longer fight The New World. His father was the real focus.

When he had composed himself, Kyle reached for his feet again. After another minute, he was too tired to continue. He had made no progress.

Kyle let himself hang again. He was so tired. He would close his eyes and rest...

When he closed his eyes, he could feel the water covering his nose, filling his lungs! He started to quicken his breath. His breaths were shallow. His mind clouded. He could not think clearly. He could feel himself drowning again!

Kyle snapped his eyes open. *I am* not *drowning. There is no water. I am alone. I am safe.* Kyle tried to free his legs again, but he could not even reach past his calf. He was too tired. *I can't make it!* Kyle gave up. He relaxed his muscles too quickly and bashed his head against the outer side of the sink.

He cursed in pain. He cursed The New World. He cursed his father. He cursed whoever had tried to drown him. They had succeeded in breaking him. His only option was to find his father and break him instead. Kyle vowed that he would focus on finding his father and avenge himself!

The last thought fueled Kyle with rage. With renewed strength, Kyle reached for his ankles. He held the pipe with one hand and released his bonds with the other. He was free within a minute.

Kyle jumped to his feet. The abandoned warehouse was a maze of rusted machinery and garbage, but he eventually found the exit. The sun was just rising. It was going to be another long day.

****

Kyle barely arrived to work on time. He lost his way twice before realizing he rode by the abandoned warehouse every day, going to and from his grandmother's house and work.

When he arrived at work, Kyle's hair was still wet. His boss glanced between Kyle and the clock as a subtle warning but did not notice that Kyle was wearing the same clothes as yesterday...and the day before. Kyle began his work immediately. He could not betray that anything was wrong. The New World might still be watching him. Kyle did not know whom he could trust.

Kyle started opening boxes and restocking the shelves. Whenever he looked up from his work, he would catch customers staring at him. More than once, he changed aisles and would continue his work, only to see a customer from the previous aisle look away.

This happened more than once. *Are these people following me? How many people are following me? Are they from The New World? The single parent with three kids probably isn't. But what about the woman who spent fifteen minutes looking at cereal? Or the man in the "feminine hygiene" aisle? Normal people wouldn't do that...* Those two unsettled Kyle.

Something crashed behind Kyle! In panic, he grabbed his boxcutter and spun around to face his attacker! A can had fallen from the shelf. No one else was in the aisle. Kyle closed his eyes and tried to calm himself. *Am I just imagining this?* When Kyle opened his eyes, the "feminine hygiene" guy walked past the aisle and looked right at Kyle. *No, I'm not imagining things!*

Kyle gripped the boxcutter even tighter and walked to the back room. He needed to be alone. Kyle kept his composure until the door to the back room closed behind him; then, he bolted for the employee restroom and vomited. He started to shake. He felt cold. Whenever he closed his eyes, he felt that someone was behind him. Kyle was in a single-occupancy bathroom but had to look behind him just in case. No one was there. As soon as Kyle looked away, the feeling returned. Kyle looked again—around the room, under the sink, up at the ceiling. No one was there, but the feeling returned as soon as Kyle looked away.

For the next hour, Kyle shivered in the bathroom, glancing behind himself every few seconds. He was literally paralyzed with fear. The New World had broken Kyle. He could not focus on anything! His only movement was to glance behind him and prove to himself that no one would drown or otherwise kill him while he was alone in the bathroom.

I don't want to die! Kyle thought. *I can't leave the bathroom! They'll get me! I don't want to be alone! What am I going to do when night comes? I don't even own a weapon! How am I going to protect myself on my way home or while I'm sleeping? They're going to get me! I'm going to die! They're going to kill me!*

Something about that last thought struck him as strange, and Kyle could not understand why. He started to focus.

The new topic was strangely welcome. His mind slowed its racing. His breaths were deeper and measured. Fear's grip had loosened. The endless loop of fear and panic had been broken. Kyle could think again, and he found his answer: *If The New World had wanted to kill me, they would have done so already. Earlier this morning, I was nearly drowned in an abandoned warehouse. They didn't have to cut me loose; they could have let me drown. No one would have found me. They could have slit my throat and dumped me in the river. But they didn't. For some reason, they left me alive. If they're as good at making people disappear as Claire said and as my research confirmed, they would have had no trouble making me disappear if they wanted. The New World doesn't want me dead; they want me afraid—afraid enough not to act. But why? Why do they want me alive?*

Kyle sheathed the box cutter and dropped it into his pocket. He returned to work, puzzling over his revelation and wondering why he was still alive.

****

Six hours and a lunch break later, Kyle was no closer to an answer. He was becoming more annoyed and concerned the longer he thought about it.

As soon as Kyle stepped outside the store, he was even more irritated. His motorcycle was missing. He parked it in the fire lane, next to the fire hydrant, every morning. After several curses and dreading the walk home, Kyle remembered the early morning events and realized that he did not drive his bike here.

Kyle tried to remember the last time he saw his bike. *I remember driving to the bar... I even remember leaving the bar. But I don't remember anything after that. Did I leave my motorbike at the bar? Rather, did my kidnapper leave my motorbike at the bar?* Kyle groaned. The bar was on the other end of the city, and Kyle did not want to walk the city at night, especially that part of the city. *I'll borrow my grandma's car and drive back there.* Kyle resigned.

Kyle began the long walk to his grandmother's house. When he passed the warehouse, Kyle made sure to stay on the opposite side of the street. The short drive was much longer on foot. By the time Kyle reached his grandmother's house, the sun had set. As soon as he stepped inside, his grandmother assaulted him with questions.

"Where have you been? Dinner was ready an hour ago!"

"My bike wouldn't start," Kyle lied. "I'm going to take the car and get it." How he was hypothetically going to drive both the car and his motorcycle home, Kyle had not considered, and his grandmother did not ask.

"Have some dinner first. I'm going to the Wednesday night service. *Then I* will drive *my* car, and we'll see about your motorcycle."

"I'll eat later," Kyle said, grabbing the car keys from the key rack.

"I said to eat first!" his grandmother shouted after him.

"I'm not hungry!" Kyle retorted, still walking to the door.

"Come back here! I have to go to church!"

"I don't care!" Kyle cursed, slamming the front door behind him.

Kyle's phone vibrated the entire drive. Kyle did not bother to see who it was; it was probably his grandmother.

Kyle almost stopped at the warehouse, but the thought of drowning there again prevented him. Kyle had not seen his bike when he had escaped that morning. He would check later if he could not find the bike elsewhere.

Kyle drove to the bar. He remembered exactly where he had parked it, by the bar entrance next to the neighboring fence. It was no longer there. Kyle spat a curse.

He threw the car into park and examined the small patch of gravel. There were no footprints. There was no sign that his bike was ever there. Kyle looked down the street. His bike was not there either.

Kyle walked into the bar. The bartender was the same from the previous night. He recognized Kyle. "Welcome back, hero!" Kyle smiled and ordered a drink. While the bartender prepared it, Kyle asked if he had seen any motorcycles in the parking lot last night. The bartender thought for a minute.

"I don't recall seeing one. What did it look like?"

Kyle gave a description and added that "It was parked by the bar entrance."

"Oh, well, I didn't see anything when I left." Kyle thanked him and paid for his drink. He would need to check around the warehouse.

Kyle's brief search outside the warehouse was fruitless. He did not want to linger there any longer than a couple of minutes, especially at night. Kyle could hardly see anything in the darkness and decided against leaving the vehicle. Kyle's phone vibrated again, startling him. Kyle cursed and glanced at the phone. His grandmother had called nearly a dozen times. Josh and Claire had both texted him; Kyle did not bother reading either of their texts. In vain, Kyle gave one final glance for the sport bike and swore again. He would check for his motorcycle again in the morning.

When he arrived home, he half expected his grandmother to have called the police on him. She had not, but when he went inside, his grandmother was livid. She screamed at him about respect. Kyle ignored her. She would run out of steam soon enough. It took longer than expected, but eventually, she did. At the end of her tirade and a long period of silence, she spoke again, "Did you get your motorcycle?"

"No, someone stole it." He answered curtly.

"Oh, thank goodness," his grandmother responded. "I never liked you riding that thing anyway."

Kyle was about to curse her out, but he held his tongue. "I'll need the car for work tomorrow."

"Like you needed it tonight?" Joan mocked. "You touch that car again, and I *will* call the police." She was not joking, and Kyle knew it. Even if Kyle could prove his innocence, he would still look bad, and he did not want to jeopardize his military career any more than he already had. Kyle surrendered the car keys and went to his room, thinking evil thoughts.

****

Kyle woke more than an hour before he usually did for his walk to work. He skipped a shower and dressed. He needed to find his bike, and that meant looking around the warehouse.

The abandoned warehouse was the last place that Kyle wanted to go. Last night had been one long unceasing dream. When he fell asleep, Kyle immediately started dreaming about drowning. He dreamt that he was being held under the water by a dark figure. Kyle woke in a cold sweat and had trouble falling asleep after that. Whenever he closed his eyes, he could feel the water filling his lungs. When he did fall asleep again, he dreamed of being chased through the warehouse. His pursuer found Kyle and drowned him again. Again Kyle started awake. The rest of the night was filled with four or five similar dreams. The only solace for Kyle was that he was still alive.

But even that bothered Kyle. *Why not just kill me? No one would have found my body in the abandoned warehouse. Why cut my bonds and let me live? The New World left me alive for a purpose. What is it?*

Kyle pondered this while he walked to the warehouse, searched for his motorbike—which was nowhere to be found—and walked to the grocery store. *Perhaps they want to scare me into submission and coerce me into helping them?* Kyle scoffed at the idea. *I'll die before I help them!*

Or would I? Am I willing to exact more "revenge" on The New World in exchange for my life? They let me live this time. The next time, they might decide that I'm more work than it's worth.

I need to focus on finding my father. That's who I really need to punish.

Kyle arrived in the back room of the store and began his shift. *The New World is my only link to Dad, but that was based merely on my conjecture. It's possible that The New World is a distant link at best. My father could have sold everything to a pawn shop before it belonged to The New World. If I were in my father's position, I would be lounging on an island somewhere, surrounded by women and partying every night. My father probably hasn't even heard about my little drug bust, much less been "hurt" by it!*

Kyle punched a wall. *I haven't hurt my father at all! And I nearly died for it! And my irrational fear of drowning on dry land has made focusing on my father impossible!*

Kyle sighed to himself. *I'm working from the wrong angle. I need to find my father and hurt him directly. The New World is not my concern.*

****

Kyle was just about to break for lunch when Josh and Claire walked into the store. They made a beeline for him as soon as they saw him.

"So you *are* alive!" Claire said. Kyle immediately had a flash of nearly drowning on the previous morning but kept his smile.

"Of course!" He leaned forward to give Claire a hug. She did not resist.

"We were worried!" she said.

"Didn't you get our texts?" Josh asked.

Kyle had forgotten. "Oh, yes! I've just been so busy, I haven't had a chance to read them."

"We were a little concerned when you didn't respond," Josh continued. "And when you missed the prayer group last night."

Kyle swore silently. *I missed prayer group! Maybe I can make up for it and spend lunch with Claire instead.*

"I just completely forgot," Kyle answered.

Claire started speaking in a low voice. "We were afraid that something had happened to you."

Again, Kyle had a flashback of nearly drowning.

"Nope! I'm all right."

"Claire told me that you had asked about The New World a few weeks back," Josh said. "We saw what you did on the news, helping with the drug bust. I'm surprised they didn't hurt you…or worse." There was a deep gravity in Josh's voice. Kyle relived a massive flashback. He could feel himself drowning in complete safety! With great effort, Kyle suppressed the nightmare and returned to the grocery aisle.

"I was just about to go on my lunch break. Do you want to join me?" Kyle looked right at Claire when he asked the question.

"Absolutely!" Claire said. Immediately, her face revealed that she had meant that less enthusiastically than her voice betrayed.

"I have to get back to work," Josh said. "I'll see you

later."

Claire and Kyle headed for the door. Josh grabbed Kyle's arm. "Be very careful," Josh whispered, his eyes serious and wide with concern.

Kyle wretched his arm from Josh's grip but nodded in agreement. "I'm done with them," he replied.

Josh's eyes grew even wider. "They did do something to you, didn't they!" Josh whispered.

Kyle glanced back at Claire. She had reached the door and was looking back at them. Kyle glared at Josh. "Don't tell Claire," he hissed. He left Josh for Claire.

"We can talk more later," Josh shouted nonchalantly after Kyle. Kyle did not bother turning around.

****

The lunch was better than Kyle had expected. He and Claire talked the entire time. Kyle was amazed at how much he had missed this over the last couple of days, especially in light of nearly dying. Claire had said repeatedly how much she had prayed that Kyle was safe and how glad she was to see him again. As soon as Kyle heard that, he promised himself that he would never confront The New World again. The entirety of Kyle's being agreed. Kyle did not want to lose Claire.

****

Kyle started awake. He had dreamt of drowning again. This time, he imagined that he was at a lake with some college friends. They had gone swimming, but Kyle had forgotten how to swim. He sank to the bottom of the lake and drowned in the cold, murky darkness. Kyle spent at least half an hour calming himself before returning to sleep.

A second time, Kyle woke in a panic. He dreamt that the Caucasian caught in the drug bust had found him at his grandmother's house and drowned him in the bathroom tub. Kyle had trouble getting to sleep after that dream. Every time he closed his eyes, Kyle could hear the water and feel it in his lungs.

Again, Kyle dreamed that he was drowning. This time, he was trapped in a glass box. His feet were caught in something that held him beneath the water's surface. Outside the container, dark figures watched Kyle drown. This time, Kyle awoke just minutes before his alarm sounded. Kyle swore into the darkness and sat on his bed. *It's going to be yet another long day.*

And another long walk to work. Why does the culture require me to take a shower before I walk all the way to work? How many days in a row can I skip a shower? I could go back to bed for a few minutes. I wonder if my boss will even notice... With my luck, he'll choose today to become observant. Kyle headed for the shower.

Kyle turned on the water and jumped into the shower. As soon as the water touched his face, Kyle suffered a massive flashback of drowning in the warehouse. Kyle collapsed onto the bottom of the tub and groped for the shower knob to shut off the water. Kyle lay in a fetal position at the bottom of the tub for a long time, trying to calm himself. *I can't even shower... I can't sleep, and I can't shower.* The mental and physical fatigue was starting to wear on Kyle. *What has The New World done to me?*

Kyle lay where he was and cried.

****

For the next three days, Kyle woke up at least once with a dream about drowning or being drowned.

For the next three days, Kyle avoided splashing any water on his face during his showers.

For the next three days, Kyle received incessant texts from Josh about meeting and talking about what had happened. Kyle did not need to talk; he needed to move forward with his life. He ignored all Josh's texts. On Sunday, Josh cornered him. Without his motorbike, Kyle was stuck carpooling with his grandmother and had to wait until she had finished talking with every single person in the congregation. This morning, she was explaining that she had missed the Wednesday evening service because her grandson had stolen her car. Kyle had slipped outside to avoid the judgmental glances during and after the story. Josh had silently followed him.

"Hello, Kyle," Josh said.

Kyle retreated further into the churchyard. "I'm fine, Josh. I don't need your sympathy."

Josh followed him. "I just want to let you know...I'm here for you, man."

Kyle spun around; he was angry now. "I got that—from all the texts you sent me!"

"I'm just worried about you. That's all," Josh said. He approached Kyle slowly and whispered, "I know how ruthless they can be."

Kyle experienced another flash from drowning. This time, he relived the whole experience, including his captor's voice. When he returned to reality, Kyle realized that he was unconsciously holding his breath.

Josh noticed. "They did do something to you, didn't they?" Josh's voice was pained.

Kyle tried to speak; his voice cracked with emotion. He nodded. "Did you tell Claire?" Kyle finally asked.

"You asked me not to," Josh answered. *At least Josh did that,* Kyle thought. Josh continued, "Kyle, I can help you. Don't go through this alone." Josh pulled out his phone. "I'm going to text you my address. Come over anytime, day or night. I'm serious about that."

"That's pretty cool, Josh. I'll think about it. But I'm not going to do anything more with The New World. I have too much to live for." At that moment, Claire exited the church. She did not see them, but the two men saw her. Kyle could tell by the smile on Josh's face that Josh understood what he meant.

"Can I pray for you?" Josh asked.

I don't need prayer! I don't need your god! Kyle thought. But for some reason, Kyle said yes instead.

Josh rested a hand on Kyle's shoulder and prayed, "Oh,

Lord, I ask that You be with Kyle. Help him to overcome the trials in his life. Help him to forget the images. Heal him from whatever happened to him. I ask that he draws close to You during this time. Be with him, God, in the days ahead. In Jesus' name, amen."

Kyle actually closed his eyes for that prayer. He looked just in time to see Claire pull out of the church parking lot. Kyle looked around the churchyard. His grandmother was probably still inside the church. The last thing he wanted to do was waste the afternoon with her; the evenings were hard enough. "Do you think I could come over now?" he asked Josh.

Josh was surprised but glad. "Sure! Should we let your grandmother know?"

Kyle pulled out his phone and shot her a text. His duty was done. "Let's go."

CHAPTER 8

"You have a nice apartment," Kyle said when they had arrived.

"It's not bad. Technically, it's my mom's place, but now that I have a job, I pay most of the bills. So take that as you will. You want anything to drink?"

"Sure, I'll have soda. I don't know how you do it. If I had the funds, I'd just get my own place." Then Kyle thought, *And I would swear out anyone who was freeloading off me.* His phone started to buzz. That was probably his grandmother. He ignored it.

"I don't make that much," replied Josh. "The rent is too expensive around here. It's cheaper to split the costs with someone else." Josh produced two cans of soda. "It's not always easy, but we have good boundaries. That reduces a lot of the tension. It also helps that my mom treats me like an adult and not a freeloader. Plus, it's nice to have someone else to help with the laundry, make dinner, wash dishes, stuff like that."

"So the roles have been reversed. That would drive me

crazy." Kyle smiled.

Josh shrugged.

Kyle looked away. *I don't want to make small talk with Josh,* Kyle thought. *Why did I even bother coming here? Oh, yeah... Because anything's better than being stuck in the same house with my grandmother.* Kyle looked about the room. Kyle glanced out the window. The view was what he least expected. Josh's apartment had a perfect view of the abandoned warehouse. Kyle recognized it immediately.

Kyle could feel his lungs filling with water. His breaths became short and quick. He was paralyzed. *I can't move! I can't free myself!* Kyle held his breath. *I can't breathe! I'm going to die! I can't hold my breath any longer!*

Kyle felt someone grab his shoulder. Kyle spun around. He clenched his soda can in his fist. *I'm not going back to the warehouse without a fight!*

Kyle almost clobbered a very startled Josh.

"Are you okay?" Josh asked rhetorically. "I called your name several times, and you didn't respond."

Kyle closed his eyes and relaxed his muscles. He took several deep breaths, but they hardly calmed him.

Kyle hated The New World. He had never been so angry at anyone in his life—including his father. His father had hurt him; they had damaged him. His father had made him stumble; they had made him fall. His father had taught him to be strong; they had made him weak. The New World had broken him.

The New World had damaged his mind. He could no

longer control his thoughts. He froze when he saw the abandoned warehouse. He could barely stand the sound of running water. He had flashbacks of dying when water touched his face.

The New World had crushed his spirit. Kyle had vowed to focus on finding his father and avenging himself. But he could no longer focus on anything other than drowning and a looming concern of death.

The New World had tainted his soul. Kyle was afraid—afraid of them. The New World had stolen his will to fight against them. They had made him cower in fear.

The New World had weakened his body. The nightmares and flashbacks had affected him. The lack of sleep and constant stress were starting to manifest themselves. The strain on his body was becoming difficult to bear.

A tear escaped from Kyle's closed eyes.

"What did they do to you?" Josh asked.

Kyle did not hear him.

A spark returned to Kyle's eyes. He was not completely undone. He was not going to bow to The New World. He would not be broken! Kyle brushed aside his vows to avoid The New World and focus on his father.

He would kill whoever had drowned him. He would destroy The New World, even if it took him the rest of his life! Revenge on his father could wait. Kyle needed to redeem his life first. He was determined to fight for it. If he did not, he would never again reach the full measure of a man, and life would not be worth living. On that, his whole being agreed. Kyle's mind, spirit, soul, and body needed to heal and overcome the trauma from the previous night. That was the first step. He needed to restore his mastery over the "Four Qualities of Man." Otherwise, he would be unable to continue his mission of vengeance against The New World and his father.

Kyle opened his eyes and brushed Josh's hand off his shoulder. "I've got to go," Kyle merely said. With that, he fled the apartment. Josh called after him. Kyle ignored the noise. He raced down the stairs. Josh continued to call, but the cries landed on deaf ears.

Kyle was thinking. *I need to disrupt The New World again. How, I have no idea. I'll think of something later. In the meantime, I need to confront my fears.* Kyle bolted out the building door and turned toward the warehouse behind Josh's apartment. A gravel strip about twenty feet wide ran between the rear of the warehouse and a wooden fence, separating the gravel access road from the apartment buildings. The area was starting to look familiar.

About halfway down the gravel path, Kyle found the door he had used to escape his prison. He only hesitated a moment before marching inside. The building was still dark, even in the middle of the day. With minimal difficulty, Kyle wound his way through the warehouse to his residence four mornings ago. Kyle felt his stomach lurch.

The place was untouched. The sink was still full with water. The duct tape was still rolled where Kyle had thrown it. The zip ties that had bound his hands were still on the floor. They were law enforcement grade zip ties and had most definitely been cut. *The New World definitely wants me alive. But why?* Kyle could feel the adrenaline rush into his system.

Kyle looked at the pipes. He could tell where his feet and hands had been bound. He could envision where his head had hung in the sink below the still water. Kyle's heart was pounding furiously now.

Kyle took a deep breath and closed his eyes. *The ordeal is over now. I'm safe. I'm alive.* Kyle's mind was still causing his body to panic. Kyle repeated the words to himself. *I'm safe. I'm—*

The phone in Kyle's pocket buzzed, startling him and undoing the effect of his calming phrases. Kyle swore and glanced at his phone. Josh was calling. Kyle swore again and shut off the device.

Kyle resumed repeating the phrases for several minutes. His fear was starting to subside. Kyle opened his eyes, and the fear returned. Kyle closed his eyes again. The fear dissipated faster this time. Kyle opened his eyes again and repeated the process. Kyle was conquering his fear.

Eventually, Kyle had to look around his former prison to summon the fear. Then, Kyle recalled the events from that night. Finally, Kyle dunked his head into the same water that had almost drowned him. Each new frontier caused a massive flashback; Kyle regained control each time. After five hours, Kyle could inhale the water in the sink without a knot forming in his stomach. Kyle coughed out the water and smiled to himself. He was healed! He had restored his mind, spirit, soul, and body! He knew that he could overcome.

Kyle turned his back to the near-death chamber and left the building. He would return tomorrow and prove that he had conquered his fears and had regained control of his being, especially his mind. Kyle stepped into the gravel alleyway. He walked down the alley toward his workplace, giving one final look around the building for his motorcycle. He circled the building and looked along the opposite wall. His bike was nowhere in sight; Kyle was unsurprised. The New World had probably sold it or scrapped the parts, just like the cars.

I wish that I could remember more of that night after I'd left the bar. Kyle lamented. *I do remember leaving the bar, but the memory is almost like looking through a fog. I think that I remember starting my motorcycle... Or am I just creating that memory?*

What happened after that? I'm usually good at holding my alcohol. Did I just fall asleep? I wouldn't have slept through being dragged to the warehouse and hung upside down...would I?

Was I...drugged?

That's a scary thought! I didn't eat anything except what was at my grandma's house, and I only drank at the bar. Maybe someone at the bar had been waiting for me!

Kyle started the walk to his grandmother's house. He had just reached the street corner of the warehouse when a police vehicle, sirens screeching, swerved off the main road onto the street Kyle was about to cross. Kyle stopped at the edge of the road just in time. The squad car did not even slow down.

If Kyle had not been satisfied with his recovery, he would have shouted and flashed obscenities at the driver. Instead, he watched the car and noticed a familiar face in the passenger seat. It was one of the cops from the bar; the last night Kyle had seen his motorbike. *Nick!* Kyle thought. *He bought me that drink! And congratulated me for stopping The New World!*

Maybe Nick *drugged me! That traitor! We're supposed to be on the same side!*

I need proof, one way or the other. I can't follow him now. I'll do that tomorrow.

Kyle arrived at his grandmother's house to another lecture from his grandmother. She yelled at him for texting her that he was leaving instead of talking to her and not even telling her where he was going. She further berated him for not answering her calls or calling her back. Kyle merely said that he had been talking to Josh and had not felt his phone vibrate. Those responses diffused part of their conversation. Joan hoped that Josh would be a good influence on Kyle.

That night, Kyle did not have any nightmares.

****

Kyle looked obviously conspicuous having to walk everywhere, but his grandmother was adamant about Kyle not using her car. As soon as he left work, Kyle skulked around the police precinct, waiting for Nick. *Finally!* Kyle spied Nick walking with his partner from the precinct to a squad car. From behind a tree, Kyle watched the vehicle start and drive from the parking lot down the street. Kyle moved from the tree down the sidewalk. The squad car turned down a side road. Kyle sped down the sidewalk as naturally as he could. He rounded the street corner just in time to see Nick's squad car make a second turn, beyond his line of sight. Kyle fell too far behind. He was not going to be able to follow Nick on foot.

Kyle quit his chase and returned to the abandoned warehouse. His heart stopped at his first sight of the warehouse and again when he saw the sink. Besides that, he was cured.

The next day, Kyle planned ahead. During his lunch break, he researched Nick. He eventually recalled what he thought was Nick's last name and found several possible matches within the city. One of the profiles rented a small apartment in the heart of the city close to the precinct. That seemed like a good place to start.

Kyle watched the clock. As soon as his shift was over, he raced to his alleged drugger's residence. The subject was on the fifth floor; the mailboxes confirmed this. Kyle paused before racing up the stairs. He rang the door buzzer for Nick's apartment three or four times. There was no answer.

Kyle found Nick's apartment door. The building hallway rounded a corner twenty feet to his left. Kyle knocked on the door and sprinted around the corner. He listened; he did not hear the door open. He peeked cautiously around the corner toward the doorway. Kyle was alone.

Nick—if this even is the right "Nick"—is definitely not at home, Kyle realized.

Kyle stood square with the door. He had not really planned this far ahead. He had wanted to break into the apartment but was now recognizing that as a bad idea. *Regardless of whether Nick really is colluding with The New World, I would be risking my Air Force career again.* Kyle laughed at himself. *I guess I've also seen too many movies with a person sneaking around someone else's apartment and getting caught when that person returns home.*

I can't call the police, at least not yet, anyway. I don't have any evidence. Am I just going to wait here until Nick comes back?

Maybe I should *break into the apartment. I can be in and out of the apartment without getting caught. Let's see... I might be able to climb through the fire escape if the window is open. I might be able to pry open the lock with my credit card—*

Kyle did not have much longer to think. Someone was coming up the stairs. Kyle hoped it was not Nick. Kyle unplanted his feet and ducked around the corner of the hallway just in time.

Kyle plastered himself against the wall and listened to the footsteps. They stopped farther down the hallway. It sounded like they had stopped at Nick's door.

Kyle gingerly poked his cell phone camera around the

corner of the hallway and watched. The footsteps belonged to a Hispanic man. He had stopped in front of Nick's door and was doing something with the doormat. Kyle could not tell what he was doing. Kyle started recording and peeked around the corner himself. The man appeared to be putting something underneath the doormat. Kyle looked at the man. He seemed familiar. Suddenly, Kyle recognized him from the other night. *He's the other man from the drug bust—the one that slipped away!*

Kyle released an uncontrolled gasp and disappeared around the corner as soon as he realized what he had done. Kyle's heart raced. He listened for sounds above that of his heart. *Did he hear me?* Kyle heard a gun being cocked. *He did hear me! If he sees me, I'm dead!*

Kyle clenched his phone and sprinted noiselessly down the hall. His ROTC field training and paintball experience were finally useful for something. The hallway turned left, and Kyle followed. Kyle could not hear if anyone was behind him. He sprinted as fast as he could. The hallway turned right. Kyle followed the hallway as it wove back and forth along the edge of the jagged building. Twice, Kyle found stairs and climbed to a higher level before continuing his race. The second time, Kyle climbed the stairs to the roof. The door was locked. Kyle did not move. There was nowhere else to go. Kyle listened. All was quiet, except for the furious pounding of his heart and his sharp breaths. A door far below him opened and closed. Kyle's heart rate increased. The steps receded; the steps were going down.

A few minutes later, another door opened. These steps grew louder. They stopped at another floor and left the stairwell. Kyle heard footsteps many times, but no one ever found him.

Kyle waited at the top of the stairs for nearly an hour. During that time, Kyle stopped recording and watched his video. He could see that the thug was putting something under the doormat. Kyle needed to find out what. Dauntless, Kyle left his hiding place.

When Kyle arrived at Nick's hallway, he became more cautious. Kyle peeked around the corner. The hall was empty. Kyle crept over to the doormat and lifted one of the corners. Four small flat packets of white powder fit snugly in the corner of the mat.

That was all the confirmation that Kyle needed. He hoped that it was all the police needed as well.

Kyle pulled out his phone. "This is 911. What is your emergency?" a voice asked.

"You have a dirty cop," Kyle began.

****

The police took some convincing, but when the internal affairs task force arrived and confirmed that the packets contained cocaine, they wasted no time. Immediately, several small, imperceptible cameras were placed in Nick's hallway, waiting for him to return home. Meanwhile, Kyle was directed to the precinct and was asked for his version of the story; Kyle stressed that the cocaine was placed by the Latino who escaped the previous bust. Kyle's phone was confiscated and the video analyzed. The investigators checked Kyle's fingerprints against the ones on the cocaine packets and the fingerprints they found in both vehicles from the drug bust. The prints on the packets matched the fingerprints in one of the cars, confirming Kyle's story. For a second time, the police vindicated him.

Several times, Kyle was instructed not to say anything about the dirty cop to anyone. Kyle easily agreed. He wanted Nick to receive the judgment coming to him.

Kyle was "allowed" to stay at the police station until Nick returned home. Kyle assumed that the police wanted him there as a scapegoat if Nick did not retrieve the cocaine. This was confirmed when he was ushered into a separate holding room and was not allowed to view the proceedings captured on the cameras.

A few minutes later, Kyle heard a chorus of groans from the other room. Nick had taken the bait.

Kyle clapped his hands and laughed. He cursed The New World. *I've stabbed them again!*

Kyle was retrieved and was asked to give his eyewitness account again as an official witness. Kyle was more than happy to do so.

****

Joan was livid about Kyle's late nights and about having to retrieve him from the police station—again. And she made sure that Kyle knew it.

Kyle knew this would happen. He had planned to walk

home and bask in his own glory, but some good samaritan at the police station had called his grandmother and asked for her to drive Kyle home. Right now, Kyle wanted to strangle them.

Being in high spirits, Kyle tried explaining the good that he was doing for society. Joan was less impressed now than she had been the first time. And she made sure that Kyle knew that too. She finished by saying that she was not going to "tolerate any more of your being arrested" and that Kyle could "walk home if you get arrested again." At that, Kyle swore at her, cursed The New World, and said that he would "do it all again if it put more of those animals behind bars!"

As soon as he had finished his tirade, Joan pulled over. Kyle was walking the rest of the way home. Kyle enjoyed the silent walk. The separation from his grandmother was almost reward enough. With every step, Kyle praised himself for another strike against The New World.

When he reached his grandmother's house, the lights were all dark. Kyle tried the door; it was locked. He used his key, but the deadbolt had already been drawn. Kyle swore at his grandmother.

Kyle tried all the windows on the ground level. They were all locked. Kyle hoisted himself up the tree and onto the porch roof and tried the window to his room. That window was also locked. Kyle swore louder. She *must have locked it!*

Kyle circled the house and pounded his grandmother's bedroom window mercilessly, but the house remained dark and quiet. Joan had probably removed her hearing aids; a bomb could detonate, and she would never hear it.

Kyle shouted a curse into the night but was met only with silence.

CHAPTER 9

Up to this point, that was the second worst night of Kyle's life. Kyle tried to sleep on the porch swing, but it was too small for him to get comfortable. The heat was unbearable. He had already started to sweat from his forced march to his grandmother's house. After only a few minutes on the porch swing, he had soaked through his shirt.

Kyle threw aside his shirt and moved from the swing to the floor. The wood was rough and radiated the heat back onto him. He kept turning, trying to find a cool spot, but still could not get comfortable.

The restless night only fueled Kyle's anger. *I'm never going to get to sleep out here! And I'm definitely not going to stay here on the front porch. I still have the key to Finneman's Market that my boss gave me. I'll crash there for the night and get some sleep. Anything's better than staying here!*

Kyle snatched his shirt from where he had tossed it and redressed. Kyle glared at the house and spat at the door. He swore that he would never speak to his grandmother again.

Despite his frustration, Kyle enjoyed his long walk

alone. He continued praising himself on a job well done. When Kyle arrived at the road near the warehouse where he had realized that Nick had drugged him, Kyle laughed and cursed him in the darkness. *No one else is going to get in my way! I can overcome them! Everything that The New World has done to me, I have undone. I'm not afraid of them! When they tried to break me, I just returned stronger. I am untouchable!*

Kyle walked through the alley behind the warehouse. He had nothing to fear. Kyle glanced at the apartment buildings to his left. He thought of Josh and remembered his kindness from Sunday. Kyle felt sorry for Josh. Kyle did not need a god to make him strong; he could make himself strong.

Kyle looked from the apartment buildings. The alley was barely lit. The only streetlights were at either end of the long gravel strip. In the limited light, Kyle could see two figures at the far end of the alley, walking toward him. Kyle's pace briefly lost its rhythm before continuing toward the silhouettes. Kyle felt a knot in his stomach as soon as he made his choice. *Who would be walking down an alley at this time of night?* thought Kyle. As he approached them, he realized the characters were two rough scrappers. Kyle looked around. The brick wall for the warehouse lined the right side of the alley, and the tall wooden fence lined the left. Kyle continued walking. He did not want to turn his back on the two "thugs," especially in the darkness. Kyle was not afraid, but the knot in his stomach continued to grow. Kyle moved closer to the brick wall. The men moved to intercept him. Kyle moved toward the wood fence. The men followed suit. Kyle became afraid.

When the groups converged, Kyle tried to walk around them, but they would not let him pass.

"Let me by," Kyle said.

"Why?" the bigger Caucasian smiled, towering over Kyle. Kyle wished he had turned around when he could. He did not want to get mugged. Kyle might be able to outrun the bigger Caucasian, but the smaller Caucasian looked like he was built for sprinting. Kyle looked behind him. Three other silhouettes had followed him into the alley. *I'm trapped!* Kyle realized. *Wait...! This isn't a mugging! This is The New World! I have to get out of here!*

Kyle looked at the warehouse. His eyes had adjusted in the darkness. *The door to the warehouse must be around here somewhere...* He found the door; it was no more than thirty feet away. Kyle flew to the entrance.

Halfway there, something caught his legs. Kyle tried to make his legs move, but they seemed stuck together. The ground raced upward to meet him. Kyle moved his hands to break his fall; they would not move fast enough. Kyle shut his eyes and braced for the impact. Kyle slid, his face, arms, and legs scraping against the gravel. Kyle twisted onto his back. The smaller Caucasian had run after him and grabbed Kyle's legs. He pounced onto Kyle's chest and started punching him in the face.

Kyle tried to defend himself. He hit his assailant. He tried to push the attacker off his chest. Then the bigger Caucasian arrived. He knelt above Kyle's head and grabbed Kyle's wrists. Kyle mustered all his strength to regain control of his arms but to no avail. The bigger Caucasian effortlessly pinned Kyle's arms to the ground above his head.

The onslaught continued. Kyle tried to shout for help, but each cry was cut short by another blow. Each punch stung the fresh wounds from the gravel. Kyle tasted blood. He felt something give in the cheekbone below his right eye. His jaw did not feel right. The other gangsters just watched.

After a minute, the posse leader spoke.

"Stop," he ordered. The pummelling stopped. "Get off him," he instructed.

Kyle's chest and arms were liberated. Kyle slowly stood. He spat at the ground. He could not see it, but he could taste a lot of blood. Kyle straightened to his full height and defiantly looked the leader in the eye. Kyle did not recognize the leader—he could hardly see anything beyond silhouettes in the darkness—but the voice matched the one he had heard the night he was nearly drowned in the warehouse.

"You've caused a lot of trouble for us lately," the leader said. "I want it to stop."

"If it doesn't?" Kyle asked. The leader looked at the others and nodded. The bigger Caucasian grabbed Kyle and locked him in a full nelson. The other grunts pounded and beat on the rest of Kyle's defenseless body. Kyle felt several ribs break. Someone jabbed Kyle in the stomach. Kyle gagged. At an unseen command, the bigger Caucasian released Kyle and let him fall to his knees. Kyle vomited twice. When he had finished, the bigger Caucasian yanked Kyle back to his feet. The leader stepped toward Kyle. He lifted Kyle's chin until Kyle looked him in the eye.

"If it doesn't stop," the leader said, "what you got today won't compare with what will happen. I may not be allowed to kill you, but everything else is fair game." He dropped Kyle's chin and walked away. The others followed. The bigger Caucasian dropped Kyle, and Kyle collapsed onto the gravel. He tried to rise, but a foot crushed his body back into the ground. The bigger Caucasian rifled through Kyle's pockets and stole all the cash in his wallet. Kyle again tried to push himself off the ground but had gravel scuffed into his face. Kyle collapsed again and listened to his attackers walk away.

****

Kyle could not move. He did not have the energy. He was in so much pain. He lay on the rough gravel. His body throbbed. Breathing was painful. The only part of his body that did not hurt was his feet. Kyle attempted to stand. He began to push himself off the ground. The throbbing changed to agony! His body screamed for him to stop! His arms buckled. He fell to the ground again. Another rib cracked. Kyle screamed. He started to sob. Kyle was angry. He cursed his father. *Why did Dad have to rob and leave us? If he hadn't, I never would have been forced to live in Florida with my grandmother! I never would have had to fight The New World! I would not be lying half dead in an alley! My father is responsible for all of this!* The thoughts were irrational; Kyle did not care.

Kyle shouted into the darkness. He cursed his father for leaving and blamed his mother for her weakness. He cursed The New World and all that they had done to him. Kyle was about to curse the God that he did not believe existed when he heard footsteps on the alley gravel. *Oh no,* Kyle resignedly thought. *They've heard my curses and have returned to finish the job.* Kyle sighed. *This is the end. At least all my problems will be over.* Kyle uttered one final curse for his father.

The footsteps stopped. "Kyle?" a voice asked. "Kyle!" the voice shouted. The footsteps raced down the alley growing louder with each iteration. The footsteps stopped next to Kyle. "Kyle!" the voice repeated. The voice belonged to Josh. "Kyle, are you all right?" The obvious answer was no; Kyle did not speak. *Why did The New World let me live? Why not just kill me?* Josh knelt on the gravel and rolled Kyle onto his side. Kyle again screamed in pain. Josh's eyes were wide. Kyle was covered with blood. "What happened?"

For the first time, Kyle spoke, "The New World." If nothing else, he could make Josh hate his attackers. Josh pulled out his cell phone. Kyle painfully grabbed Josh's hand. "No. No police."

"You need a *doctor*," Josh argued.

"I'm fine." With renewed energy, Kyle attempted to stand. This time, Kyle supported himself on his hands and knees without collapsing back onto the ground. Kyle gritted his teeth and ignored his body's anguish. Josh pocketed his phone and helped Kyle stand. Kyle was shaky on his feet. He was unable to take a single step without Josh's support.

When Kyle fled Josh's apartment on Sunday, he had arrived in the alley in less than a minute; now, even with Josh's support, they did not arrive back at the apartment for another twenty minutes. Even at that pace and with Josh's help, Kyle needed to rest at the end of the alley. Josh knew that Kyle was worse than he had claimed. When The New World threatened anyone, they hurt them...or worse.

Josh only spoke to applaud Kyle's progress to his apartment and to ask if Kyle needed a break. When they finally reached the apartment, Josh found a towel and gave it to Kyle. Kyle sank into the couch and dabbed the wounds on his face. Josh sat on the other end of the couch and watched.

In the absence of the suffering brought by walking and of the concentration to conceal his injuries from Josh, Kyle began to process the events of the previous nights. *Twice, I've fought The New World. Twice, I've injured them. Twice, they've attacked me. Twice, they've let me live.*

That bothered Kyle. *Why not just kill me and be done with it? The New World has no issue with killing. There has to be a reason.*

Kyle closed his eyes. The dizziness in his head began to dissipate. Kyle needed to concentrate. As much as he wanted to forget every moment of the past hour, he tried to recall as much as he could about the latest attack. Kyle remembered everything. *I remember the dark alley. I remember the two bruisers blocking my path. I remember them and the other thugs from The New World hurting me.* Kyle could feel their wounds now. *No one said anything—nothing meaningful, at least—except for their leader. He wanted me to stop provoking The New World. What were his words, exactly? "You've caused a lot of trouble for us lately. I want it to stop."*

More pain. They hurt me again. Kyle's body throbbed with the recollection. His mind skipped ahead. *What else did the leader say? "If it doesn't stop, what you got today won't compare with what will happen. I may not be allowed to kill you, but everything else is fair game."*

"I may not be allowed to kill you." That's a telling statement. But what does it mean? Is someone else making the calls? Someone above this "leader"? Whoever it is, they want me alive for some purpose. Kyle silently swore at the unknown enemy. Kyle hated the idea of being anyone's pawn.

Kyle remembered the rest of the quote. *"But everything else is fair game." I don't like that part.* Neither did Kyle's mind or body. *If what I've experienced so far was just a warning, I'm headed for more pain and injury if I do anything other than leave The New World alone.*

Kyle finished wiping his wounds. Even in the dim apartment light, Josh noticed that Kyle's wounds were worse than he had initially thought. Kyle looked like he had been in an accident with his motorcycle. All Kyle's exposed skin was covered with abrasions. Blood poured from his nose and mouth. Kyle's face did not even look symmetrical. He seemed to have difficulty breathing—and it was not due to exhaustion!

Josh pulled out his phone again and dialed three numbers.

"Put the phone away!" Kyle ordered. Josh ignored him and relayed his address and the situation to the operator.

"They're on their way," Josh said, covering the mouthpiece. Kyle painfully snatched the phone from Josh and ended the call.

Josh swore. "Sorry. I didn't mean that. The operator was still on the line!"

"Don't apologize," Kyle spat. He hesitated, wondering if his snappy retort had revealed his true disdain for Josh's religion. At the moment, Kyle no longer cared if Josh knew or not, and Kyle had no desire to conceal his feelings. Kyle swore at Josh. "I don't need you, and I don't need your god!" Kyle shouted. The ruse was finally over. Kyle did not need to pretend anymore.

Josh gave a slow sigh. "I know," he said.

Kyle shrugged. "You did? When'd you find out?"

"I always knew. Ever since you first joined us at the college prayer group."

That surprised Kyle. "You knew all this time?" Kyle asked. Josh nodded. *Josh knew all this time? But he treated me the same as everyone else?* Kyle thought. *Why did he do that?*

Josh looked like he had something to say, but he said nothing. Neither spoke for several seconds, allowing Kyle to ponder the new information, but no answer came.

"I'm always here for you, man," Josh finally said. "I want you to know that. If you ever want to talk about anything—Christianity, work, your father—" Kyle froze.

"Who told you?" Kyle demanded.

"Claire," Josh answered again. Kyle remained indignant. He was glad it had not been his grandmother; he had forgotten Claire had heard it from her. Still, Claire had no right to tell others about his life.

"She's worried about you," Josh continued. "And so am I."

Kyle turned, revealing that he would later develop a black eye, and stared at Josh. "Seriously?" he clarified.

"Yeah, we're your friends. We care about you. Claire and I have been praying for you since we met you."

"Yeah? Well, your prayers seem to be working," Kyle patronized. Josh dropped his gaze. "Tell me this," Kyle continued. "Claire told you my story. She told you about how my father robbed and left me and about how my mom was weak and killed herself. I was nearly kicked out of ROTC and lost my home, college, friends, girlfriend, and my old way of life. But god did nothing. I'm stuck down here with my grandmother, for lack of a better option, and the police have had no luck in finding my father. And, on top of all that, I've almost been killed by The New World...*twice*! Now, have you been praying for all that, or has your god been ignoring your prayers and choosing to torment me?"

Josh did not speak for several minutes. "I believe...that God allows bad things to happen...to show us that this isn't how life is supposed to be. And that those bad things are to point us to God."

Kyle scoffed. "Yeah, right!" He looked to the ceiling and shouted, "Well, it's not working!"

Josh hesitated briefly before continuing. "I don't tell this story to many people… I used to be just like you. I didn't care about God. My life was fine without Him. But there was one friend, John, who was different. There was a constant happiness or joy around him. When I asked him, he said that 'it was Jesus,' but I didn't care.

"One day, all that changed. John and I were driving together, and a drunk driver, a member of The New World, ironically, ran us off the road. Medically speaking, both of us died, but we had vastly different experiences. John went to heaven, and I…" Josh shuttered at the recollection. "…and I…went to hell." Kyle saw the truth in Josh's eyes; he could see that Josh believed his near-death experience was true, regardless of what Kyle thought. Josh continued, "The worst part wasn't the pain or the heat or the flames; the worst part was feeling completely and utterly alone and knowing that I would never feel joy or happiness ever again."

Josh stared into space and absentmindedly rubbed a spot on his right arm. "God brought me back to life and literally rescued me from hell. John and I spoke about our experiences, but he later died and is now in heaven with Jesus. Before he died, John explained everything to me, and I, too, asked God to forgive me for my sins.

"Every day, I wish that I never had to experience hell; I

wish that John wasn't dead; I wish that we had never been run off the road by The New World. But I know now that if none of that had happened, I never would have come to know God."

"But your friend is still dead," Kyle interrupted. "Your god just let him die, and you're okay with that?"

"No, I'm not okay with that. I still ask why. But every time I ask that, I realize that God allowed John to die so that I could spend eternity in heaven with both Him and John and not in hell away from them both."

"So your god loved you more than John? John and I are expendable, and you're not."

"No, God loves all of us—you, me, and John. God just knew that if I experienced hell and if John died, then I would realize how much God loved me and would choose to follow Him. On the flip side, God also decided not to have John suffer through any more pain or sickness or sadness on earth after the car accident; so, God decided to take John to heaven."

Kyle mused on what Josh had said. He had never heard Christianity explained this way before now. If nothing else, it was an incredibly interesting mythology.

The ambulance siren wailed briefly down the street. The paramedics would arrive soon.

"Kyle," Josh started. "I don't know why all this is happening to you. I don't know why God let it happen. But I think He is trying to get your attention—the same way He used John's death and my experience in hell to get my attention. He loves you, and He wants you to know that He loves you enough to die for you. He died so that you could escape hell and live in heaven, just like I did. All you need to do is choose to love the Lord with all your heart, soul, mind, and strength."

Kyle's heart stopped. *What!* thought Kyle. *Those are the "Four Qualities of Man"! How did Josh know them!* Kyle tried to ask, but the words stuck in his throat. "Why'd you say that?" Kyle demanded, finding his voice. The siren gave one final announcement of its arrival, drowning Kyle's question. Josh had moved to open the door for the paramedics; he had not heard the question, but he knew that Kyle had spoken.

"We're up here!" Josh shouted down the stairway. Kyle could hear the paramedics on the floors below. Josh turned back to Kyle. "What was that?" Josh asked Kyle, half distracted.

"Who told you to say that?" Kyle demanded again. He stood from the couch to emphasize his question.

Kyle immediately regretted trying to stand. His joints were stiff; his body throbbed; he was in so much pain! Even with the adrenaline in his veins, he was having difficulty standing. He knew that he should sit down, but he needed Josh's attention.

The commotion on the stairs below was louder now. "We're up here!" Josh shouted again. He turned to Kyle again. "To say what?"

Kyle did not feel well. His mouth was suddenly dry, and he felt short of breath. His mind started to cloud. He had lost too much blood. But he would not let Josh ignore his question. "About your mind…soul…" Dark shadows filled Kyle's vision. "…and…and…" Kyle's legs buckled, and he felt himself falling.

He heard himself hit the carpet, though he could not feel it.

A great distance away, he could hear Josh screaming for help.

CHAPTER 10

Mind. Spirit. Soul. Body.

Heart. Soul. Mind. Strength.

Mind. Spirit. Soul. Body.

Heart. Soul. Mind. Strength.

The lists are very similar. Both have "Mind" and "Soul." "Body" is close to "Strength." And I guess that "Heart" and "Spirit" could be the same thing.

Why had Josh said that? My father came up with the "mind, spirit, soul, body" mantra. The only way Josh could have heard it would have been from my father! Were they both working for The New World?

Maybe it is a different phrase. The words are different, and so is the order. Josh was so sincere last night. Maybe he didn't know. Maybe it was just a coincidence…

Mind. Spirit. Soul. Body.

Heart. Soul. Mind. Strength.

Mind. Spirit. Soul. Body.

Heart. Soul. Mind. Strength.

The same thoughts repeated.

****

The first sound Kyle heard was a slow, rhythmic beeping. He did not bother opening his eyes; he was still so tired! The pain had disappeared, but his body ached.

Kyle wiggled his fingers. He felt his hands lying at his sides, not tied behind his back. *Good. I'm not in any danger. Maybe I can rest for just a little longer...*

Something grabbed Kyle's hand! *I am in danger!* Kyle thought.

Kyle sat bolt upright and wretched his hand to safety. He searched wildly around the room, trying to recognize his surroundings.

A startled Claire was sitting by his bedside. Kyle was in a hospital room, connected to several machines. He was safe after all. Kyle collapsed back onto his pillow and closed his eyes again. The rapid movement had caused him so much pain! He tried slowing his breathing and heart rate; the staccato beeping annoyed him.

"Are you all right?" Claire asked. Kyle opened his eyes slightly.

"Yeah." He gave a weak smile. His jaw ached, and he stopped. "You just startled me. That's all."

"Sorry," she smiled sheepishly. "I didn't think you'd react that way. It was the first movement we've seen since last night."

Kyle looked toward the window. The curtains were drawn. "How long was I out?"

Claire shrugged. "About twenty hours."

Kyle almost swore but turned it into a whistle. "Now I see why you grabbed my hand."

"I was worried about you... *We* were worried about you. Josh and your grandma were here all day. They left a few hours ago. Josh and everyone else at the prayer group are praying for you right now."

Kyle ignored the second half of Claire's words. "*You* were worried about me?" Kyle pressed.

"...Yeah... *I* was worried about you *too*..."

"Hmmm. Well, when I get out of here, maybe we can have dinner sometime, and you can tell me why you were worried."

"Kyle—" Claire stopped. A doctor had knocked and entered the room.

"Hello, Kyle. Glad to see you're awake." The doctor examined Kyle and asked several questions before announcing that Kyle had "three cracked and two broken ribs, a cracked cheekbone, and a dislocated jaw." Surgery was not required. There was nothing the doctor could do for the ribs; he requested that Kyle "rest for the next few weeks." The doctor had carefully repositioned Kyle's cheekbone and popped Kyle's jaw back into place with instructions to eat soft foods for a week. Kyle genuinely promised that he would try. The doctor also mentioned that a nurse would be taking Kyle for additional x-rays later that evening.

The doctor left.

Kyle preempted before Claire could say anything else. "Don't say no. I just got stuck in the hospital."

"Kyle," Claire began again. She sounded like a "Dear John" letter. "I like you. I really do. But…I can't get into a relationship with you. I'm a Christian. And I'm not supposed to date someone who isn't…"

"So I didn't fool you either?" Kyle asked in disbelief. "How long have *you* known?"

"I've always known…"

"Josh told you, didn't he?" Kyle sighed in disgust.

"No, I found out on my own—"

"That's what Josh said! How did you two know?" Kyle was shouting now.

Claire replied slowly and softly, "You just…didn't act like a Christian."

"How's a Christian supposed to act?" Kyle retorted.

"A Christian obeys God. They do what He commands us in the Bible."

"You mean the 'thou shalts' and the 'thou shalt nots.'" Kyle rolled his eyes.

"Sort of," Claire admitted. "But that's just part of it. Christianity is not a 'to-do list.' Doing a certain number of good things or not committing certain sins doesn't make you a Christian. A Christian is someone who recognizes that they have done wrong and asks God to forgive them and tries to do good instead of evil."

Kyle considered. "So if I'm actually a Christian but still sin, does that mean we can go out?"

"Kyle! This is serious! A Christian shouldn't be looking for ways to sin! The entire focus of Christianity is love for God and love for others, and a Christian's motivation for doing good is their gratitude and love for God. True Christians love the Lord, and their actions show it. In fact, that is one of the only 'rules' that we have to follow: 'love the Lord your God with all your heart and with all your soul and with all your mind and with all your strength.'"

"Josh told you to say that, didn't he!" Kyle exploded. He was sitting upright again.

Claire was taken aback. "To say what? The Bible verse? Josh—"

"It's a Bible verse?" Kyle interrupted.

"Yes..."

"Show me."

Claire flipped through the Bible she had been reading. She came to a page with many lines in red. *The words of Jesus.* Kyle remembered. Claire handed him the Bible and pointed to an underlined passage, written in red. "Love the Lord your God with all your heart and with all your soul and with all your mind and with all your strength" (Mark 12:30, NIV).

This is just too weird, thought Kyle.

"Have you ever heard it reordered 'mind, spirit, soul, body'?" Kyle ventured aloud.

"No," Claire said slowly. "This is the only way that it's written."

"Have you heard anyone else say the order 'mind, spirit, soul, body'?" Kyle asked again.

"No..." Claire said just as slowly.

"This is just too weird," Kyle repeated aloud.

"What is?"

"Someone I used to trust said that phrase—mind, spirit, soul, body—that it was the measure of a man."

"Maybe God is saying this *is* the measure of man," Claire mused.

A knock on the door prevented her from saying more and prevented Kyle from correcting the quote. Two police officers entered the small hospital room.

"Kyle Baker?" the female officer asked.

Kyle welcomed the escape from the talk about God. Although intrigued that an ancient culture had used the concepts of mind, spirit, soul, and body to capture the full measure of a man, he had no desire to continue the current conversation with Claire. She would probably try to convert him.

"Yes, that's me," Kyle answered.

The questions started.

What had happened? He had been attacked.

Who attacked him? The New World.

How did he know it was them? They kind of admitted it.

Could he prove it? No, but who else would attack him?

Did he have a description of the attackers? Not really; the alley was too dark. There was a big White guy, a smaller White guy; the leader was either Hispanic or eastern European; the other two might have been Black.

Would he swear to that in court? Only if the police caught them.

The police questions continued. Kyle was getting good at answering their questions.

"One last thing," the female officer asked. "You said you thought this was The New World. Are you still willing to testify against the members we have in custody?"

"Absolutely," Kyle emphasized. His mind, spirit, soul, and body would not even consider the alternative. Revenge on his father and on The New World was too important.

"Are you sure?" Claire asked. This was the first she had spoken since the police arrived.

Whose side are you on? Kyle thought to himself.

"Yes," Kyle answered, shooting Claire a quick glance. "It's going to take a lot more than this to keep me from testifying."

"The feds will be glad to hear that," the other officer added. "They're involved now, and they're willing to place you in witness protection."

Kyle considered the offer. His being was immediately divided. His mind and body urged Kyle to accept the witness protection and protect himself; his spirit and soul argued for Kyle to stay where he was and to continue fighting The New World.

Kyle's mind desired the safety of witness protection. Although The New World had admitted that they would not attack Kyle again as long as he stopped threatening The New World, Kyle's mind reasoned that he should not expose himself and tempt them more than he already had. The trauma from nearly drowning was still fresh in his head, and his mind refused to endure any similar situations.

His spirit pushed Kyle to continue. Kyle could not give up! He had sworn vengeance on his father and The New World. If he allowed either of them to escape justice, Kyle would never forgive himself. Leaving The New World alone was out of the question.

Kyle's soul abhorred the idea of hiding like a coward. Kyle had no reason to be afraid! He had almost completely healed his mind from the trauma of nearly drowning in the warehouse. His body would heal as well! There was nothing The New World could do to him that Kyle could not undo. Kyle was not weak. He had overcome their torture twice; he could overcome again.

Kyle's body, although sore, relished the thought of meeting any of the thugs from last night—one on one, of course—and having a fair fight. Still, Kyle's body recalled the trauma and retribution from Kyle's last attacks on The New World and objected to experiencing any more physical abuse.

The vote was two to two.

Is there a way to break the tie? Kyle considered. *My mind and body desire safety from further pain and injury; my spirit and soul desire further action against my father and The New World. Getting revenge has been worth all the pain so far—my whole being agrees with that. But my being also agrees that further action is not prudent until I've had time to heal. Using witness protection might keep me safe, but it would also prevent me from acting against The New*

World until after the trial, maybe later!

On the other hand, testifying at the trial would be the best revenge; if I can't testify, little else will matter. A conviction against The New World will be a true blow, more than interrupting a drug deal or finding a dirty cop. Testifying will culminate my work so far and solidify my damage to The New World. I can be safe and *exact revenge at the same time!*

Besides, The New World has hurt more than just me. The fight's getting too big. Maybe I do need a higher power; maybe I should talk to the feds.

The vote from his being was unanimous.

"Yes, I'll go into witness protection," Kyle announced.

"Great! We'll let the feds know. They should be in touch with you shortly," the officer said. She and her partner left the hospital.

"Witness protection?" Claire asked. "This sounds more serious than you've told me."

"I'll be fine. Besides, I didn't think you cared about me," Kyle jabbed.

"Kyle! I do care about you. I care about you enough that I don't want you killed by The New World!"

"But not enough to go out with me," Kyle argued.

Claire became angry. "Kyle, I don't want anything to happen to you. I care about you—as a friend." Kyle felt like he had been punched in the stomach again. He turned his head from Claire and stared at the wall. Claire's tone softened. "Kyle, I'm worried about you. You know how ruthless The New World is, how many people they've killed. What makes you think that The New World won't come after you again, even in witness protection? What makes you think that you won't end up back in the hospital, or worse? I…I don't want to lose you."

That was enough for Kyle. Just as his mind, spirit, soul, and body all agreed that he should keep fighting The New World, they all agreed that Kyle should do whatever he needed to please Claire in hopes of their friendship becoming more.

He turned back toward Claire.

"Do you really mean that? That you don't want to lose me?"

"Yes."

"But only as a friend?" Kyle asked.

"Does that matter?"

The non-answer spoke volumes. "Claire, I don't want to lose you either. I care about you more than just as a friend." Kyle placed a hand over his heart and held his other hand in the air. "I swear that I will do anything for you, Claire, regardless of how you feel about me." Kyle relaxed his hands. That simple gesture had been painful. "I'll do anything for you, Claire. I love you."

Claire did not respond.

CHAPTER 11

The FBI was elated with Kyle entering the witness protection program; they did not want anything to happen to their star witness, and they said so. Kyle would fly to the safe house on the following evening; in the meantime, agents would be stationed in front of his house. Kyle was surprised at how quickly he would be moved. The only response Kyle received to that comment was, "With all that has happened to you already, we aren't going to take any chances." Kyle shook his head to himself. They did not know half of what had already happened to him, and Kyle intended to keep it that way.

Against the doctor's initial wishes, Kyle was immediately returned home to pack. The FBI could not tell Kyle where he was going or how long he would be there. So Kyle packed all his clothes and the rest of his meager possessions that he might need. Joan complained about Kyle leaving on such short notice; Kyle wondered if she secretly enjoyed that he was leaving and would no longer be around to break her rules. Whatever her true feelings, Joan was gone for the afternoon, visiting a friend from church across town. That was perfectly fine with Kyle; he was counting down the hours until he could leave "that old buzzard" behind.

Kyle enjoyed his peace and quiet until the doorbell rang.

Kyle was not expecting any visitors, and his grandmother had a key. *Where are those bodyguards?* Kyle thought. *They're supposed to be watching the house!* Kyle peeked out the window at the black unmarked car parked conspicuously across the street. There was no activity. *Has The New World come for me? Have they killed the guards in order to reach me? In broad daylight, no less?* Steeled by his soul, Kyle grabbed a large kitchen knife and stalked toward the door.

The doorbell rang again. Kyle could not see who was at the door from the side window. He cautiously opened the door, holding the knife behind it.

The person standing on the porch was one of the last people he expected to see. Kyle stood there looking with a puzzled expression on his face.

"...Jill...?"

"Hello, Kyle."

"Jill!" Kyle shouted. He had forgotten how much he had missed her! He almost jumped out of the doorway to hug her when he realized that the knife was still in his hand, hidden behind the door. He dropped it point down; it landed with a dull thud; Jill did not seem to notice the sound. The two embraced. Jill was smiling. *That's a good sign!* Kyle thought to himself. *Why did I allow myself to lose contact with her? When she stopped calling, I should have called her! Maybe there's still hope. Maybe we can fix our relationship.*

The hug lingered for several minutes. Eventually, Jill released him and held him at arm's length. She looked him over.

"You look awful!" Jill stepped forward and felt Kyle's face. He had forgotten about his black eye and myriad bruises. Painkillers were a wondrous invention. Kyle tried to laugh off her comment, but the light chuckle pained his ribs.

"Don't worry. I'm fine." He reached for Jill's wrists and moved her arms toward his chest. Jill moved her hands back to his face and gave a quizzical look to his remark.

"What happened?" Jill asked.

Kyle groped for an answer; he had been ordered, in no uncertain terms, not to tell anyone that he was entering witness protection. "A couple of guys and I were horsing around, wrestling each other," Kyle finally said.

"Your *friends* did this?" Jill shouted. A slow smile spread across her lips. "What do *they* look like?" Kyle laughed but quickly groaned. His ribs throbbed. He grabbed his side. Jill's eyes widened. She had noticed the cuts on Kyle's arms. "Did your friends do that too?" she asked. Kyle shook his head.

"Motorcycle accident."

"You have a motorcycle?" Jill looked at the driveway behind her, trying to find it.

"It was stolen," Kyle clarified.

"That's awfully convenient," Jill said, giving him another sly smile. "Losing your motorcycle right before I arrive."

Kyle smiled. "Speaking of which, what are you doing here?"

"I just wanted to say hi. I feel awful for losing contact with you."

"How did you find me?"

"Well, I was visiting my cousin Jennine—you remember my cousin Jennine? I visited her for spring break one year. Anyway, I was visiting her this summer to go to the beach and the Everglades and Key West. She lives in the city, and we saw you on the news! I felt bad that we didn't stay in touch, and I wanted to come by and say hello. I looked through my texts, but you never gave me your grandmother's address. I was going to text you, but the look on your face was worth the surprise! It took a few days, but I finally found you!"

"Yep! You found me," Kyle said. "I guess that means I should move again!" Kyle could not keep from laughing. Jill punched him on the shoulder. Kyle groaned in agony.

"Are you sure you're all right?" Jill asked.

Kyle desperately wanted to tell Jill the truth. His entire being agreed, but his mind also kept arguing no. Claire knew; the police knew; his grandmother knew; the federal agents knew—they had even cautioned Kyle against telling anyone else, even Josh. Too many people knew already.

Kyle's mind continued to reason. Jill also deserved the truth. She had been looking for him in the largest city in Florida. She had finally found him! Kyle could not disappear again. She deserved more than that. And now they had a chance to restore their relationship. They could return to the way life was before Kyle's father robbed him and his mother died. Claire had made it clear that a relationship with her could never be like the relationship Kyle had with Jill.

"You'd better come inside," Kyle said at last. Jill stepped into the house. Kyle smiled and waved to the unseen agents in the dark vehicle and closed the door behind him. "These aren't from my friends," Kyle whispered, motioning to his injuries.

"I figured," Jill responded. "What happened?"

"I was beaten up…by a gang."

"What?" Jill asked in a hushed shout. "Why?"

"I got in their way."

"You mean with the drug bust on the news?"

"That was part of it. They'd also bought a cop, and I exposed him."

"Wow! How did you know?"

"I saw someone leave drugs at his apartment."

"Wow," Jill repeated.

"I have to testify in court," Kyle continued. "And to keep me safe, the feds are putting me into witness protection."

"Okay. When are they doing that?"

"Tomorrow night."

Jill swore in anger, and Kyle sympathized with her. "So you weren't kidding about moving as soon as I found you!" Jill shouted. "You left me in Boston, dropped communication, and now that I've found you, you're going to leave again!"

"Okay! You're right! You're right," Kyle interrupted. "You deserved better than that, and I'm sorry. But I have got to do this. It's about more than just putting gangsters in prison."

Jill scoffed, only partly pacified with Kyle's apology. "Oh, really?"

"Yes. You remember that my father robbed me. He stole the house, the cars, the money, everything of value. He even emptied my personal bank account."

"Yeah," Jill recalled.

"My father is still out there somewhere, and I found out that he might be connected to the gang The New World as a supplier or something."

"So since you can't find your father, you're going after the gang," Jill finished. Kyle nodded frankly. "Oh, Kyle! That's awful! I am so sorry." Jill gave Kyle another hug. "How have you been holding up?"

"I've been fine. That's really been the only downside since I've been here...that and my prison warden of a grandmother!"

Jill laughed. "Sounds like you've done all right. I'm sorry that my parents were jerks and that you couldn't stay in the spare bedroom. Maybe I could have taken the couch, and you could have taken my room... Actually, my parents probably wouldn't have allowed that either."

Kyle laughed despite the pain. "I love you," he said.

"I love you," she replied. "I guess you're happy to get out of here?"

"Absolutely. I counted down the days until I got my orders, and now, I'm counting down the hours until I get hidden in witness protection."

"When do you have to leave? Exactly?"

"Tomorrow night, about midnight."

"Is your prison warden around?" Jill asked.

"She's visiting a friend. She won't be back for a while."

"Well, since I won't be seeing you for a long time, I should probably give you a proper goodbye."

Kyle drew the deadbolt on the front door and led Jill to his room, and the two said goodbye.

****

Later that afternoon, Kyle received word that an unmarked vehicle would arrive at his house at 12:37 a.m. the following night. When the agents arrived, Kyle would have a thirty-second window before they needed to leave. He would need to have his bags ready to go.

For the second time in six months, Kyle reduced his life into two large suitcases. He finished packing just as his grandmother arrived home. Her first words were, "Now, you had better go to church while you're in witness protection."

Kyle could not wait to leave.

****

Several weeks later, Kyle was settled into his new home. He had been relocated to somewhere in South Dakota, near the Black Hills. At first, living so far from anything familiar had bothered him, but he had slowly become accustomed to the flat land and the lack of people.

The sky was so large! He could see for miles! At night, the sky was no longer black—but tan with stars! There was no other light to hide them.

Kyle was in the best shape of his life. At dawn, he would choose a direction and run. There was no one to see him in the vast open plains and no one to threaten his life. His only company was prairie dogs and antelope. He had never seen so much wildlife! When he was tired of running, he would turn around and run back to his cabin.

Kyle had started to sleep outdoors. On most nights, he would unroll his sleeping bag near the cabin and fall asleep in the open air. Sometimes, he would travel into the Black Hills and camp; he enjoyed living out of only his backpack.

Kyle had purchased another motorcycle. Every day, he would ride it on the long deserted roads. With no one else around, he tested how fast he could go. His top speed was 189 miles per hour. He was determined to beat it.

The best part of all was Jill. The federal agents had allowed her to come as long as she lived under the same rules as Kyle and stayed at the cabin until the trial. Kyle and Jill never missed anyone; they never thought of contacting anyone else. All they needed was each other. Their favorite times together were riding Kyle's motorcycle on the open road. Kyle would drive for hours at a time, and Jill would hold onto him. Jill would always squeeze him or rub him to remind him that she was there. But Kyle needed no reminder. They were alone. No one could catch them. No one would bother them. They needed no one else. They had each other.

And they celebrated that every night.

****

Kyle awoke from the vivid dream.

He was still in Florida. His suitcases still stood by his door, waiting for the agents to arrive late tomorrow night. He still had one more day of his grandmother imploring him to go to church while he was in witness protection.

Kyle longed for the life in his dream. That was all he had ever wanted! His mind, spirit, soul, and body yearned in perfect unison for that life. It was not yet a reality, but it soon would be. He would ask the agents if Jill could come with him into witness protection.

Kyle could not sleep for the rest of the night.

****

The sleepless night passed without incident, and the day looked the same. The agents had ordered Kyle to stay home during the entire day. Two of them had personally visited his boss at Finneman's Market and informed him of the situation. His boss had not been happy, and neither was Kyle, but the paycheck for the last few days almost remedied the situation.

Kyle just had to wait one more day, and then he was free from his grandmother. With any luck, he would stay in witness protection until he received his orders. Then he would never have to see her again. The trick was dealing with her all day today. She seemed especially full of unnecessary advice. *Is there nowhere else she needs to be today?* Kyle wondered.

Evidently not. Kyle was relieved when his grandmother finally fell asleep in her armchair. She occasionally did while reading her Bible. At last, the Bible proved to be good for something.

Kyle hoped that Jill would come again today. He could use someone else to talk to…or otherwise occupy his time. Though, they probably would not have as much fun as they had the previous day.

Kyle had asked the agents about Jill joining him in witness protection. The agents unequivocally declined the suggestion or any possibility of communication. Yesterday, Kyle had promised Jill that he would stay in contact, and Kyle intended to keep his promise, despite it being against the rules. He had not figured it all out, but he had some time. He would probably send her a postcard with a phone number.

Kyle stared at his phone. The day was growing late. He desperately wanted to talk to Jill before he left, but he had no idea what to say. With the agents' refusal, he definitely could not tell her his dream. He longed for her to call him, even if it was to berate him for ignoring her. *Maybe she's ignoring me now*, Kyle thought. *Maybe this is payback for letting our relationship die when I moved to Florida.* Kyle groaned inwardly. He deserved it but hated the thought.

Kyle's phone buzzed with a text—from Jill! Kyle's body shook with excitement. Evidently, Jill had not forgotten him!

"Hey, cutie!" Her text read. "Can you meet me someplace? I have a surprise for you!"

"What's the surprise?" Kyle texted back.

"I can't tell you that. It's a surprise! ;)" she replied.

"Hmm. I don't think I can make it. I'm kind of under house arrest." Kyle teased. "Not unless it's a GOOD surprise," he added.

"It'll be worth it. If you hurry, we might get some time alone before tonight."

Kyle's whole being agreed to that!

"Where do you want to meet?" Kyle texted.

"That's part of the surprise!" She texted back. "When you leave your house, turn left and keep walking. I'll tell you when to turn again."

Kyle smiled. It was like a treasure hunt, and Jill was the prize!

Kyle almost ran out the front door before remembering the agents' command to stay at the house. There was no way the agents in the car would let him leave, and Kyle certainly did not want them to accompany him on Jill's quest. *Is there a way for me to leave the house without being seen?* Kyle thought. Kyle raced to the second story and looked out a rear window. The little yard behind his grandmother's house rolled into a shallow swamp. *If I crawl through the grass to the water's edge, I can sneak into one of the neighbors' yards without being seen*, Kyle thought to himself. *That'll work for my bodyguards; now I need to fool my grandmother.* Kyle scribbled a quick note saying that he was taking a nap and taped the notice to his now closed and locked bedroom door. Kyle slinked down the stairs and spied his grandmother still dozing in the living room armchair. Noiselessly, Kyle sneaked out the back door. Kyle dropped to his stomach and crawled to the edge of the swamp, being careful to keep the house between him and the vehicle housing his bodyguards. Crawling with broken ribs was much more painful than Kyle had thought; he was relieved when he reached the neighbor's house and could finally stand. He cut through several more backyards before looking back at his bodyguards' vehicle. There was no movement. They had not seen him leave. Kyle figured he was safe and continued his journey on the sidewalk.

As soon as Kyle stepped onto the concrete, Jill sent him another text. "Turn left at the intersection. You'll be on this road for a while."

Kyle obeyed. "When will I know if I need to turn again?" He texted back.

"Don't worry. I'll let you know when you get close."

"How will you know?"

"Because I've got my eye on you. ;)"

Kyle stopped and looked around. He did not see Jill anywhere. Kyle chuckled to himself and continued walking. Jill always had been good at stalking him. Back when they were at college in Boston, Jill would send Kyle texts like this all the time. He had found them adorable, which was probably why Jill had continued. When Kyle finally found her somewhere on campus, she would award him with a kiss and some trivial item that she had stolen from him. As he walked through Jacksonville, Kyle knew he would catch a glimpse of her eventually; he always did.

Kyle followed the familiar road. He had driven up and down this street more times than he could count. He had driven it into the center of town every day for work and even further for his college classes. And of course, over the last few days, he had walked this same road to Finneman's Market. The road seemed much longer today. Kyle longed for his motorcycle again. *That's another reason to go after The New World,* Kyle thought. Kyle cursed The New World under his breath and spat on the sidewalk. *Wherever I land in witness protection, I will definitely need to buy another motorcycle—just like my dream.* Kyle quickened his pace.

His phone buzzed a moment later. "So you CAN go faster. I thought you might be getting tired," Jill texted.

"Not a chance," Kyle texted back. *How much farther is this?* Kyle wondered. But he could not ask that; he would not sacrifice his dignity that quickly. "I can't wait to see you!" Kyle texted instead.

Jill interpreted the message. "It's not much farther. I'll let you know when to turn again."

I hope that the turn comes before I reach the center of town, Kyle thought. *Finneman's Market is on the other side of the street, but if my boss sees me... Let's just hope it doesn't come to that. I still have a few miles before the store.*

Kyle walked for another mile and a half. The entire distance, Kyle kept discretely glancing at his surroundings, expecting to catch a glimpse of Jill following him. This time, she was doing a much better job of staying out of his sight.

Kyle's phone chimed with another text from Jill. "All

right! You're here! Turn left." Kyle turned left.

A cold shiver ran down his spine. He was staring at the abandoned warehouse.

CHAPTER 12

Kyle stood on the sidewalk in horror. His entire being balked. He could not think. Kyle just stood there, staring in disbelief at the building in front of him. Kyle did not blink; he could not breathe; his mouth dropped open in terror. Kyle had a flashback of downing. He could feel the water filling his nose and lungs. He could feel his mind clouding. He was drowning again!

Kyle snapped back to reality. He was taking quick, shallow breaths. Kyle slowed his breathing and closed his eyes. The vision of drowning returned. Kyle snapped his eyes open. *I am not drowning! I am safe. I am still outside the warehouse...*

Outside the warehouse. On the other side of the building lay the scene where Kyle was badly beaten. His blood and vomit still stained the gravel in the alley! Kyle could feel the pain of every broken bone—each bruise—every punch The New World delivered to him. The agony was unbearable!

Kyle arrested his mind from the wild thoughts. *I am safe. I am in no danger.*

Kyle had to think rationally.

How does Jill know about this place? Kyle asked himself. *Why does she want to meet me here?*

"Are you inside?" Kyle finally managed to text back. He could not will himself forward unless he received confirmation from Jill.

"Yep! I'm at the door around back," was Jill's reply.

Kyle's mind was screaming at him: *Don't do it! Don't take a single step! Something is wrong!*

The rest of his being was also speaking.

"You want Jill more than anything," his spirit reminded. "Are you willing to go into the warehouse for her?"

"There's no need to be afraid of the warehouse," his soul goaded. "You aren't afraid of anything! Don't be a chicken!"

His body whispered, "You are strong enough to overcome any trials, even if you are still injured. You don't need to be afraid! Remember the pleasures of last night. Today, again, they are yours for the taking!"

The vote was three to one. Kyle, resolved, walked to the back of the building.

Kyle could still see the remains from the last time he had been behind the warehouse. He could see the events so clearly: the long groove where he fell, his vomit and blood, the place where dirt and gravel had been scuffed into his face. Despite his desire for Jill, Kyle's mind screamed louder for him to stop. But the rest of his being remained resolute.

Kyle continued for the same door he tried to reach that fateful night behind the warehouse. He had already made his choice.

Kyle opened the door. He poked his head into the opening.

"Jill?" he asked the darkness. No one answered.

"Jill?" he asked again, louder. He was met with silence.

Kyle opened the door fully. He still could not see anything. Kyle took three brave steps into the warehouse. His eyes had trouble adjusting to the darkness.

"Jill?" he called loudly into the darkness. Silence.

The door behind Kyle slammed shut. Kyle spun around. He saw nothing in the darkness except for an even darker shadow filling his vision. Kyle tried to fight, but he still could see nothing. The shadow effortlessly forced Kyle back and, with a single hand, pinned Kyle's right arm and head against the wall. Kyle felt a sharp blade against his neck.

"Don't say a word," the shadow ordered. Kyle's eyes were adjusting to the darkness. He recognized his attacker; he was the Hispanic man who had escaped the drug bust and who had delivered the drugs to Nick's apartment.

"Where's Jill?" Kyle asked. Kyle felt the blade dig into his neck.

"I said, 'Don't say a word,'" his attacker sneered. "Blondie's fine—for now. And if you want her to stay that way, you're going to do exactly what we tell you. You are going to go to the DA's office, and you're going to tell them that you're no longer willing to testify against any of us. Understand? Then, you're going to talk to your federal agent friends, and you're going to decline witness protection. If either one of these things doesn't happen, we're going to send you Blondie's head in a box. Do you understand?" The attacker lowered his knife enough for Kyle to nod. "Good. Bring us Nick's special doormat as proof. You have twenty-four hours. We'll be waiting." The thug released Kyle and started to walk away. "Oh," he said, turning around to face Kyle again, "and if anything happens to me or if you try to do something stupid, you'll never see Blondie again." With that, he disappeared deeper into the abandoned warehouse.

****

Kyle had debated for hours on whether or not to tell the agents that Jill had been kidnapped.

In his mind, Kyle knew that The New World would not hesitate to murder Jill if he did anything other than what they had asked—and that meant he needed a doormat and no cops. He could not get the doormat without their help, but the only way to avoid police involvement was to do this himself. Could he talk the agents out of bringing in the police? Probably not. But they certainly had more resources. Maybe they would help. Was their help worth the police involvement he knew was coming? Probably. His mind—tentatively—chose to work with the federal agents but balked at being the deciding vote.

Kyle's spirit reminded him that he always kept his promises and finished his tasks. Kyle had sworn that he would exact revenge on his father and, by extension, The New World, for destroying him. But he had also promised himself that he would never forsake Jill again. She did not deserve being dumped; he did not deserve her searching for him after all the months apart or a second chance at their relationship. Kyle believed that the FBI held the same values: that a person's life was more valuable than imprisoning a criminal. The choice was easy; his spirit advocated telling the federal agents.

Kyle's soul was determined not to abandon Jill. His only fear was losing her permanently. The New World might forgive him if he met them without the mat, but if he arrived with federal agents…there would be no deal. If Kyle was *lucky*, Jill would remain unharmed, and they would be right back where they had started; worst case…Kyle would lose Jill forever. His soul voted against speaking with the authorities.

Kyle felt the fresh cut on his neck. Kyle knew that he was not strong enough to fight The New World and rescue Jill without the mat. He also knew that he was not strong enough to fight all of the security guards and retrieve the mat on his own. The only possible way to rescue Jill was for him to talk to the federal agents. His body sided with the FBI.

The vote was three to one.

The agents were furious when Kyle spoke with them at the local police precinct. They were irate that Kyle had ditched his security to go on a "scavenger hunt" and demanded that Kyle not leave the building without protection. They were even more enraged when Kyle explained that he would no longer testify.

"Are you kidding me!" the female FBI agent shouted. "This is the only shot we've had in years to put *any* of The New World behind bars! And now, we can put *two* away! This is a golden opportunity! Either one of them could cave, and we could deal some serious damage to The New World!"

She was right. Kyle knew that she was right. The drug dealer and Nick could both cave. The feds might unravel the whole gang. They might even get Kyle's father and destroy him for good. They were right; Kyle's mind agreed with them. But his mind, as well as the rest of his being, also agreed that he could not lose Jill—not again.

When Kyle mentioned that Jill was a hostage, the change was instantaneous. They demanded the full story and interrupted only to ask clarifying questions. Kyle, again, stressed the demands from The New World: that he no longer testify, that he decline witness protection, and that the agents surrender Nick's doormat. The agents glossed over the ultimatums. They reviewed the texts from "Jill" and sent a team to look around the condemned warehouse.

"Don't do that!" Kyle screamed. "They'll kill her!"

"No, they won't," the male agent said. "They kidnapped her for leverage. They want something in return."

"Yeah, they want us to drop the case," Kyle reminded them.

"That's not going to happen," the male agent said.

"They also want us to give them Nick's doormat," Kyle continued.

"That's also not going to happen."

Kyle became even more exasperated. "Then what *is* going to happen?" Kyle yelled.

"What *is* going to happen is that *we* are going to wait for further instructions from the kidnappers. Regardless of what they might have told you or otherwise implied about the exchange being made in the warehouse, they're not going to go anywhere within a three-mile radius of that place. That's just not going to happen. They know we're going to be watching the warehouse." Kyle looked around the police precinct. No one had listened to his plea to stay. The agent continued, "The New World isn't going to have one of their men sitting on their hands at the warehouse for the next twenty-four hours waiting for you to show up. They're going to give us a different location."

"So what do we do now?" Kyle asked.

"We get ready to move at a moment's notice."

****

Two hours later, Kyle received another text from "Jill."

"The timetable has been moved up. Meet us behind Finneman's Market. Midnight. Bring the mat. Come alone." The text read.

"They know I'm working with you," Kyle spat. The agents ignored him.

"Ask them if Jill will be there," the female agent ordered.

"Will Jill be there?" Kyle texted back.

"Remember our agreement" was the simple response.

"What *exactly* was the agreement?" the female agent

asked. The male agent ruffled through his notes.

Kyle beat him to the answer. "That I'll never see her again if I do anything stupid." Kyle sighed. "They know I'm working with you," he repeated. Then he thought, *What have I done?*

"Ask for proof of life," the male agent ordered. Kyle texted The New World.

"None is coming" was the response.

"Then no deal," the male agent concluded.

"I'm not texting that!" Kyle screamed.

The female agent sighed and pointed to the phone. "Insist on proof of life, but act like the deal is still on. We need them to come out so that we—"

"Act like—!" Kyle interrupted. "You're going to let them kill her!"

"I have no proof of life, and they're not willing to give it," the female agent bellowed. "So my—"

"You're going to let them kill her!" Kyle reiterated.

"They might have already!" the female agent shouted. "And if they have, caving to their demands would compromise our cases against them for nothing!"

While she regained her composure, the male agent continued, "Even if we had proof (from a separate source) that Jill was alive, current law prohibits us from (a) dealing with abductors refusing to give 'proof of life' and (b) engaging in deals that compromise 'equal or higher priority criminal investigations.' Jill is just one person compared to the hundreds that The New World kills every year in this city alone. And your testimony gives us the chance to stop them."

"Besides," the female agent resumed, "this whole thing smells fishy. If Jill really is alive and they still refused to give proof of life, then they aren't after your testimony or the mat; they're after something else. And I'm not going to make any deals until I find out what they're really after." She turned to the police officer standing nearby. "Since we know where the trade is going to take place, I want snipers stationed on roofs with clear shots. As soon as someone sets foot in that alley, I want to hear about it."

"I was told to come alone," Kyle reminded her.

The agent shot him a dirty look. She had no intention of sending Kyle.

The officer responded, "That area was a possible exchange location. We've already checked; there's no suitable roof anywhere in the area."

"Then find us a studio apartment that we can use!" the female agent ordered.

"Do I at least get the mat?" Kyle asked rhetorically. The male agent shot him a glance that said, "That's not going to happen."

The female agent looked Kyle square in the eyes. "Send the text," she seethed through her teeth.

****

After sending the text, Kyle stormed from the room in disgust. If he had believed that it would help Jill in any way, Kyle would have killed someone. Instead, he raced through the halls of the precinct, venting his frustration. *What is The New World going to do to Jill if I don't bring the mat?* Kyle pondered. *I guess that doesn't make much of a difference now, does it? Jill is as good as dead. There is no way The New World will bring Jill to the exchange. They're too smart for that. And with all the agents surrounding Finneman's Market, there won't be any deal. The snipers might as well have shot Jill themselves.*

Kyle's whole being ached. He felt sick. *I've murdered Jill.*

No. Kyle corrected himself. *I have not murdered Jill— The New World has.*

No. Not "has"—"will." The New World will murder Jill. If The New World murders Jill, I will spend the rest of my life fighting and killing—yes, killing—members of that gang!

But for now, Jill is (I hope) still alive, and that means that I need to do everything in my power to keep her that way, even if that means stealing Nick's doormat.

Someone touched Kyle on his shoulder. He turned to face a young female police officer.

"Hi," she said tentatively. "I couldn't help but overhear. Were you looking for 'evidence'?" Kyle hesitated at the question. The woman pressed. "To get something for the FBI agents?" Kyle nonchalantly looked around. *Am I being watched?* Kyle thought. *Did I say that I was going to steal the doormat out loud?* The officer seemed in earnest.

Kyle had nothing to lose if this were a trap. "Yes," Kyle responded. "I am looking for the evidence room."

"I thought so," the officer responded, smiling. "A lot of people get lost looking for 'evidence.'"

Is this for real? Kyle thought. *I'm not dressed like a cop. What's going on here?* Kyle pushed the thoughts aside. The female cop started rattling off the directions to the evidence room. Without hesitation and little gratitude, Kyle followed her instructions. He was determined to try anything to save Jill. Kyle followed the officer's verbal directions through a doorway and into a basement and ended at a gated window.

A male cop stood behind the bars. Kyle's spirit and soul urged him forward; his mind concocted a believable lie; adrenaline flowed through his body. He had come too far. He was not going to desert Jill now.

Before Kyle even opened his mouth, the male officer produced the mat for Kyle and shoved it noiselessly through the opening in the door. Kyle gave the guard a quizzical look as he held the mat. The officer glanced at the security camera. Kyle looked at the camera and back at the officer.

"It's not recording. She said you'd be coming," the guard grinned; he gave Kyle a wink.

Kyle felt sick to his stomach. *Nick is not the only dirty cop on the force!* He realized. Kyle concealed the ransom as best as he could and left the basement without a word.

As he navigated the traitor's directions in reverse, Kyle glanced at the other cameras. He had a feeling that none of them were recording. *How long have they been like this? If The New World wants Nick's doormat so badly, why not remove it themselves?* Kyle knew the answer in spite of his questions. Kyle had created the case; he would undermine it. The New World could not afford to lose any more moles; Kyle was expendable. The FBI, police commissioner, all the cops—they were suspicious of each other; Kyle was the perfect scapegoat. No one would believe him that two more police officers were working for The New World—especially while he was holding evidence.

Kyle conceded that the female FBI agent was right; The New World was after more than just the mat.

Kyle conducted another vote based on the conversations earlier that afternoon and the current situation. The vote was unanimous. Kyle strode resolutely for the door without his bodyguards. He was going to save Jill.

****

Kyle had barely turned the street corner before receiving another text. In his disgust at the federal agents, he had unconsciously pocketed his phone after sending the second text insisting on proof of Jill's life.

"Smart move," the text read. "Meet at the warehouse. Midnight."

"There are agents there," Kyle responded.

"Not anymore," The New World texted back. Kyle knew that the agents had all regrouped behind Finneman's Market.

Kyle felt sick. *The New World had planned this all along. The police, the federal agents, me—all of us played right into their hands. And I'm probably walking into a trap. Jill probably won't be at the warehouse either. The New*

World will just take the mat and keep Jill; I definitely won't testify then. I'll be right back where I started. No, I'll be back farther. I would have regressed because The New World would still have taken what I loved. I'll never see Jill again. Kyle's eyes watered. He was starting to cry.

Kyle had no choice other than giving the doormat to The New World. The New World had outthought him, the police, and the federal agents time and again. They had planned for every situation. Kyle could do nothing except play their game. Kyle wiped his eyes. He would give them the doormat. If he did, the worst that would happen is that they would keep Jill; at best, Jill would be safe. That was the priority; his being heartily agreed.

After that, he would need to devise some way to destroy The New World. Starting with his father's robbery and ending with Jill's kidnapping, there was no end to what they deserved. His whole being ravenously delighted at the prospect.

****

Kyle wandered aimlessly. He could not stop at home carrying evidence. He definitely could not return to the police station. He did not want to wait at the warehouse for the next few hours. Despite retraining his mind and overcoming his fear, the warehouse still held bad memories for him. In his directionless quest, Kyle actively avoided all locations that he knew well. His grandmother's house, the college, the bars, Finneman's Market—he refused to even walk on their streets. The agents were probably searching for him now. For Jill's sake, Kyle could not afford to be found by the police. Kyle clutched the doormat even tighter.

Yet, even in his random path, the warehouse drew Kyle closer to itself. The warehouse was the next step on Kyle's journey. Kyle knew that it was his destiny. He knew that his path would eventually end there as it had earlier that day. Still, Kyle resisted. He did not want to arrive at the warehouse any earlier than needed. Kyle continued to wander, but he marched significantly closer to the warehouse with each hour. The urge was becoming stronger.

At eleven o'clock, Kyle surrendered to his fate. He did not know where he was, but he could feel himself being led to the warehouse. He stopped resisting and let his feet move freely. He slowly began to recognize his surroundings. He noticed several large crumbling apartment buildings. The warehouse was just beyond them.

But the urge that Kyle had been following was seemingly eclipsed by another one. The stronger urge was no longer taking him to the warehouse. Instead, Kyle felt that he needed to go to one of the apartment buildings. He stopped moving. He still knew that he was destined for the warehouse and that he needed to give the mat as ransom for Jill. But he also felt a "Voice" from outside his being. This "Voice" was telling him to go into one of the apartment buildings *before* entering the warehouse.

Kyle was confused. He quickly evaluated the "Four Qualities of Man."

His mind ordered him to continue to the warehouse. He was too close to loiter in the open until midnight and too far to duck inside if he were spotted.

Kyle's spirit willed him forward. He had promised never to leave Jill again, and he was going to keep his promises. He could not afford to let her down. Not again.

His soul goaded him toward the warehouse. He was not afraid of The New World; he was only afraid of what they would do to Jill if he missed the deadline. Kyle could not take any chances.

His body urged him to rest at the warehouse. He was too tired from the injuries and from moving all evening and just wanted to rest.

Kyle's being agreed. There was no dissenting opinion.

Kyle's confusion deepened.

What is telling me to go into an apartment? What exists beyond my being? My father said that there was no measure for a man other than the mind, spirit, soul, and body. Is there a fifth aspect that he'd missed?

The "Voice" swelled in strength. It was nearly equal in strength to the four parts of Kyle's being. Yet, Kyle still chose to remain where he was.

Slowly, Kyle could feel the "Voice" affecting the decisions of his being.

His mind allowed him to enter an apartment building. He would not be seen and could leave when he needed.

Kyle's spirit conceded that he stall his movement. He would not leave Jill, but he would still need to wait until midnight. Investigating where the "voice" was drawing him would occupy the time.

His soul agreed to halt his progress. He would not arrive late to the exchange; he would watch the time. Besides, The New World might become suspicious and void the trade if he arrived too early.

His body suggested that he rest. He could rest just as well at the apartment building as at the warehouse.

Kyle marveled. *What is this "voice"? It has the power to change my being!*

Kyle still hesitated. *How can I trust the "voice"?* Kyle stood immobile for several minutes, weighing his decision. Finally, he decided, *If the "voice" is strong enough to change my whole being, it deserves to be followed.*

Kyle strode, resolutely, for the apartments.

CHAPTER 13

Kyle could feel the "Voice" directing him to a specific apartment building. He walked past several and stopped at the building closest to the warehouse. The building looked familiar. He thought he remembered it from a dream. *Have I been here before?* Kyle could not tell in the darkness. As soon as Kyle opened the door to the lobby, he remembered. *This is Josh's apartment building. What are the odds?* Kyle thought.

The "Voice" led Kyle up several flights of stairs to a designated floor. Kyle vaguely remembered that Josh lived on this floor. An awful thought struck Kyle. *Is the "voice" leading me to Josh?* Kyle almost laughed at the thought. *If the "voice" really is stronger than my mind, spirit, soul, and body, it would know better than to direct me to Josh!* Still, the thought remained.

The "Voice" led Kyle down the hall. Josh also lived in this direction. Kyle looked down at the ground as he walked. *The "voice" is leading me somewhere else. I'm sure of it,* Kyle thought. *I don't have time to be distracted by Josh. Not now.*

Kyle continued walking until the "Voice" instructed him to stop. Kyle had arrived! He could feel it. Kyle looked from the ground in anticipation. This was Josh's apartment. As soon as Kyle saw the apartment number, he knew that he was supposed to go inside.

Kyle sighed in disgust. *Josh is a nice enough guy, but he talks about god all the time. He'll probably say something like, "God has a plan for everything that's happened" to me and then try to convince me that it's true. I can't deal with that right now, not with Jill's life still in the balance.* Kyle waited for the "Voice" to lead him to another door. The "Voice" gave no other direction. The "Voice" urged Kyle to open that door; Kyle needed to open that door.

Kyle refused.

Kyle clouded his mind, hardened his spirit, calloused his soul, and deafened his body to the "Voice." He could hardly hear the "Voice" now. Kyle had resumed control, though he had been in control the whole time. *I am only going to do what I want to do. And I don't want to talk to Josh.*

Kyle turned to go. As he did, the door behind him opened a crack.

"Kyle?" a voice asked. Without turning around, Kyle knew that the voice belonged to Josh. "I knew you'd come," Josh continued.

Kyle spun around to face Josh. Josh had opened the door fully and stood in the doorframe wearing only a pair of shorts and his jewelry. "How did you know that?" Kyle accused. "I didn't even know that I was coming here until five minutes ago." *This is all too weird,* Kyle thought. *I've got to get back to rescuing Jill.*

Josh shrugged at Kyle's words. "I just knew you'd be coming."

This is just too weird, Kyle's thoughts repeated. "Well, I'm sorry I woke you," Kyle said, turning again to go.

"You didn't wake me. I couldn't sleep. I felt a...a 'Voice'...telling me to pray for you."

Kyle could not believe Josh's words! Kyle's thoughts ran wild. *This is too much! How did Josh know to say that? Did he have ESP?!*

Kyle faced Josh again with their eyes only inches apart.

"What did you say?" Kyle seethed.

Josh stammered. "I...felt...that I needed to pray for you."

"No, 'voice'! You said that you heard a 'voice' telling you to pray for me!" Kyle said. He was nearing derangement.

"Yeah..."

"Why did you say that!" Kyle shouted.

Josh stepped into the hallway and shut the door. "Shh. My mom's sleeping. Why'd I say that? Because that's what happened."

"But why did you say 'voice'? How did you know to say that?"

"Because that's what happened. I felt that God was calling—telling me to pray for you. Kyle, what's going on?"

Kyle felt deflated. "So your god told you to say that?"

Kyle clarified.

Josh considered. "God told me to pray for you…"

"But you said you heard a 'voice.'"

"Yeah, I felt that God was speaking to me—telling me to pray for you. That's what we say when we hear God talking to us."

This religion gets weirder and weirder all the time, Kyle thought. Then he said, "God talks to you?"

"Oh, very rarely," Josh answered. "Claire hears God speaking sometimes too. Mostly God just speaks through the Bible. Sometimes, though, He speaks to us through His Holy Spirit."

Kyle's mind was spinning frantically. *How did Josh know to say that? Josh had said the "mind, spirit, soul, body" thing in a different order, and that was a Bible verse, according to Claire. Now Josh said he heard a "voice" after I was led by a "voice" to Josh's apartment. Was that just a coincidence? Or was Josh really told that by…his god?*

Josh spoke again, "What's going on, Kyle? …Is that a doormat?" Kyle realized that he was still holding the doormat. Kyle, in vain, hid it behind his back.

"I was just led here by something that I had thought was a 'voice.'"

"So that's how you got here," Josh mused. "I knew you'd come."

"But how?" Kyle moaned. "I was outside five minutes ago minding my own business when a 'voice' told me to come in here and led me to your apartment."

"Really?" Josh mused. "God told me that you would be coming. And I think that the Holy Spirit told you to come here too."

Kyle swore and thought, *How is that possible? None of this makes any sense!*

"So you think your god brought me here?" Kyle asked aloud.

"Yes, unless you have a better explanation."

"But why?" Kyle asked.

"Kyle...Claire is worried about you, and so am I. My heart breaks for you! I—"

"I don't need your pity!" Kyle snapped.

"It's not pity; it's sympathy."

"I don't need your sympathy either!"

"Kyle, I know what it's like to have my father abandon me—"

"He didn't just abandon me! He stole from me and sold everything of value to The New World!"

Josh froze. "Your father sold everything to The New World? Claire never told me that."

"None of this is hers to tell!" Kyle shot Josh a look, implying that he should die with the information.

Josh stared at the ground. "I never knew that," Josh repeated, then muttered to himself, "That makes so much more sense...your father robbing you..." Josh looked back at Kyle. "That's what my father did too. He changed the locks on the house one day. Before we could get the authorities involved, he had already sold the house, emptied the bank accounts, stolen the cars, everything. This was back when I was in high school.

"A few weeks later, he met me and my younger brother and sister at school. He told us that he had joined The New World and that we could come with him and that we could be together again. My brother and sister went with him. I turned him down. I didn't want anything to do with him.

"Every day, even now, I have to decide whether or not I want to hate him and let that consume me or if I am going to move on with my life. For years, I made the wrong decision. I hated my father, and I let that drive everything I did, even when I wouldn't admit it. Instead of trying to destroy The New World, I tried to forget it. I drank; I used drugs; I turned to other pleasures. It wasn't until I met John that my perspective began to change. He told me about God. He said that God was a Father. Of course, that didn't mean anything to me. It meant less than nothing. It meant that God was someone to be avoided and despised. And I told John that. I told John everything.

"So instead, John told me about a God who loves me and forgives me and is a friend who sticks closer than a brother. And John chose to show me exactly what that meant, through thick and thin. I did some awful stuff, and John knew about it, and he still became and remained my friend. Even when I or someone else hurt John, he would forgive us. I asked him once how he could forgive others. His response was that Jesus helped him to forgive and that Jesus wanted us even to love our enemies and pray for those that persecute us."

"I don't think I could do that," Kyle interrupted.

"That's exactly what I said to John. John told me that we are all enemies of God. John explained to me again the gravity of the wrong things that I had done. Jesus gave only two rules: love the Lord with all your heart, soul, mind, and strength, and love others as you love yourself. Whenever we break either of those laws, we show that we are not worthy of God and that we deserve to be punished by being separated from God and, by extension, everything that we consider 'good.' Every time I hated my father, I broke the second rule. It wasn't until after I died that I understood just how serious that was."

"But our fathers deserve that! They deserve our hate! How can that be wrong?" Kyle shouted.

What am I still doing here? Kyle thought. *Why am I even staying to have this philosophical conversation with Josh?*

"Kyle, we all deserve that and so much worse. Just like The New World deserves to be punished because they have broken human laws, we deserve to be punished for breaking God's laws. If we do not love God or others, it is as if we have committed treason against God by trying to steal His power and wealth and home and use it for our own gain. This is the exact same thing that our fathers have done to us.

"But God, in spite of all that we've done, still loves us. He loved us enough to take our place and endure the punishment that we deserved so that we wouldn't have to be separated from Him forever. God chose to endure what I deserved so that I could enjoy what He deserved."

Kyle was stunned. His mind was racing. *What does all of this mean? Is there any truth to what Josh is saying? Josh has made some good points. Maybe he's right...*

No! I can't *stop hating The New World! I* can't *just ignore them! I have no choice! I* won't *allow myself to stop! I still have to save Jill.* Kyle's being, in a united effort, shut out Josh's words. His being could not fully repress the conversation, but his being did slide it to the deep recesses of his mind.

"And you believe all that?" Kyle asked, trying to trick himself into believing that he would consider the thoughts later. Josh's words and their implications tried to surface; Kyle held them in check.

"Yes. Jesus has had a profound impact on my life. He freed me from my hate. He healed me from my additions. He gave me a job, helped me pass the GED, save for college, earn a degree, and get a better well-paid engineering job. Every day is still a struggle for me to forgive my father, especially when I think about what life could have been like if he had stayed. But every day I choose to forgive, I feel as if a giant weight has been lifted off me." Josh hesitated. "Kyle, I'm sorry that I didn't say this before now. It's one of the hardest things for me to talk about. You are the only person, besides John and my family, to know this story."

"Do you ever wish that you could be with your father again?" Kyle asked genuinely.

"My father has made it clear that we could only be together if I aided The New World. That price is too high.

The New World is evil, and there is nothing that would ever make me want to join him."

The thoughts had almost broken free! Kyle was about to ask another genuine question when he thought of the time. It was already midnight!

"I've got to go!" Kyle shouted. *I hope that Jill's all right,* Kyle thought. The strange concepts from the conversation had all but disappeared from Kyle's mind.

"Before you go," Josh asked, "can I pray for you?"

I don't have time for this! Kyle thought. But for some reason, he answered, "Sure." He reconsidered his gut reaction. *What can the prayer hurt? Maybe it will help get Jill back.*

Kyle did not hear any of the prayer. His only thought was, *I hope that Jill is still alive.*

****

Kyle uttered a hasty goodbye to Josh before leaving the apartment. Kyle, still clutching the doormat, thundered down the crumbling stairs. *I'm already late! I'm so late! I never should have listened to that "voice"!* The forgotten words spoken by Josh began to resurface. Kyle pushed the thoughts down again. He would think about them later—if "later" ever came.

Kyle sneaked into the gravel alley, where he had been left for dead several days ago, and arrived at the door he had used earlier that day to enter the building where he had almost died…several times. Kyle could hardly see where he was walking. The moon offered barely any light, but Kyle could see enough. He looked around the alley. No one was following him. *That's all that matters,* Kyle thought. Kyle tried the door handle to the warehouse. The door opened easily. Kyle gave another furtive glance around the alley—he was still alone—and ducked inside the warehouse.

"You're late," a voice accused before Kyle had even closed the door. Kyle recognized the voice from earlier that day.

"I came alone," Kyle returned. The little light from the moon was gone. He could not distinguish anything in the abandoned warehouse.

"If you hadn't, we wouldn't be having this conversation." Kyle was unsure where to look. The voice seemed to come from everywhere. Kyle heard the ceiling boards above him creak. "Where's the mat?" The voice came from directly in front of Kyle, startling him. Kyle could barely distinguish the outline of a man. Kyle slowly moved the mat closer to the shadow. Without warning, it was snatched from his hand. Kyle could tell that the thug was inspecting the mat.

"Where's Jill?" Kyle asked. Kyle could barely discern the form looking back toward Kyle.

"Patience. We'll take you to see her now."

Kyle heard motion behind him and felt a sharp pain on the back of his head.

That was his last memory from the warehouse.

CHAPTER 14

Kyle first noticed that he was freezing. He tried warming himself with his hands and tried opening his eyes to determine where he was, but he could do neither. He could feel himself standing, almost hanging, vertically with his hands chained high above his head. He tried moving his feet only to find them bolted to the floor. He could not see any light, only darkness. He could move his head and feel that there was something over his eyes, but he could not remove it. Despite knowing that he was a captive of the enemy, Kyle futilely called for help only to realize that something was stuffed in his mouth to prevent him from making any noise.

The temperature continued to drop. Kyle felt the cold wind blow directly against his body. He could feel that he was no longer wearing anything except his pants. Kyle flexed his muscles in an attempt to stay warm. He was successful for a little while, but his muscles began to fatigue. Kyle gritted his teeth and pushed through the exhaustion. He continued for another eon. Kyle could not tell how much time had passed. He had no way of knowing. Kyle felt himself become warmer, but when he stopped flexing, the cold returned even more fiercely than before. Still, Kyle continued. His body, despite the tiredness, agreed with the rest of Kyle's being: if he stopped, Kyle would slip into hypothermia and die. Kyle could not continue forever, and he accepted that. But the cold continued, and that meant Kyle would continue as long as he could.

Finally, Kyle succumbed to the pain. Despite the urgings of his mind, spirit, and soul, Kyle's body could no longer move. His muscles were just too tired. His mind conceded that his body could no longer move. Kyle's spirit and soul refused to give up their pleas. The vote was two to two. But his body, since it was burdened with the work, received the weighted vote. Kyle would rest in spite of the cold. When he had enough strength, he would continue.

Kyle let his body hang by his hands and allowed his mind to wander while he rested. *Why is The New World doing this? What's the point? They have the mat. They've kidnapped Jill to stop my testimony. Why kidnap me? Why not kill me and silence me forever? The New World has done the same to many others before me. What makes me different?*

The room suddenly became quiet. For the first time, Kyle realized that a loud motor had been running in the background, most likely producing the frigid air. He heard the sound of air blowing and felt the room become warmer. When the room had reached a comfortable temperature, the blowing stopped. Kyle waited in silence for several seconds. Then, a door opened.

"I'm impressed! Even with your injuries, you lasted fifteen minutes longer than Bull!" a male voice said. Kyle heard the speaker's footsteps, along with several other pairs, move closer to him. "No one else thought that you had the guts to do it, but I never doubted you." A pair of footsteps, who had continued to walk behind Kyle, removed the gag from Kyle's mouth.

"What do you want with me?" Kyle accused the voice.

Immediately, the blindfold was released from Kyle's eyes. As soon as it fell away, Kyle was blinded by the brightness of a small empty white room. Kyle's visitors were only shadows. When he could finally see again, he looked straight at the speaker. Kyle could hardly believe his eyes. It was his father. He seemed colder and harder than the man Kyle once knew.

Kyle spat into his father's face. He had been waiting for this moment for so long! Kyle swore at his father. How many times had he thought about the words to say! Now Kyle could unleash them!

Long before Kyle was finished, the big Caucasian from the warehouse alley stepped from behind Kyle and punched him in the face. Kyle felt the same bone in his cheek break. Kyle spat blood onto the floor. He stopped talking.

"That's no way to talk to your father," James patronized as he wiped his face. "Especially after not seeing each other for a while."

"*You* left *us*, remember?" Kyle shouted, expecting another blow.

The big Caucasian was more than happy to give it, but James Baker stopped him. "That's enough, Bull." Bull obeyed. Kyle watched in disbelief. "So you're their leader?"

James shrugged. "Always have been."

That makes perfect sense! Kyle thought to himself. *That's why my bonds were cut instead of me being drowned in the warehouse! That's why the posse leader had said that he wasn't allowed to kill me! My father has been orchestrating the events and has been watching me all along!*

"So…what?" Kyle asked aloud. "You crawled down here begging for a job, and they just made you their king?"

This time Bull punched Kyle in the stomach, knocking the wind out of him. James did not intervene. When Kyle could breathe again, James answered.

"You misunderstand. I was always a part of The New World. My father brought me into The New World when I was twelve years old. It was the family business. I learned everything he knew and taught him a few things along the way. In my prime, I stole billions; I killed thousands; I extended The New World into every major city in North America and beyond. I transformed The New World from a simple gang into a global mafia. The New World has become the standard for the next stage of evolution in organized crime. We make our own weapons, print our own money, develop our own drugs, recruit new members from schools…we even have scientists, lawyers, and politicians researching new breakthroughs and pushing our agenda. When the government legalizes drugs, we corner the market as legitimate businesses. If weapons are outlawed, we can build our own. When someone stands in our way, we apply leverage and gain an ally or remove them and replace them with a friend.

"We have maintained global connections and operations with our fellow brothers and sisters without compromising our security. We have infiltrated thousands of police stations and have hundreds of federal investigators on our side. We have spies in strategic places around the city. By the way, I assume you went after Nick because you believed that he was the one who tainted your drink. That was a lucky guess. The bartender was one of ours as well. He was the one that spiked your drink and gave us your bike for resale. You wouldn't believe how many people, especially high-profile people, have come to that bar that he's drugged. He's consistently been one of our best assets in the field."

Kyle was in complete disbelief.

James continued, "We have perfected money laundering and identity creation. As soon as someone is discovered, they are given a new identity and moved to a different city."

Kyle was alarmed. "Is that what happened to you?" Kyle asked, trying to disguise the surprise in his voice.

James nodded. "When I was your age, I was discovered. I took too many risks. Within the day, I was given a new identity and moved up to Boston. For years, my job was to disappear, gather intel, and report back what I had learned. I even took your mother as an additional cover. Handy, she moved up to Boston just before I was discovered."

Kyle swore at his father and cursed his name. "So it was all an act!" Kyle screamed.

James motioned for Bull to stop before the big Caucasian even had time to react.

"First, 'James' isn't my name. Not anymore. When I was inducted into The New World, I lost my old name and received a new one. My name is 'Augustus'; I am the 'divine ruler' of the Jacksonville division of The New World. I left Boston when it was time for me to assume my power.

"And it was not all an act. I taught you everything I know. I taught you to hone your mind, spirit, soul, and body. I taught you the importance of those four aspects of a man. I built you into a man worthy of my blood. Then I left, and your world fell apart. You could either abandon my teaching and wither or embrace my teaching and survive. You chose to survive. You were forced to cling to those aspects of your being and mold yourself into a man that could endure all things. And you succeeded beyond my wildest imagination!

"Before I could ask you to join me, you came yourself, and you tried to destroy what I had built. We attacked your mind, and you restored yourself. We attacked your body, and you returned to fight against us. And with the final test, against both your body and mind, you surpassed even our strongest member in Jacksonville. You have truly achieved the four qualities, especially the spirit and soul, which are the hardest to master.

"And now, finally, we are together. And I am going to ask you the same question that I meant to ask you many months ago. Will you join us? Join The New World, and in time, you will become the new Augustus. Join us, and we can be together again."

Kyle did not have to think twice. "No," he responded in much more colorful terms.

Bull did not move. Augustus smiled and chuckled to himself as a parent would at the foolish actions of a child. "You don't need to be afraid, Kyle. We're all your friends." Augustus proceeded to introduce the three other individuals who were in the room. "This is Bull," he said, pointing to the big Caucasian from the alley. "This is Onyx," Augustus said; Kyle recognized him as the Latino from the drug bust and from Nick's apartment. "This is Dingo," Augustus introduced, motioning to the small Caucasian from the alley. "And you already know Jill."

"Jill?" Kyle gasped. Kyle had forgotten that he had come to save her. He berated himself for forgetting her.

The only door to the room opened, and Jill appeared. She was fine but seemed to have been crying. Jill ran toward Kyle and embraced him. Kyle was unable to do anything to return the affection. "Jill! Jill, are you all right? Did they hurt you?" Jill did not say anything. She just shook her head. "Let her go," Kyle commanded Augustus. "I've given you all that you've asked for."

Augustus shook his head. "She is free to leave whenever she wishes. She stays because she is one of us."

"What!" Kyle screamed at the man he hated. He turned to his old girlfriend. "Jill?"

"My name's not 'Jill,'" the woman said. "Not here. Out there, my name is 'Jill.' Here, my name is 'Delilah.'"

Kyle recalled hearing the story of Samson and Delilah either during church or during the prayer group. He swore. "So you played me this whole time too," he said, shooting a glare at Augustus.

"No! All that was genuine," Delilah pleaded. "Everything that we had together was real! I love you! When I visited my cousin, I came to see you because I love you! I didn't realize that you were Augustus' son. Not until yesterday. "

"Don't lie to him. He'll see right through you," Augustus complained. He turned to Kyle. "I called her here. The 'divine ruler' of Boston owed me a favor. Still does."

"That's not true!" Delilah insisted. "Kyle, you believe me. Don't you?"

Kyle turned his head away from them both. He did not know what to believe.

"Thank you, Delilah. You may go," Augustus ordered. The woman who used to be Jill left without another word. Augustus continued, "Kyle, I only threatened Delilah because we needed you to come to the warehouse alone. I'm not going to threaten anyone to make you join The New World. And that includes Claire." Kyle stiffened at the name and turned to face Augustus.

"If you do anything to her, I swear—"

"You are in no position to be making threats," Augustus commanded. "I just want a simple answer. Are you going to join us?"

Kyle adamantly refused. He threw a curse into the refusal as well. Again, Bull did not move.

Augustus became angry.

"You don't understand, Kyle. The only reason I didn't kill you was because I wanted you at my side. You will be part of The New World either as a brother and a member of the family or as a prisoner until you choose to become one of us. What is your final decision?"

Again, Kyle refused, even more vigorously than his last two refusals.

As soon as the words were out of his mouth, a sharp crack like lightning split the air. Kyle felt a sharp pain like a burn across the length of his back. He cried in pain. He tightened his back muscles in an attempt to reduce the residual sting. He could feel blood dripping down his back.

Augustus spoke again, "Wrong answer, Kyle. If you continue to refuse, you will receive worse—much worse. I will ask you again in a little while. If you refuse again, we will continue to break you until you accept our offer. There is no other choice." Augustus turned to leave, and his comrades followed suit.

"You'll never break me," Kyle called defiantly.

Augustus turned back toward Kyle and smiled. "Of course, I will. I'm your father."

As soon as the door was closed, the motor started again, and the air became colder.

****

Kyle was livid at—he could not even call him "his father" anymore. That man was now "Augustus," a man that Kyle never knew. Kyle denied that he was related to Augustus. That man was a monster worthy of hate. Kyle screamed curses at Augustus. While they did little to warm him, they made Kyle feel better.

Kyle channeled anger into his being. He would not be broken by Augustus so easily. Kyle did all that he could to keep warm. But his muscles were still tired from his previous and newly inflicted injuries and from his previous fight against the cold. Still, Kyle resisted. He flexed every muscle and enjoyed the warmth before it was stripped away. His body reached the point of exhaustion much faster than the first time. Still, Kyle resisted. His mind and body knew that failure to persist would most likely result in another lash that stung in the frigid room. He moved and flexed until his mind agreed with his body and screamed for him to stop. Still, Kyle resisted. Kyle hung limp. But his body, unable to move with fatigue, shivered tirelessly.

Kyle could feel the hypothermia crawl into his being. His mind began to cloud. He was nearing unconsciousness. Kyle's wrists and ankles had been numb since he had originally woken in the empty white room, but now, he felt the numbness spread down his arms into his shoulders and chest and up from his ankles into his calves and thighs. Sharp needles of pain dug at all points of his body. The shivering was no longer effective. As soon as Kyle realized that, the shivering stopped.

As if Kyle's shivering had driven the loud motor, the creation of the cold air ceased. The air in the room slowly warmed. Kyle's shaky breath disappeared. Kyle did not notice. He let himself hang by his wrists. He no longer had the strength to stand.

Kyle only heard a voice that sounded like it was coming from infinitely far away.

"I'm impressed! I checked twice to make sure that you were still alive. I thought for sure that they'd forgotten to tell me that it was time to ask you again." Kyle did not even move in response. But with every word the voice spoke, a fire rekindled within Kyle's being. Kyle hated Augustus with all that he had! Augustus continued, "What do you say, Kyle?" Kyle's chin was raised to look Augustus in the face. Augustus was smiling. "Escape from this place and join me."

The effort required to speak was laborious, but Kyle finally managed the strength to respond.

"You'll have to kill me first," he said with all the venom he could rally.

Augustus stepped back just in time for Bull's whip to slice Kyle's back. Kyle screamed in half-hearted agony. Without warning, the whip returned, lacerating Kyle's right side. Kyle could only grunt in pain. He noticed that several drops of his blood provided a stark contrast to the icy white floor.

Augustus lifted Kyle's eyes to look into his. He was no longer smiling. "The whipping will increase for each refusal. Choose wisely."

Without another word, Augustus and Bull exited the igloo.

When they had left, the temperature dropped again.

****

Kyle could not track the passage of time. He had no way to tell how much time had passed. How many days had he been a prisoner of The New World? Kyle could not tell.

So he counted the times that he was subjected to the freezer. But the cold played with his mind. He had lost count several times. He had been through the cycle maybe six…or seven times. He was unsure.

So Kyle counted the times that he was whipped. But he discovered that he would fall unconscious between lashes only to wake when he received the next strike. He never remembered more than five between cold spells. Kyle knew it was more; a small pool of blood had formed around his feet.

Through his delirium, Kyle knew that Augustus was playing with him. The torture was designed for someone who strove to embody the four qualities of mind, spirit, soul, and body.

Mind: Kyle knew that nearly freezing to death and the whipping would not only continue but also continue to increase. At what point would his mind decide that the pain was not worth his resistance?

Spirit: Kyle's iron will could only endure so much; his spirit could only fight for so long. When would it choose to quit and answer "yes" to joining The New World instead of "no"?

Soul: Kyle was determined to hate Augustus and reject his offer. His soul was willing for him to die in defiance, but would the defiance be worth the coming pain?

Body: Kyle's body had borne the brunt of the torture. Kyle was parched, but no one gave him water. His body was stiff with cold, and his skin had a blue tint to it. He had lost blood, and his bare flesh stung with every breath of icy wind. How much longer could he endure?

Kyle had tried to beat the master at his own game. *When will I cave?* Kyle wondered. *Is my refusal worth the inevitable acceptance?*

No, not yet. Kyle hated Augustus. He hated The New World. If nothing else, the torture had forged Kyle's resolve stronger. If at all possible, his hatred had grown. Yet, in spite of his hatred, Kyle recognized the danger of caving to Augustus' demands. He had every intention of resisting, but in a moment of weakness, he might fail. The spirit was willing, but the flesh was weak... *Where have I heard that saying before?*

Suddenly, Kyle heard the door open. *Why are they coming?* Kyle still felt as cold as ice. He breathed but did not see his breath. Kyle could no longer feel heat.

Someone yanked Kyle's hair. Kyle saw that it was Bull. Augustus stood directly in front of Kyle. He looked rabid. He tried to say something, but he was too angry to speak. He punched Kyle instead. Kyle was too tired to react.

Finally, Augustus found his words, "No one has ever resisted the freezer! I have whipped you fifty-five times"—Kyle tried to figure out how many repetitions that had been. He could not determine the answer; he was too tired—"and still you reject me!" Augustus punched Kyle again. "I'm going to give you one last chance—"

Kyle casually refused with several expletives. Augustus punched Kyle again.

"Don't be so rash!" Augustus seethed. "You may be stronger in mind, spirit, soul, and body than anyone else, but there is not a single man that I haven't been able to break!"

The door behind Augustus reopened. Onyx entered, carrying a small cauldron; he set it several feet away. The cauldron was filled with glowing orange coals. Slowly, Kyle began to feel the heat from the coals. Onyx buried one end of a long metal rod deep into the cast iron bowl; only the wooden handle was still visible.

Kyle had a bad feeling about this.

"The only way you leave this room is either dead or as a willing member of The New World!" Augustus lowered his voice to a whisper. "And we won't let you die." Augustus' eyes were ice cold. The eyes were filled with hate!

Kyle could hardly move in his current position, but Bull held him so that he could barely squirm. In one fluid action, Augustus wretched the iron device from the cauldron, scattering orange coals across the floor. Kyle recognized the device. It was a branding iron. The heated end was almost the color of the remaining coals in the bucket. Kyle did not have the time or the energy to react. Without hesitation, Augustus stabbed the brand onto the left side of Kyle's chest.

The pain was excruciating! Kyle screamed! What little adrenaline remained in him fueled his attempts to escape, but Bull was too strong. Without other options, Kyle continued to scream in pain. In his anguish, he cursed The New World, and he cursed Augustus. Finally, Kyle exhausted his energy. Only when Kyle had stopped screaming did Augustus remove the brand. Kyle hung limp. He did not have the energy to raise his head.

Kyle looked at his wound. The entire left side of his chest was burned red. In the middle of the raw wound was a symbol made of black charred flesh. Kyle could not tell what it was. Kyle could feel the burn sapping the little energy he retained.

Augustus grabbed Kyle's hair and looked him in the eye.

"You are now property of The New World. There is no escaping us, Kyle. There is no escaping me. You will be a part of our family either now or later. There is no other option. If you continue to resist, you will be unmade in the most horrific ways possible."

Kyle was incensed. He did not need to consult his being. With one voice, his mind, spirit, soul, and body openly raged against Augustus and The New World. His being rallied enough energy to stand on his feet without hanging by his wrists.

"I...hate...you," Kyle managed to say.

Augustus screamed in frustration and punched Kyle's

face. Kyle let every muscle in his body hang limp. He had no energy left to stand.

"Then you have made your own choice," Augustus said. He turned his back toward Kyle. Augustus' last sentence almost sounded pained. Augustus turned around and looked at the man behind Kyle. "Bull, destroy him as you will, but leave him alive."

When Kyle heard those words, his measureless anger and hatred toward Augustus only increased. Augustus was handing him over to Bull for even more suffering!

Bull wandered into Kyle's vision. He was wearing a hideous grin on his face and cracked his knuckles. A bottomless, black fear, greater than Kyle's hate, welled from his soul and poured through the rest of his being. *Bull is a sadist! He is going to enjoy nearly killing me!* Kyle was sickened at the thought. His whole being was sickened at the thought!

"No, please!" Kyle croaked. With a burst of energy, he stood on his own to emphasize his entreaty. Augustus had already turned around and started walking toward the door. "Please," Kyle groaned slightly louder. Still, Augustus continued for the door. Despite his revulsion at saying the words, Kyle said, "Dad, please no." Each word required enormous strength to even speak. Even still, Augustus left the room and closed the door behind him.

****

Three hours later, Bull left the room. He had replaced

Kyle's blindfold and gag. The room had remained warm. Without any visual distractions or life-threatening conditions, Kyle was left alone in his anguish.

Bull had unleashed his full power against Kyle. Kyle recalled every blow. Kyle felt his bones break and pop out of joint. His back was an open wound, sensitive to every breath of wind, and sent waves of agony through his body whenever Bull kicked him. Kyle felt his ribs break and scrape against his lungs even when he barely breathed.

At first, Kyle screamed at the new pain. Then, he could only yell. Soon, he could only groan. Finally, Kyle would make no noise at all in spite of his indescribable torment. He had no energy to do anything else other than silently sob.

Kyle was utterly broken.

His mind recognized that his pain was no longer worth resisting The New World. Kyle recalled the words spoken to him in the alley, "If it doesn't stop, what you got today won't compare with what will happen. I may not be allowed to kill you, but everything else is fair game." As unimaginable as it was, Kyle knew that his pain would only increase as long as he continued to resist. His mind voted to surrender to The New World.

Kyle's spirit could no longer fight against Augustus. As much as he loathed submitting to The New World, he had endured too much. Augustus had broken his will; Kyle had no choice but to submit.

His soul was unimaginably afraid of what would happen to him next if he refused the offer to join The New World.

He had endured too much already! Kyle's determination to resist was gone. He could not die in defiance; The New World would not let him. His only option was to become a servant to Augustus.

Kyle's body screamed for death! Death would have been preferable to the unending agony of his injuries. Kyle could feel his blood pooling at his feet. A fate even worse than death awaited him if he continued to resist. Kyle's body agreed to finally surrender.

Kyle had decided—his whole being had decided—when he was asked again, Kyle would accept the offer to join The New World. Kyle held no reservations. Nothing was worth more abuse—either verbal or physical—from Bull.

Kyle wept, alone in his thoughts, unable to escape the trauma of his time with Bull.

****

Hours passed. Kyle's posture remained unchanged. He could not escape the memory of his time with Bull and the pervasive sharp anguish that tormented his body.

Where was god this whole time? Kyle wondered. *Everyone in the prayer group claimed that god is good and righteous. How is god good if he allows a monster like Bull to nearly kill me and enjoy it?* Kyle cursed Josh and Claire's God through his gag. *Either god has abandoned me, or he is not as good as everyone believes.* Kyle gave several more curses for good measure. *Their god, if he even exists, deserves it for Augustus' robbery, my mother's death, Joan's mistreatment of me, me being beaten down multiple times, Delilah's betrayal, letting me nearly freeze to death, and Bull—*

The door opened. *Bull is back!* Kyle immediately started to panic.

Are they going to let me talk? Kyle thought. *I'm ready to submit! I am willing to be a part of The New World! I don't have any reservations! My whole being agrees!*

Kyle mumbled through his gag. None of his words were understandable.

"Kyle?" a female voice said. Kyle barely calmed; the voice belonged to Delilah. "I didn't want this to happen," Delilah said. Kyle cursed her vehemently. She could not understand his words, but Kyle hoped that the hostility in his voice conveyed the message. "I didn't want this to happen," Delilah repeated. "I didn't want any of this to happen. I asked to see you. I wanted to talk with you about…all this."

Kyle relaxed slightly but remained guarded. *What is she doing here? What does she want?* Kyle thought.

Delilah continued, "I know it couldn't have been easy learning that we were all a part of The New World. Or that your father was the leader." Kyle stiffened when she said "your father." Delilah noticed. "I know your father."

I have no father, thought Kyle.

"He would never hurt you—"

Then take a look at my chest and my back and anywhere else on my body.

"—unless he thought that there was no other way."

There was until he stole from us and left us on the street.

"I hate seeing you like this. I begged them not to hurt you. Every time they came out, I begged them to let me talk to you! I didn't want you to endure any more torture. Even after Bull, they still wouldn't let me see you. I had to sneak in here now. I still care about you, Kyle. I always have. You know that…right?"

Kyle was not sure what to think. Despite being broken in his resistance toward The New World, he still held great animosity toward Augustus and reluctance toward his ex-girlfriend. *Maybe this is another trick?* Kyle wondered. Kyle was unsure how to respond. He hung silent and motionless.

Delilah did not like that. "Kyle, I still love you. That part of our relationship was always real. I've loved you ever since we first met. Don't you believe me?" Kyle did not know if Delilah was telling the truth. Again, he made no sign.

Delilah touched him. Kyle later reasoned that she had probably just meant to reinforce her words and to show that she cared. But the images of the three hours together with Bull filled Kyle's blank vision. Kyle recoiled from the touch. He groaned and shook, trying to escape the memories, pain shooting through every broken bone, every dislocated joint, and every open wound. Again, his being agreed that he should avoid another lifetime with Bull, regardless of the cost.

The door opened again. "Hey! You're not supposed to be in here!" a male voice accused. Kyle shuddered. The voice was Bull's.

Delilah had no explanation. "I'll go."

"If you did anything, I'm coming after you next." Kyle stiffened at the thought of that monster doing anything to Jill, but he did not say or do anything to defend Delilah. She deserved it.

Kyle heard Delilah walk to the door and close it behind her.

"Don't count on her being able to save you, Kyle," Bull began. "Whatever she promised, she can't deliver. She begged for your release and for your old man to spare you from torture." Bull chuckled. "And look how that turned out. Augustus knew you weren't that soft. He knew that he'd made you stronger than that. And he's never wrong. That's why he calls the shots here. And my orders are to make you submit to us by whatever means necessary.

"When I first came to The New World, Augustus, even from Boston, saw my potential as an interrogator. I have killed almost as many as your father, but I have turned twice as many to The New World.'" Kyle felt a knife at his throat. He lifted his head to alleviate the pressure, but the pressure only increased. Kyle continued to lift his head until he would have been looking Bull in the face. The pressure ceased; the knife had stopped moving. "Everyone that I have tortured has chosen to swear allegiance to The New World. If you refuse again, we get to spend a few hours together." Kyle shuttered. The suffering from his culminated afflictions flooded Kyle's mind. "So Kyle," Bull asked, "have you had a chance to think about our offer again?"

Kyle knew the alternatives. He did not have a choice. His being had already decided.

Kyle nodded his head slowly to avoid the blade.

Kyle felt the knife leave his throat and heard Bull sheath the blade. First, Bull removed the blindfold; then, he removed the gag.

"What's your answer?" Bull asked. Bull wore the same hideous grin from before the torture. Kyle hated Bull, The New World, and Augustus more than he ever had before now! Still, Kyle knew and agreed that he had no choice other than to surrender. His choice hardly mattered. Whatever answer Kyle gave, Bull would win.

"I—" Kyle croaked. His mouth was suddenly dry. He had been thirsty for as far back as he could remember being a prisoner, but he had always been able to talk. Now, he could not speak. He released several hoarse, dry coughs.

"I—" Kyle started again. Without warning, Kyle felt a familiar power wash over his body. The "Voice" had returned. It overcame Kyle's mind, spirit, soul, and body and beseeched Kyle to resist just a little longer. Kyle rejected the "Voice" without consideration. It had led him astray to Josh's apartment, and if it had anything to do with God, as Josh had suggested, Kyle did not want anything to do with it. The "Voice" was going to kill him. Kyle had to join The New World.

Bull was growing impatient. So was Kyle. He had quenched the "Voice" and could finally speak.

"I submit."

Kyle's surrender was never heard. The door slammed open, drowning Kyle's words and startling the two men. Augustus appeared. He looked even more enraged than the last time Kyle had seen him.

"Cut him loose," Augustus ordered.

"What!" Bull roared. "He was about to cave!"

"Do it, Jake! Or you'll be the next person we put in here!"

Bull grudgingly obeyed. He unlocked Kyle's feet and then freed his hands. Kyle collapsed to the floor. He was too weak to stand. His dislocated shoulder prevented Kyle from catching himself. Multiple scabs on his back ruptured. Several broken ribs dug into his lungs. Both broken collarbones twisted violently. Kyle groaned in pain; he did not have the energy for more of a response. *What's happening? Why am I being unchained?* Kyle wondered. Bull yanked Kyle off the floor. If he had the energy, Kyle would have screamed. Bull's "help" only caused more pain. Kyle struggled to balance on his feet.

As soon as Kyle stood, Augustus punched him in the face. Kyle sprawled on the ground. Kyle had no energy left to react.

"Get up," Augustus yelled. Kyle could not respond. Augustus kicked him. *"Get up!"* If Kyle had the energy, he would have obeyed the man he had sworn never to obey again. Kyle could do nothing else. The pain and torment were too much. They had broken him. Kyle had surrendered. In spite of his hate, Kyle would join The New World. Augustus had won.

Again, Bull roughly and reluctantly stood Kyle on his feet.

Kyle looked at Augustus. Augustus hesitated. He appeared to be deciding whether or not to hit Kyle again. Kyle noticed that Augustus' hands were balled into fists. Grudgingly, the hands opened, and the loathing, wrinkled expression softened into mere hatred. Augustus tried to speak. He had difficulty forming the words, almost as if he regretted speaking them. "You…are free. You can go."

Kyle did not understand. *Free?* Kyle thought. *Are they going to release me? Why would they do that?*

"*What!*" Bull roared, swearing. "We were this close! He was *this close* to breaking!"

"Shut up, Bull!" Augustus demanded.

Bull refused to be silenced. "He was going to give up right before you arrived!"

"*Shut up!* I said shut up!" Augustus was red with fury. He softened his tone only slightly. He addressed Kyle, but he was speaking to Bull. "We were offered a trade for your life. Someone has offered to join us in exchange for your freedom," Augustus spat.

None of this made sense to Kyle. *Does The New World really live by that code?* Kyle thought. *Will they really release me? Is this another trick? Are they just trying to break me further by dashing my hopes of freedom?*

More importantly: *If all this is actually true, who would exchange their life for mine?*

Bull swore at Augustus' explanation. "And you took *that*

deal?" Bull accused.

Augustus glared at Bull. "I chose a willing brother instead of breaking a stranger into submission."

"But we broke him! He won't dare to cross us now!"

"The other one showed up on our doorstep and dared us to take him in exchange for Kyle, or he would call the police!"

Bull swore. "And you actually believed him? Just put a bullet in his head!"

Augustus cursed him. "Watch it! I don't need to explain myself to you! If you don't like it"—a weapon pointed at Bull appeared in Augustus' hand—"*you'll* get a bullet in *your* head!" The weapon remained pointed at Bull, but Augustus' tone quieted again. "Onyx concurred with my decision. We don't know what safeguards our visitor put in place. We're going to talk to him now. I want *you* there. This other guy was—is—a wild card. Best to keep a close eye on him." Augustus motioned to Kyle. "Breaking Kyle will prevent him from speaking to the authorities about us. And we'll make sure he doesn't know where we are." Augustus holstered his weapon. "Sooner or later, Kyle will come back to us. Everyone you break does. You did good." Augustus turned back toward Kyle and poked the fresh brand. Kyle winced in pain. "You will always be a part of us," Augustus whispered to Kyle.

Augustus left the room, not waiting for Kyle to respond or follow. Bull waited. He glared at Kyle and muttered under his breath. Kyle took a hesitant step forward and nearly fell in the process. He glanced at Bull for approval. Bull crossed his arms and gave Kyle a sneer but made no move to stop him. The decision for Kyle's freedom was beyond Bull's control.

Kyle took several more steps. His joints were stiff from cold and lack of movement. One of his ankles felt like it had been at least sprained. Kyle reached the doorframe and leaned against it as he caught his breath. Even walking those few steps had been exhausting. The hallway outside his prison was a welcome sight. Further down the hallway, Kyle could see Augustus talking to someone in another room. Kyle despaired. He could not walk all the way down the hallway. He did not have the energy.

Someone shoved Kyle through the doorway and into the opposing wall. Kyle lost his balance and fell onto the ground. Several more wounds tore on his back.

"Get up," Bull sighed. Kyle could not move. He needed to catch his breath. When Kyle did not move, Bull dragged Kyle to his feet by the hair. Kyle found his balance with great effort and rested against the wall. Kyle heard Bull unsheath his knife and felt a sharp prick on his wounded back. Kyle reluctantly crept forward. When he could no longer continue, Kyle received another prick and continued another few steps. Whenever Kyle stopped, Bull goaded him forward. Kyle had to stop several times, but Bull moved him almost as fast as if Kyle had been walking normally. Kyle grasped the doorframe to the room where Augustus stood.

Onyx stood at the other end of the room with another

man. Through his clouded mind, Kyle recognized the third person in the room: Josh.

CHAPTER 15

What's Josh doing here? thought Kyle. Then, a horrible idea struck him. *Josh has been captured! Just like me! He will be imprisoned in the white room, just as I was. He will nearly freeze to death, be whipped repeatedly, be branded, and if he continues to resist, will be beaten almost to death— all, just like I was—until Josh is broken.*

Kyle surrendered to his despair. Both he and Josh were permanent prisoners of The New World. Worse, they would be allies, accomplices of The New World until they died.

Another thought surfaced. *Maybe Josh is a member of The New World! I've been played all along! First, Augustus! Then Delilah! Now Josh! I can't trust anyone! Everyone I've ever trusted belongs to The New World!*

Then, Kyle remembered. *Augustus did say that "someone" was substituting their life in The New World for mine. Is that "someone" Josh?*

Augustus, looking grim, turned toward Kyle and motioned harshly toward Josh at the other end of the room.

"He will take your place," Augustus spat, as if to answer

Kyle's silent thoughts.

"Josh," Kyle gasped.

"Quiet!" ordered Bull, who was standing behind Kyle.

Kyle did not hear; he was too choked to say more. Josh nodded in response. Josh did not say anything. The same mortified expression upon first seeing Kyle remained on his face. "Why are you doing this?" Kyle asked Josh.

"Quiet!" ordered Bull. He shanked Kyle's left flank with his knife. Kyle yelped in pain and struggled to keep his balance with one hand on the doorframe and the other on the new wound. He felt the blood trickle through his fingers.

Josh said nothing. Instead, Onyx started to speak.

"Josh, do you choose to join us as part of The New World?"

"Yes, I do," Josh replied.

"And why do you choose to join us now?"

"I want to join you in place of Kyle. I want to be a substitute for him."

"And why would we allow that?" Augustus asked.

"Because I left a letter with our location. If one of us doesn't retrieve it, the entire Jacksonville SWAT team will descend on this place."

"So why the trade?" Onyx asked. "Why not demand Kyle's freedom and keep your own?"

Josh stuttered, "Well…uh…it's…um…I…wanted to give you a sign of good faith."

"I don't buy it," Bull announced. Augustus and Onyx looked his way and nodded their heads in agreement.

"Did you search him?" Augustus asked Onyx.

"Yes," Onyx said, exasperated. Onyx turned to Josh. "I've asked you for years to join me, your brother, and your sister. So that we could be a family again. And—"

"You forgot Mom," Josh interrupted venomously. Onyx punched Josh and sent him reeling into a wall.

Kyle stared in disbelief. *Onyx is Josh's father! That makes so much sense! I can see now that they look alike.* Kyle marveled: *Josh is willing to work with his father— something that he said that he would never do—so that I can escape The New World! Why would he do that?*

Onyx pulled Josh off the floor by his throat and pinned him to the wall. Onyx continued to speak, "I asked you for years to join us, and you refused! And now, you walk in here and want to join us to save your friend! I don't buy it!" Onyx shoved his son into the wall again before releasing him.

No one said anything.

"So...where does that leave us?" Josh asked, still massaging his neck.

After a few moments, Augustus calmly responded, "We have no reason to believe what you are telling us is true."

"Then I guess we'll wait and find out," Josh said. Onyx moved to punch Josh again, but Augustus motioned for him to stop.

"No," Augustus began just as calmly as previously. "We are going to give you a chance to verify your words. We will put you through the same tortures that Kyle experienced."

"No!" screamed Kyle. Kyle felt Bull's knife dig into

his side again, and he released a short groan. *Josh doesn't deserve that! Any of that!* Kyle thought silently. *Especially not for me!*

Augustus continued, "If you are still willing to become a part of The New World and if you still insist that you are telling the truth even after all that, then we will release Kyle. Do we have a deal?"

Josh looked at Kyle. Josh cringed. Kyle knew that he must look awful. Aside from what Josh could see, Kyle's back and side had continued to bleed. Kyle was standing in his own blood yet again. Josh hesitated. Kyle shook his head violently. *No, Josh! No!* Kyle thought.

"We have a deal," Josh said. Kyle groaned. Bull pushed past Kyle. He grabbed Josh and started to drag him to the white room.

"One last thing," Augustus said. Bull stopped. Augustus was addressing Onyx but intended Josh to hear as well. "Give the orders. Move everything to our secondary location. I don't want a scrap of evidence indicating that we were ever here."

Onyx nodded and followed Bull and Josh, being forcibly pushed from the room.

Kyle was left alone with Augustus.

"Come, Kyle. Let's see if your friend is as resilient as you are."

****

Kyle felt sick. He was not just nauseated. He felt a large

knot deep in his stomach.

He was distraught and grieved with Josh's decision.

He empathized with Josh in his pain because he had experienced exactly the same suffering.

He hated Josh for agreeing to the torture only to free Kyle after he had become willing to submit to The New World.

He despaired and groaned, knowing what Josh would have to endure.

But above all, Kyle could not shake the feeling of pure evil. Augustus, Bull, Onyx, The New World—they were evil. They were enjoying what they were doing to Josh. Kyle wondered if they enjoyed what they had done to him. Perhaps not Augustus, at least not at the end, but the rest probably did.

As soon as Josh had been pushed out of the room, Augustus ushered Kyle into a nearby control room with gauges and monitors to watch the proceedings. Josh was nowhere near Kyle's "pre-capture" level of physical fitness; he lasted only a slight fraction of the time that Kyle spent in the freezer before he fell unconscious. Bull noticed and mocked Josh openly. Augustus even remarked that he was weak. Onyx failed to defend his son.

Kyle did not want to watch any of what Josh endured. But Augustus forced him to watch the proceedings. For a while, Kyle pretended to watch. He would try to close his eyes or look elsewhere. Augustus caught him once and ordered that he watch or Josh would suffer certain tortures twice. As hard as it was to watch, Kyle dared not look away. It was the least he could do for Josh. Instead, Kyle tried to stare blankly, looking without seeing. Kyle was mostly successful, but Josh's cries or the mocking of The New World would force him back to reality.

In the end, Kyle saw everything. The motor would pour ice-cold air into the room. Josh would nearly faint. The room would warm. Augustus and Bull would ask if Josh was still willing to join The New World and if he was telling the truth about his letter to the SWAT team. Josh would agree. Bull would use the whip. Then the process would repeat.

The ten cycles of freezing. The interrogations. The whipping. Every time Kyle saw the next phase in the cycle, his anxiety and grief increased. He knew what was coming.

Finally, after Augustus and Bull entered, Onyx joined them with a bowl of hot glowing coals. Augustus branded Josh. Then, Bull nearly killed Josh. Those were the second-longest three hours of Kyle's life. Kyle never forgot what he saw. Kyle remembered his own torment. The knot in his stomach grew exponentially until he could barely breathe. Kyle hated to watch, but Augustus threatened to hurt Josh more if Kyle refused. Kyle could see Josh clearly on the monitors. Josh had been broken long before Bull had finished, but now Josh had been destroyed. Bull had shattered whatever power Josh possessed in his mind, spirit, soul, and body.

The New World had done worse than kill Josh; Kyle knew that was by Augustus' design.

And Kyle knew that Josh was doing this for him.

****

The waiting began. For another eon, Kyle and The New World waited for Josh just as The New World had waited for Kyle to dwell alone in silence and consider the "correct" answer to the same question that he would be asked again.

Why did god allow all this? Kyle thought again. *Surely a good god would have prevented Josh from suffering as he had!* Kyle still cursed the God he did not believe existed. Josh deserved so much better from the powers that actually did exist.

Finally, the time came for the final question. Bull and Augustus entered the room. Kyle accompanied him, guarded by Onyx. Bull removed Josh's blindfold and gag. Josh cowered at his first sight of Bull. Bull obviously delighted at that. He waited for the initial fear to dissipate from Josh's face. Then, he asked his question.

"Do you still want to join The New World?"

"Yes," Josh finally croaked.

"Did you really leave a letter for the authorities with our current location?"

"Yes," Josh agreed.

"What about Kyle? Do you swear to join The New World in his place?"

Josh did not speak for some time. When he did, his voice was slow and cracked. Josh sounded like he had no reason to live. "I am here for Kyle. I will trade my life for his. I swear allegiance to The New World." Josh hung his head in shame.

Bull turned toward Augustus and Onyx. Augustus

nodded in approval.

"Release Josh," Augustus said. Bull removed Josh's bonds. He collapsed to the floor and lay in his own blood. Kyle knew that he must have torn several wounds on his back, but Josh did not react.

"Get up," Augustus ordered. Josh did not respond.

"*Get up!*" Augustus shouted. He kicked Josh. Reluctantly, Bull dragged Josh from the ground, and Josh, with great effort, stood on his feet. "Clean him and prepare him for the ceremony," Augustus ordered.

Onyx led his son, not harshly, out of the room. Kyle watched them leave. Augustus did the same. When they were gone, Augustus turned to his son. "You don't have to go," Augustus began with unusual pleasantness. "You could join us. We could be together, just like Josh and Onyx. They have been reunited as father and son. If you joined us, we could all be together—be father and son again."

Kyle almost accepted the offer. Kyle's fear of what The New World would do to him if he refused again was evenly matched by his ravenous hatred for Augustus and The New World.

But from somewhere outside himself, Kyle knew that he could not accept. Josh had suffered too much for his freedom. Kyle knew he had to reject their offer so that Josh would not have suffered in vain.

"No," Kyle finally said, after a long pause. "I have to leave."

The deference fled from Augustus' face. "You will stay

for the ceremony." Augustus turned to leave, hesitated, and turned back toward Kyle. "Whatever you choose, you will always be part of us." He poked Kyle's burnt wound. Despite the pain, Kyle did not react.

****

The next time Kyle saw Josh, Josh was clean and wearing the clothes that he wore when he had arrived. Kyle noticed that Josh had changed so much since then. Josh looked vacant, broken, and defeated—much like how Kyle felt. Josh's injuries were so extensive, he hardly looked like the man Kyle knew from college; Kyle knew that he must look the same way. Kyle now understood why Josh had looked so shocked after seeing Kyle freshly released from captivity.

Josh and Kyle had been led to the room where Kyle had first learned of Josh's part in the exchange. Only Bull and Onyx accompanied them in the room. The first was to guard one prisoner; the other was to encourage the second prisoner.

A large camera on a tripod had been added to the room since they were last there. The camera was facing the far wall where Onyx and Josh stood. There was no way to tell if the camera was on.

Finally, Augustus arrived. He stepped to the front of the room, shook hands with Josh, and started speaking to the camera.

"Thank you all for joining us. I apologize for the unusual methods for conducting the ceremony, but current circumstances have prevented us from letting you be seen."

Augustus glanced away from the camera and shot Kyle a daggered expression. "As you are all probably aware, we have a new brother joining us." Bull gave a celebratory shout. Augustus chuckled. "It's just not the same without everyone here," he smiled. "We have been hoping for this particular recruit for some time. This is one of the sons of Onyx." Augustus gave a dramatic pause, presumably for applause, which Bull provided. "Some of you already know the story, but Onyx was under deep cover for many years. When he returned to The New World, two children, his son Death and his daughter, Artemis, joined the ranks beside him. But his wife and other son chose to reject his offer and live in squalor instead."

"Boo!" shouted Bull from off-camera.

Augustus continued, "Today, after years of waiting, we add a new chapter to that story, for the other son of Onyx has chosen to join our family!" Bull cheered, and Onyx clapped. Josh looked as sullen as death. "Josh, extend your right hand," Augustus commanded. Josh obeyed. Onyx produced an ornate dagger and passed it to Augustus. With a single fluid stroke, Augustus slit his right palm. He handed the blade to Josh. Josh hesitated. He looked at Kyle, then cut the palm of his right hand. Augustus and Josh shook hands. Smiling, Augustus addressed the camera again, "Ladies and gentlemen, please join me in welcoming Steel, our newest member of The New World!"

Onyx and Bull clapped. Together, they started chanting, "Steel! Steel! Steel! Steel!" Kyle tried to drown out the noise. He did not want to think about how many people were chanting the name along with Bull and Onyx. As far as he was concerned, that man was still Josh.

Suddenly, the chanting stopped. Augustus dropped his act and left the front of the room. The broadcast was apparently over. "The deal is done," he said pleasantly to the man who was now Steel. Augustus turned to Bull. "Get *him* out of here," Augustus sneered; he did not bother looking at Kyle. Bull did not hesitate to obey the order. He shoved Kyle down the hallway. Several of Kyle's wounds reopened.

Kyle was eventually pushed into a room full of mirrors. The mirrors seemed different and darker from regular mirrors. They seemed to have no purpose. Kyle wondered if the walls of the room were made of one-way glass. Kyle's belongings were in the middle of the floor. "Change. Now," were Bull's orders. He closed and bolted the door, sealing Kyle inside the mirrored room. Kyle wondered why Bull bothered to leave. Kyle changed as quickly as he could. Kyle realized that many of his belongings were missing. His cash, his credit and debit cards, his watch, his cellular phone, his driver's license—everything of value was gone.

The door opened. Bull was waiting. Kyle did not mention anything.

Kyle stepped out of the room and looked at Bull. Kyle was not sure what to do next. Suddenly, Bull grabbed Kyle's shoulders and neck and started squeezing. Kyle tried to fight him, but he could not; he was too injured and fatigued under the circumstances and too weak in general to fight Bull. Bull smashed Kyle into a wall. He kept feeling and pushing with his fingers. Kyle realized that Bull was looking for a pressure point just as he lost consciousness.

****

Kyle woke with a start. He felt frigid water drench him. The room was completely dark. He could not see anyone. Kyle immediately tested his arms and legs. He could move both. *Am I really free?* Kyle wondered. *Is this even possible? It can't be that easy. Nothing is that easy—not that my captivity has been easy by any stretch of the imagination. The New World doesn't just let people leave... Maybe I'm the special case because Augustus is the leader in this city?*

"Hello?" Kyle asked the darkness. No one answered. Kyle heard nothing. *Perhaps I really am alone,* he thought.

Kyle was not going to wait. He looked around himself again. Kyle noticed walls and a ceiling. They looked familiar, like he had been there sometime previously, but it was impossible to tell without any light.

Kyle stood. The space did look familiar. Crates and pallets decayed against the walls; trash and debris littered the floor. He was somewhere in the warehouse. Kyle was sure of it. This was near the place where he had been abducted so long ago. The exit to the warehouse should be somewhere close. Kyle saw the door.

He walked toward the door and opened it. The moonlight poured into the dark building. He stepped into the alleyway. *It's so great to be outside!* Kyle thought. *I never thought that*

I'd ever be glad to see the empty alley where I was beaten.

Kyle looked beyond the fence. The lights were on in many of the apartments. *Josh lives in one of them... No. Josh no longer lives there. He is now a slave, a willing captive, of The New World. What will happen to Josh's mom?* Kyle had no answer.

Kyle walked toward his grandmother's house. The initial excitement at freedom worn away, Kyle tired. He barely made it to the end of the alley before collapsing from exhaustion. The pain of his wounds had returned and spiked with the fall.

Kyle rested his face on the gravel. He closed his eyes. *I'll rest. Just for a moment. Then I can continue. I really want to get into my own bed tonight.*

Kyle did not get up. Sleep slowly overpowered him.

CHAPTER 16

Kyle gradually became aware of his surroundings despite being mostly asleep. Kyle heard his breathing greatly magnified. It did not feel like it matched his breathing, almost as if he were having an out-of-body experience. As Kyle gained awareness, the sound of breathing slowly matched the feeling from his body.

His body felt different. His limbs felt leaden. He could hardly move. Kyle chose not to test whether his hands were tied. No need to alarm himself until he was fully rested.

Kyle felt physically numb. He had grown accustomed to constantly feeling the sharp pains from his back and chest and side and ribs and face and jaw and arms and wrists and feet and hands and a dull ache throughout his entire body. Now, Kyle only felt the ubiquitous dull ache.

Kyle also finally felt warm. He had forgotten how warmth had felt.

Kyle heard a sharp beeping noise in the background. He recognized it as a heart monitor. Kyle relaxed himself and drifted back to semi-consciousness. He was probably safe. A hospital was probably the best place for him anyway.

Kyle did not move. If he truly was in a hospital, then someone was probably watching him. The last thing he wanted to do was to answer questions or talk to anyone. He was not ready yet. Kyle needed a little more rest.

That decision became a poor choice.

Kyle let his mind wander. Involuntarily, his trauma as a captive returned to mind. Kyle could feel the ice-cold room, the lashes on his back, and the burn from the glowing brand.

Worse still, Kyle experienced every minute of his time alone with Bull. Kyle tried to shake the images from his mind. The hateful grin, the mocking tone, the pounding fists, the breaking bones—Kyle attempted to think of other thoughts. He tried to focus on the aches in his body. Nothing worked. Kyle could not redirect his attention. The heart monitor quickened its pace.

For what seemed like ages, Kyle suffered, reliving every moment of his time in what he termed hell. He was trapped between desperately wanting to avoid reality and desperately wanting to escape the memories of his past. Kyle silently wept the entire time.

Kyle knew he was not going to get any more rest. Finally, he opened his eyes.

Claire was sitting at his bedside, reading a large book with onion skin pages. It was the Bible. Kyle cursed silently. *Does she read any other books?* Kyle silently cursed her God. *He, if he even exists, has certainly abandoned me for— for—I have no idea how long—forever! If a god truly does exist, he would never have let Augustus or Onyx betray their families, sell their possessions to The New World, leave their families destitute, and give orders or choose to allow the torture and near killing of their sons. If Claire were in my position, she would have abandoned her god long ago.*

Kyle must have made some noise. Claire looked from her reading.

"Kyle! You're awake! Your grandmother and I have been worried sick! Let me go get her."

"No. No," Kyle said. He grabbed Claire's arm to anchor her. *Joan is the last person that I want to see right now,* Kyle thought. *Actually, she's probably fourth on that list.*

Claire returned to her seat. "How are you feeling?"

"Fine, I guess." Kyle noticed several IVs stuck into his arms. *That explains why I feel so good,* Kyle thought. Then he asked aloud, "How long was I out?"

"Eighteen hours or so. Your grandmother called me when they found your body."

"How long was I gone?"

Claire seemed startled that Kyle had to ask. "Kyle... You were gone for weeks." Kyle deflated. He was completely flabbergasted. He could not believe that. His captivity had felt like an eternity, but his memories could hardly fill an entire day. *What else did The New World do to me that I can't remember?* Kyle shuttered. Claire saw the dread and confusion on Kyle's face. "Kyle, how long did you think you—"

"How long, exactly?" Kyle interrupted. "How many

weeks?"

Claire counted silently on her fingers, trying to remember. "You were gone for over three weeks. I remember we prayed for you at three separate prayer groups." Kyle could not believe it. "I believe your grandmother called me the day you were supposed to leave for witness protection. The FBI had called her and said that you were with them at the police station but that you'd disappeared. Someone found you early this morning in the alley near Josh's apartment." Kyle recollected. Then he remembered Josh.

Josh! Why had he been so stupid! Why had he surrendered himself to them! Kyle silently cursed Josh and the organization that he had joined.

Claire spoke again, "The doctors wouldn't tell me anything because I'm not a relative, and your grandmother didn't say anything before she left. Kyle, what happened?"

Kyle recalled every detail of the experiences that he had suffered. He remembered all that he had been forced to watch Josh endure. Kyle's hatred for Augustus, Bull, and the rest of The New World flooded into Kyle's mind, and Kyle burned with hatred and contempt for Claire's God.

Kyle glared at Claire and summoned all the venom and malice he could muster. "Your god abandoned me! That's what happened!" Kyle did not give Claire a chance to react.

"I'm not talking about how, seven months ago, Augustus—my father," Kyle spat the words, "who, by the way, happens to be the leader of The New World, stole all our valuables, my mom committed suicide, and I was left destitute in Boston—but your god did *nothing*!

"I'm not even talking about how The New World tried to drown me and scare me into submission or how they pummeled me half to death as punishment—and your god still did *nothing*!

"No, I'm talking about the last few *weeks*! They did everything they could to break me! I was chained in a cold room until I no longer had the strength to shiver! This was done *ten* times! After each refusal, I was flogged! I was whipped *fifty-five* times! Do you want to see my back?" Kyle painfully twisted in his bed, revealing his entire back covered in gauze and black with dried blood. Kyle turned to look Claire in the eye. "But your god abandoned me! And The New World did more!" Kyle ripped his hospital gown and pointed to a large bandage on his chest. "The New World branded me as one of theirs! They said I would belong to them, either as a member or as a piece of property! But your god was not finished with his apathy! As a final push, I was nearly killed by a sadist! I felt my bones being dislocated and broken! My ribs were shattered until it hurt to breathe! They *destroyed* me! And your god did *nothing*!" Kyle was close to tears, but he retained control of his voice. "Your god *abandoned me*!"

Claire was silent for a long time. She did not seem to have an answer. She slightly crinkled the pages of her Bible. Kyle felt justified. *I've finally stumped Claire,* he thought. *She no longer has an answer. She has to admit that her god abandoned me.*

"I am so sorry, Kyle…" Claire finally said. "I don't even know what to say… I am so sorry."

"Do you admit it?" Kyle pressed. "Do you admit that your god abandoned me?"

Claire thought for a few moments. "Kyle, you just got back. Why don't you get some rest? We can talk about this tomorrow—"

"No! Answer the question! Will you finally admit that your god abandoned me?"

Again, Claire was silent for several seconds. She seemed to be debating with herself on how to respond. Finally, Claire spoke, barely above a whisper, "Did you ever think of God before this?"

"What?" Kyle scoffed.

"Did you ever think about God before all this horrible stuff happened to you?"

"Not really. My ex-girlfriend's parents were jerks and religious Christians. Oh, my grandmother. Her too."

Claire pursed her lips. She looked like she was going to rebuke Kyle. "I'm not going to address what you've said about Joan. But it sounds like you didn't really think about God before your father robbed you. What if God allowed all this so that He could get your attention?"

Kyle cursed the God of heaven. "Then he is evil!"

"Would you rather have Him leave you alone—"

"Absolutely!"

"—and let you suffer a worse fate?"

"A worse fate? You mean 'hell'? I just lived through

hell!"

Great sadness choked Claire's voice and filled her eyes. "What you lived through was awful and terrible and something that nobody should ever have to live through. But it was only a small taste of hell. You had a horrible experience that I would not wish on anyone, and I am so sorry that you lived through that, but you have years ahead of you for laughter and happiness and love, even if you don't feel that's possible right now. Hell is the complete absence of God and, by extension, the absence of His nature, which is the laughter, happiness, and love that you will experience in the future."

"So you think that god made these bad things happen to me so that I could escape from worse things?" Kyle scoffed.

Claire considered. "Well, the Bible says that nothing evil comes from God. So He didn't *make* these things happen to you; He *allowed* them to happen to you. Other than that, yeah. That's the gist of it."

"That doesn't make any sense," Kyle complained.

"Then think of it this way. Have you ever had surgery?"

"I might after what your god *allowed* to happen to me."

"Well, if you do need surgery, would you let the doctors do it?"

"Probably, if my insurance covered it." Claire gave him an annoyed look. "Okay, yes, I would do the surgery."

"Even if it meant them cutting you open to do the surgery?"

"Yeah."

"And bed rest for a few days?"

"Yeah."

"And a few weeks or months of minimal physical activity?"

"Sure."

"So you would be willing to endure something 'bad' to avoid something 'worse.'" Claire stated.

"That's different!"

"How?"

"Because this is my life we're talking about! My life was at stake…and I'm going to carry some of this stuff with me for the rest of my life!"

"Surgery can threaten your life!" Claire commented.

"That's different!"

"If you're willing to risk your life on a complex surgery and a few weeks after that on your recovery so that you can live out the rest of your life, how is that different from risking this eighty years of your life when the rest of eternity hangs in the balance?"

Kyle hesitated; *Claire does have a point—if she's right.* Kyle silently conceded.

"That's still different!" Kyle insisted aloud. "Besides, if the surgery is too complex, I might choose not to risk it!"

Claire sighed and dropped the argument. "Do you at least see the logic in what I'm saying?" Claire asked.

Kyle nodded reluctantly.

"But I still don't believe it. Or believe in god," Kyle added hastily. Kyle thought and added, for good measure,

"Or think that he's good."

Claire shrugged. "Josh said that he told you his testimony. Do you really believe that he made that up?"

Josh! Kyle cursed him, almost aloud. *He should never have surrendered to The New World!*

Kyle wrenched his attention away from Josh's current situation and thought back to his first conversation at Josh's apartment. Kyle remembered the bizarre story about Josh going to hell and back. Kyle did not believe the story was true for a second. But Kyle believed that Josh believed that the story was true.

"Oh, Josh!" Claire said, breaking into Kyle's thoughts. "I almost forgot! Josh left you a note!" Claire replaced a bookmark in her Bible and flipped to the inside cover. She produced a white envelope with the name "Kyle" scrawled on the front.

Kyle snatched the letter. He was stiff and sore. The envelope was still sealed. Kyle ripped the envelope open. He could barely read Josh's handwriting.

Hi Kyle,

I sure hope you're reading this.

As soon as you left my apartment, I knew that something was wrong. I felt called to continue to pray for you, even after you left. I looked out the window and saw someone go into the warehouse. Somehow, I knew that it was you. When I went to the warehouse, no one was there.

I looked for you the next day, but the police and I couldn't find you anywhere. I was afraid that you were taken by The New World. And I was right.

Since my father is part of The New World, I still have connections. They said that you are a prisoner.

I know they won't just let you go, even if I asked. There's probably nothing that I can do to get you released, but I know that I have to try.

My father's wanted me to be a part of The New World for years. I'm going to try to trade my life for yours.

I don't know if this will work. I don't even know if they'll let me talk to you. By now, I'm pretty sure that you know what's happened.

I know you'll probably think that it was stupid for me to even try.

But I <u>had</u> to do this. You don't deserve this. Neither of us do. You need a second chance. And if trading my life for yours is the only way to do that, then I'm going to try.

God did the same for me, and He wants to do the same for you, Kyle. Please remember that.

Josh
PS: Please take care of my
mother for me. I'm not sure

how much I can help her now.

Kyle's face flushed with rage. *Josh never should have surrendered himself to The New World!* Kyle thought.

And then he had to bring god into his reason for doing it! Josh is a bigger fool than I'd thought! Why can't Josh just leave me alone?

If Josh had miraculously appeared in the hospital room, Kyle would have strangled him.

Without hesitation, Kyle crumpled the letter into a ball and threw it at the trashcan. The activities shot great bursts of pain throughout his body. The paper wad missed the trashcan and bounced along the floor.

"Kyle!" Claire exclaimed. She twisted in her chair and snatched the letter from the ground. "Josh wrote this before he left. He said to give this to you when you came back. He said it was very important."

"There's nothing important in that. Just throw it away."

Claire did not move. "When he gave this to me, Josh was acting very strangely. He kept on acting like he was going somewhere and that he wouldn't be here when you were found—if you were found. He also said that if I didn't see either of you after a few days, I should give this to the police." The letter remained a crinkled ball in her hands. "Do you know what happened to Josh?"

Kyle felt a knot grow in his stomach. *So she has no idea...* Kyle thought.

Kyle tried to explain, but he was too furious, sad, and upset at Josh. Finally, Kyle vented his emotions. He cursed

Josh for his actions and cursed Josh's God for allowing them. Kyle did not stop with them. He continued through the attendance list of all he had seen while in captivity. Kyle paid special attention to his words for Delilah, Augustus, Onyx, and Bull. The shouts ended with cursing Josh and his God repeatedly.

Claire's face during the tirade spoke volumes. She obviously did not understand the whole story. She waited patiently for the end but could not find the words to clarify what she had just endured.

"I was a prisoner of The New World, and Josh took my place," Kyle clarified. "He traded himself for me." Kyle cursed Josh again.

Claire jumped in her chair. "He *what*?!"

"He bargained with his father and Augustus to trade himself as their prisoner. And they accepted him." Kyle cursed Josh again.

"Wait! You know about that *too*?" Claire asked. Kyle did not hear her. Claire's question was lost in Kyle's second obscenity-laden speech to the entire hospital. Claire shouted over Kyle, demanding that he answer her question. Kyle eventually quieted. Claire began again. "You know about Josh's father being a member of The New World?" Claire asked.

"He told me the minute before I was abducted," Kyle answered.

"He didn't tell me about that until he gave me your letter," Claire said.

"He's not going to tell it to anyone else. At least, no one that's going to care," Kyle sighed.

"And he traded his life for you too?" Claire asked. Kyle nodded. "Wow," Claire mused. "That's just what God did."

Kyle swore at the general situation. *Will these religious fanatics ever leave me alone!?*

"That's exactly what Josh said in the letter!" Kyle screamed. "What is it with you people! You cling to a god who allows—"

Kyle could not think of where to begin. Would he recount, again, all that he had lived through during the last few days? Would he explain to Claire that Josh had endured the same punishments and tortures? Or would he start earlier with the way that Augustus had left him and his mother for dead? Or remind Claire that The New World killed several people in the city alone each night? Would he explain the broad death caused by the genocides, holocausts, and wars that occurred in the past and continued to happen and were happening now and would occur in the future? Or would he be broad and explain about the fires, floods, famines, hurricanes, earthquakes, volcanoes, and other natural disasters around the world?

Kyle could not decide.

"—all this evil in the world! Why do you even follow him?!"

Claire understood. "So you're saying that if God is all good, then He can't be all-powerful, and if God is all-powerful, then He can't be all good. Many people have that question. I've even asked that question myself. But I think I have an answer. If you were God, what would you do with evil?"

Kyle did not hesitate. "Destroy it! And destroy every evil person along with it!"

"Who do you think is evil?"

"The New World." *For starters,* Kyle thought.

"Okay. Why?" Claire's face contorted. She realized that she should have worded that question differently. "What's the standard for calling someone 'evil'?" Claire recovered. Kyle appreciated Claire's thoughtfulness in rewording the question.

"Doing evil," Kyle spat. He could not see where this was going.

"And as God, how would you define 'evil'?"

Kyle thought for a moment. "Causing pain for others."

"What about people who do both good and evil?" Claire asked.

"They cancel each other out," Kyle decided.

"I figured you'd say that, but that's not true in real life. In real life, one bad thing can wipe out all the good things that someone has done…or many good things might be needed to undo just one bad thing."

As soon as Kyle heard the words, he knew that Claire was right.

Kyle thought back to Augustus and Delilah. *I have many good memories of my father before he became Augustus; James Baker had made me into a man strong in mind, spirit, soul, and body. Even though Augustus did break me, I was strong enough to resist Augustus' tortures until Josh arrived. Augustus even admitted that no one else was as strong as I was in the four attributes. Even now, I've regained much of my strength in the four areas, though I will probably never be as strong as I was before the tortures. Regardless, he taught me how to throw a baseball, manage finances, drive a car, get a job, and many other skills that have not and cannot be taken away. Still, I can never trust my father again, and Augustus has forever negatively impacted my life. His actions over the last few months, even the last few weeks, have more than undone the years of good.*

The same is true with Delilah. She loved me, or at least, she said that she loved me. I believe that what we had together was genuine. Delilah said that she had tried to save me from torture; she'd said that she wanted to keep me safe. Assuming that this was all true, and I believe that it is, Delilah has a lot on the "good" side of the scale. I guess— no, I believe—that she wasn't really responsible for letting her name and phone be used to lure me to the warehouse. What did Delilah really do wrong? Kyle tried to recall every painful moment and interaction with Delilah since they had reconnected. *The only thing Delilah did wrong was withhold that she was a part of The New World. But how much good will she have to do to make up for her mere association with The New World? That amount of good is infinite; I don't think I can ever trust her again.*

Claire saw that Kyle understood her point.

"According to God, it would take more than an infinite amount of good deeds to eliminate one evil act. Evil cannot be undone. Good cannot undo evil. That is why God had to die for us.

"God *is* going to destroy evil and every evil person like you said He should. And that includes all people that have ever done any evil. That includes you, me, The New World, your grandmother, Josh—" Kyle tensed at Josh's name. "—everyone. You see, God can't see beyond our sin, our evil deeds. And as much as He loves you and wants to spare you from destruction when He destroys evil, He cannot ignore evil, just like He cannot ignore what The New World has done…to you or anyone else.

"But God found a way to save us. He would still need to punish our evil, but He could transfer the blame to another person. The problem was that only someone who had not sinned could take our sin and suffer destruction in our place. That person was Jesus. Jesus was God Himself. Jesus never sinned. He had no evil that needed to be removed. God chose to die so that He could take our sin and our destruction, and we could take His goodness and His reward."

Up to this time, Kyle had been listening intently. He agreed with his previous assessment that Christianity was an extraordinarily interesting work of fiction. It was deeply interwoven with the realities of the real world and was even applicable to the real world. He thought back to a "World Mythology" course that he had taken in college to satisfy an elective. Christianity was unlike any other religion he had ever studied.

That also concerned Kyle. Claire had answered all his questions and concerns, with the exception of proving satisfactorily that her God existed. *Assuming that her god does exist or that Claire has a convincing enough answer, what are the ramifications? What does that mean for me and my life? How will that affect my future? If god really does exist, I can't just ignore it...*

No! I cannot *allow that! I am* not *willing for my life to change! My spirit and soul will* never *allow it!*

So when Claire mentioned that the punishment could be transferred, Kyle voiced his refutation.

"That doesn't happen in real life. You can't just have someone else take your place and cancel each other's punishments. That isn't justice."

Claire mused, "It doesn't happen often in real life, but the justice system does allow for it to happen in certain situations. A righteous judge cannot arbitrarily remove a penalty from a person; if he does, then that wouldn't be justice. The full penalty has to remain. As long as the penalty is paid, justice is served, right?" Kyle agreed, but Claire did not wait for him to answer one way or the other. "Let's say you were guilty of speeding, and you go to court. A just judge has no choice other than to fine you for the amount of the ticket. To wipe out the ticket would not be justice. But, if you got the ticket, you could pay it, or your grandmother or I could pay it. You could not force us to pay it for you, but instead, we offered to take the penalty for you. Since *we* could do that, what is preventing the *judge* from paying the fine for you? The "just" judge could set a "just" fine for your ticket and, at the same time, write a check out of his own funds to pay for the fine. That is what God did for us. All we have to do is ask."

"What about jail time? That's not transferable," Kyle said.

Claire shrugged. "The justice system only allows for so much. But you just lived through one example: what Josh did for you."

Kyle had an epiphany. Instead of cursing Josh, Kyle finally understood. He finally understood what Claire was saying about Jesus' sacrifice.

Claire was talking again. "It's not a perfect comparison. We are all in bondage, trapped in our sins, waiting for a punishment that we deserve. We chose to enter that life. We all did. And even if we wanted to escape, we couldn't. We will always remain slaves. One way or another, we are all trapped, and there is no way for us to escape. That is why Jesus had to die. Someone had to take *our* punishment; Someone had to endure the pain that *we* deserved. And that Someone was Jesus. Jesus endured all of that, and more so that you could be free."

Kyle put out his hand. "Can you hand me Josh's letter?" The tight wad of paper was still in Claire's lap. "Josh said the same thing in his letter," Kyle continued. "He said that was why he traded himself for me." Kyle gingerly opened the crumpled ball. Kyle read the last lines of the letter aloud,

"And if trading my life for yours is the only way to do that, then I'm going to try. God did the same for me, and He wants to do the same for you, Kyle."

That's what Josh and Claire have been saying! Kyle thought. *I understand now! Josh has given me a picture of what their god has done for them. Maybe Claire is right...*

No! I refuse to accept that! My whole being refuses to accept that! I still have questions that need answers. I... I desperately want to believe that what Claire and Josh have said is real... I really do, but there is no proof that their god even exists.

"I still don't believe god is real," Kyle finally said. "This is all very interesting, but...I...I just can't believe any of it."

"Even after Josh told you about his experience in hell?" Claire asked.

"He could have hallucinated it! I need something more concrete."

"What about the Holy Spirit—or the 'Voice' as you call it?"

Kyle gave her a skeptical look. "Did Josh tell you about that?"

"Yes," Claire said, nodding her head. "He said that you felt drawn to his apartment and that you went there despite not having any desire to see him at all."

"I didn't say that!" Kyle defended himself.

"That's how he interpreted it," Claire countered.

"Well, he's not wrong. I was trying to rescue Del—uh, Jill, a friend from Boston, who had been kidnapped by The

New World, when I got led on a wild goose chase to Josh's apartment in the middle of the night."

"And the 'Voice' led you there."

"Yep."

"And you didn't hallucinate that, did you?" Claire pressed.

"No," Kyle sighed. He was running out of excuses. "But that's still not very concrete," Kyle concluded.

"We don't always see some concrete evidence for the existence of God," Claire said. "When Jesus was on earth, His followers saw Him before He died and after He rose from the dead. Most modern historians, even secular ones, believe that Jesus' tomb was empty and that the disciples saw *something* that they thought was Jesus. All of them were willing to suffer and even die believing and preaching that Jesus rose from the dead." Claire motioned to Kyle. "Would you have been willing to fight against The New World and endure that pain if you didn't believe that you were doing what was right?"

Kyle considered. "I guess not... But you said that Jesus rose from the dead. That's not possible."

"God is doing miracles all around the world. Nothing is impossible for Him. Talk to David or my sister Abby after prayer group sometime. They'll tell you some incredible stories about how God worked in their lives. Talk to J—uh... you already know Josh's story," Claire recovered.

"I'd need to see a miracle for myself," Kyle stressed.

"I can't help you there. Only God can do miracles, and

He doesn't usually do them on demand."

"Then he can heal me anytime he wants. If he did that, then I'd believe in him."

Claire managed a toothy smile as if she were forcing herself from responding.

The two sat in silence for several minutes.

Kyle could think of nothing else to say. He wanted to discuss Christianity more, though he could not think of any other questions. *Besides,* Kyle thought, *the whole topic is moot for the time being. I can't decide anything until I receive a miracle. Actually, what I really need to do is think through everything Claire has said. I can't jump into this blindly.*

Kyle tried to think about his discussion with Claire. He forced himself to think through the arguments, but he could not concentrate with Claire sitting silently beside him.

Kyle listened to the ticking of the clock. He glanced around the room, but more often than not, his eyes would eventually settle on Claire. She too examined the room, looking at nothing in particular; as far as Kyle could tell, the only place she did not look was at him.

They waited in silence for several more minutes.

Still, neither of them said anything.

Kyle continued to look around the room. He heard Claire make a noise. She was reading again and had turned a page in her Bible.

"So what? You're just going to sit there and ignore me?" Kyle asked.

Claire looked from her reading. "Did you want to

continue our conversation?"

"I don't think there's anything left to say."

"Okay then," Claire said. She resumed reading her Bible. Kyle stared at Claire. Evidently, she felt his eyes looking at her; she looked back at him, smiling. "What? Did you want to talk about something else?"

"No, I guess not."

"Should I let you get some sleep?"

"No…I don't know…I don't know what I want," Kyle said and added, silently, *I just want you with me. Maybe Claire can read to me. Of course, she's reading the Bible, but it's better than sitting alone.* "Can you read to me?" Kyle asked aloud.

"Sure," Claire said. Kyle settled back into his pillow and closed his eyes.

Claire began reading where she had stopped:

There was a rich man who was dressed in purple and fine linen and lived in luxury every day. At his gate was laid a beggar named Lazarus, covered with sores and longing to eat what fell from the rich man's table. Even the dogs came and licked his sores.

The time came when the beggar died and the angels carried him to Abraham's side. The rich man also died and was buried. In hell, where he was in torment, he looked up and saw Abraham far away, with Lazarus by his side. So he called to him, "Father Abraham, have pity on me and send Lazarus to dip the tip of his finger in water and cool my tongue, because I am in agony in this fire."

But Abraham replied, "Son, remember that in your lifetime you received your good things, while Lazarus received bad things, but now he is comforted here and you are in agony. And besides all this, between us and you a great chasm has been fixed, so that those who want to go from here to you cannot, nor can anyone cross over from there to us."

He answered, "Then I beg you, father, send Lazarus to my father's house, for I have five brothers. Let him warn them, so that they will not also come to this place of torment."

Abraham replied, "They have Moses and the Prophets; let them listen to them."

"No, father Abraham," he said, "but if someone from the dead goes to them, they will repent."

He said to him, "If they do not listen to Moses and the Prophets, they will not be convinced even if someone rises from the dead."

Luke 16:19-31

Kyle's eyes snapped open. *That passage fits perfectly with Claire and my discussion. Did Claire choose that passage on purpose?* Kyle thought. He chose not to ask; he was afraid the answer would be no.

"What are you reading?" Kyle interrupted, feigning ignorance that Claire was reading her Bible. "Are you reading the Bible?" he asked rhetorically. "Don't read that."

"It's the only book I brought," Claire replied.

"I don't want to hear that," Kyle said.

Claire closed her Bible. "Maybe I should let you get some rest."

"That's fine," Kyle said. He decided that he would prefer to be alone than to be read the Bible.

"I'll try to visit again tomorrow."

"I'll let you know if any miracles happen while you're gone," Kyle joked.

"Just…think about our conversation," Claire pleaded.

"I'll believe it when I see a miracle."

CHAPTER 17

The miracle Kyle desired never came.

…or perhaps it did. The nurses administered a hearty cocktail of sleeping medicine to Kyle. But Kyle could not fall asleep. Though he was exhausted, every time he closed his eyes, his mind would voluntarily search for a refutation to Claire's arguments. The pace of his thoughts accelerated faster and faster until he would open his eyes and they would disperse. When he closed his eyes again, his mind would resume the sprint even faster than previously.

Kyle used every trick he knew, trying to calm his mind. He made up stories in his head. He thought about what he would do to any member of The New World if he crossed paths with any of them. He thought of his time with Jill before their relationship ended. He thought of his good life before Augustus destroyed it. He put his fingers over his eyelids and forced his eyes to focus on the same spot. He painfully stood from his bed and walked around the room until he was tired, which was only once. He even tried counting sheep, which he swore never to do and always scoffed at people who did.

None of his attempts worked.

So Kyle just lay wide awake, exhausted, staring at the ceiling.

After what felt like an incredibly long period of time, Kyle realized his being was in turmoil. He had not heard much from his being since Bull had—

Kyle assessed his being.

Kyle's mind was leading the charge. It did not like what Claire had said one bit. She had explained her position well, but it was too difficult to believe. Kyle's mind would not let him believe it. His mind, however, was still frantically searching for a hole in her arguments. Until it did, it screamed for Kyle to assume that she had lied and that her facts were false.

Kyle's spirit objected as strongly as his mind. Kyle was in control of his own destiny! He would not be subject to some god! He could not! He would never subject himself to someone or something that had allowed such horrible circumstances to happen to anyone that it claimed to love! Kyle had been burned too many times to trust something that claimed to love him and, in the end, did not. Kyle was determined never to let that happen again.

Kyle's soul agreed. Kyle was sufficient. Kyle did not need anyone else, especially someone that would allow evil to destroy Kyle in the way that Claire said that her god would. Besides, what else would that god force him to do? Once Kyle had decided to follow that god, how else would it shape his life? What else would it demand? His soul would not surrender anything to that being as long as it had a vote.

As far as Kyle's body was concerned, it refused to believe anything until it had seen, touched, or heard anything to make him believe that something greater than Kyle even existed. Until then, it would just be an unverified hypothesis or figment of Claire's imagination. Claire passing information second hand was not good enough. Kyle needed to experience it himself.

Well, that's that, Kyle thought.

His being had decided, without dissent, that he could not accept Claire's arguments for God. Kyle closed his eyes. Immediately, his mind raced. *For what?* Kyle sighed. *I already have an answer. Even if my mind can't concoct a reason for rejecting her arguments, the rest of my being will not let me choose Christianity until they are satisfied.* Kyle's eyes remained shut.

Still, his mind frantically searched for an answer, counterargument, hole, anything in response to Claire's arguments.

Kyle opened his eyes. As tired as he was, he was not going to get any rest until he had resolved this matter. *It shouldn't take too long to concentrate on Claire's arguments and refute them.* Kyle decided.

Kyle focused on his being's concerns.

He thought back to all that Claire had said. *First, I need to counter Claire's argument that god has done—no, allowed— that god has allowed all the evil in my life to get my attention.*

Kyle's mind, spirit, and soul rejected that notion. They could not rest without a solid counterargument.

Kyle considered his opposing position. *Claire's god, assuming that he even exists, should never have used that evil to get my attention. He would not need to use evil for his purposes! He just needed to send me a message saying, "Pay attention! The world is filled with evil! You are not doing what is right! Focus more on me!"*

The thought that God had used evil to send that message to Kyle crossed Kyle's mind. He could not determine if the thought came from something Claire had said or from outside his being. Kyle brushed the thought and its origins from his mind and resumed his contemplation.

After god has sent the message, he would just need to send the message repeatedly until I responded or changed my ways or something.

Another thought with unclear origins crossed his mind: *What if that is why God allowed the attacks to increase?* Again, Kyle pushed the thoughts away and resumed his reasoning.

If I still did not respond after those continued messages from god, then god would eventually need to completely break any distractions; then, I would have no choice other than to focus on him.

At that moment, Kyle distinctly heard from the same "Voice" that he had heard outside Josh's apartment: *But that is what God did.* This thought definitely seemed to come from beyond Kyle's being. Kyle tried to push the thought from his mind, but it stubbornly refused to leave. Instead, the other thoughts returned and insisted on being considered.

Kyle grew frightened. He had not only stumbled upon a rationale for how God had acted but also heard again from the "Voice." Josh had already claimed that the "Voice" was God, and Kyle did not have a better explanation. And this time, as at Josh's apartment, Kyle was not hallucinating the "Voice."

Kyle tried to think of other counterarguments to answer Claire. He could not think of anything beyond the three answers he desperately wanted to ignore. Kyle only grew more panicked. All the answers made sense, even if he did not believe it.

I'll think of a better rationale later, Kyle thought. *In the meantime, I have other arguments to craft.*

Kyle did not spend too long on the middle portion of Claire's case. He saw Claire's point about good not being able to cancel out evil and how the penalty can be voluntarily transferred from one person to another. He did not need to look for a refutation; he believed that Claire was right. Even the current justice system did not give someone a free ride just because they had done more good things than bad in their life.

With that, Kyle turned to the last part of their argument: the existence of God. *Claire's main argument was that modern historians believe that Jesus' body was gone. Why had I assumed that she was right? I should have questioned her right then and there! Still, it doesn't matter. I won't believe until my senses are satisfied.*

His mind, on its own accord, remembered its interactions with the "Voice."

How can I rationalize that? Kyle thought. *The "voice" seemed so real to me!*

And her other point: Jesus' disciples had seen something that they thought was him after he had died, and they were willing to die believing that he had risen from the dead! How can I rationalize that?

Kyle could think of neither explanation. Again, Kyle grew uneasy.

He attempted to recover and rationalize the situation. *No one in modern-day actually does that; no one is willing to sacrifice themselves for what they believe.*

Despite his efforts to suppress contradicting thoughts, Josh slipped into Kyle's mind. Unintentionally, Kyle found the answer to both questions.

Josh had heard the "Voice" on the same night, at the same time that Kyle had. Kyle had not hallucinated the "Voice"; it had been corroborated on the same night by a source that was completely unaware of Kyle's own situation!

On top of that, Josh was willing to give himself for Kyle! He did not hesitate to trade himself to The New World so that Kyle could be free!

Why would he do that?! Kyle scoured his mind for an answer. Some words from Claire returned to his mind. An answer formed: Josh sacrificed himself and the rest of his life because he knew that Kyle's eternity hung in the balance.

Kyle despised the answer he had found and searched for another. He writhed on his bed. *I don't want to accept that answer! I need another!* But he could think of no other explanation.

Josh had provided the same explanation in the letter. And he had said that God had done the same for them.

Kyle's being was suddenly overwhelmed at Josh's sacrifice. He wept. *So that's what the gospel means.* Kyle finally understood. The tears flowed down his cheeks.

His mind was confounded. It scrambled to find another reason but could think of no other explanation.

His spirit was deflated. Despite its resistance, there were no other objections. His spirit could no longer resist. There was no other logical option.

His body was not satisfied, yet it had received the proof it demanded. Kyle had seen and heard, in unforgettable detail, the "voice" and Josh's example of the gospel. It, too, had no choice.

Kyle's soul still resolutely rejected the conclusions. Accepting Jesus and believing that he was god would affect the rest of his life. This could not be entered into lightly.

That did not matter. Kyle had not made the decision easily. The vote was three to one.

Deep inside, Kyle and his whole being knew that all that Claire and Josh and his grandmother and their pastor and the people at the prayer group and anyone else had said was true. Kyle knew that he was evil. He knew that, because of his evil, he was destined for an endless life of pain and suffering and death, just as he was as a captive of The New World. Kyle knew that he needed Someone, Jesus, to take his place, just as Josh had done. Despite his soul's objections, Kyle knew that Jesus deserved his entire life, not only because He had sacrificed His life but also because He was God.

At that moment, Kyle became a child of God.

To verbalize his commitment, Kyle merely said, "Jesus, save me."

With that, Kyle finally fell asleep.

****

Kyle awoke with a start. He had another nightmare, reliving his torturous hours as a prisoner of The New World. Kyle was deeply grieved with the memories. All he wanted to do was forget about his torment and heal from his wounds.

Though, this time, Kyle felt different somehow. Deep inside himself, Kyle knew that his captivity in The New World was no longer the defining moment of his life. There was Something greater in him now. He felt a deep peace and calm through his entire being, including his soul. And that made the saga slightly, very slightly, easier to relive.

****

When Kyle awoke again, his grandmother was sitting beside his bed.

"Good morning, Kyle!" She spoke in the soft, soothing tone that all grandmothers develop for use on their grandchildren. "We were so worried about you!" She set aside her knitting and wrapped Kyle's closest hand in both of hers. "Claire said that she spoke with you last night and that I should come see you today. How are you feeling?"

"Ugh. Awful."

"The doctors said that you had quite a few injuries. What happened to you?"

Kyle was not sure how much he should or even wanted to relay. "What have the doctors told you?"

"Nothing. You're over eighteen and didn't give permission for the doctors to tell me anything," she guilted.

Kyle almost cursed her right then. *I've been gone for weeks and have returned unconscious, bloody, bruised, and burned!* thought Kyle. *Cut me some slack!*

Joan continued, "Josh said that something bad had happened to you. The police stopped by the house looking for you and asking questions. They said that you have been kidnapped or something. But we didn't have a ransom note or anything." Joan obviously did not know anything that had transpired. Claire kept her mouth shut this time. Joan did not press the point; she probably expected Kyle to offer the information. Kyle did not say anything. He was too mad to say anything, even if he wanted to do so.

They sat in silence for several minutes.

"Oh," Joan said. "You received a letter while you were gone." *Another letter?* Kyle thought. Joan reached into her purse and produced a crisp, unwrinkled letter. The letter bore an Air Force insignia on the envelope. Kyle snatched the letter, despite the pain, and ripped the envelope open.

Through all the military jargon, Kyle read that he had to report for duty by the end of August—that was only a few weeks away—at Eglin Air Force Base. That was just on the other side of the state. Kyle would be stuck in Florida for the next few years. He had plenty to do. *Maybe I can reconcile with my grandmother and find a way to save Josh and get to know Claire better,* Kyle thought.

"I'm going to be stationed at Eglin, near Pensacola," Kyle relayed to his grandmother. "They need me there by the end of August. Do you mind if I take the car and look around the area?"

His grandmother stared at him with corpse-like seriousness. "You are not touching my car, not after the last time you took it."

Kyle was about to answer with a swear when he remembered how his grandmother had reacted the last time she heard him curse. He, irrationally, did not think it was beyond her to dump his belongings on the porch and change the locks to the house while he remained trapped in the hospital bed. Kyle bit his tongue.

Kyle and his grandmother sat in silence for another few minutes.

At length, the doctor visited and saved the couple from silence.

"Good morning, Kyle. How are you feeling today?"

"Fine. Just achy."

"If that's all, then that's good. Kyle, you're very lucky to be alive right now. When you were brought to us, you had lost a considerable amount of blood, both to open wounds and internal bleeding. We started with a transfusion and emergency surgery to stabilize you before addressing your other injuries, which were also very extensive." The doctor looked down at Kyle's medical file. "I don't even know where to begin... Nearly every single rib in your chest was broken or cracked. Quite frankly, I don't know how you didn't puncture a lung. We're still monitoring your ribs, but the brace should be sufficient for now.

"Your left ankle was sprained; we gave you a short-term cast so that it doesn't move. Your right shoulder was dislocated and has been maneuvered back into position. We have also given you a support cast for while it heals.

"Both your collarbones were broken. The sling should be all that is needed, but right now, it looks like you'll be wearing the sling for at least three months.

"Your jaw had been dislocated again, and a few of your facial bones had been cracked. Right now, I don't think we need to do anything other than slide your jaw back into place, which we've already done.

"We stitched up the gashes on your side. We treated your back, but I'm afraid you're still going to have some nasty scars. Same thing with the burn on your chest; it's pretty deep and will definitely leave a scar."

Kyle swore silently. *Another permanent reminder of Augustus*, Kyle thought. Though, the doctor's explanations confirmed one fact: Augustus never wanted him dead. Kyle still loathed him and the rest of The New World, with all his being.

"So," the doctor continued, "my orders are to stay here for the next few weeks; we'll continue to run some tests, and we'll reevaluate then. In the meantime, no strenuous physical activity of any kind. Stay in bed and get some rest. I don't want you to *think* about leaving that bed without buzzing for a nurse first."

Kyle accepted the doctor's recommendations without complaint and chose not to mention his late-night lap around the hospital room. His grandmother stormed out of the hospital. She did not visit Kyle for the rest of the day.

****

Claire visited again in the afternoon. As soon as he saw her, Kyle started speaking.

"I did it! I accepted Jesus! Everything just clicked for me last night. And I understood what you and Josh were trying to say!" Kyle was beaming.

"Wait! What!" Claire said. "You're a Christian now?"

"Yep! I was lying awake last night. I couldn't sleep. I thought through all that you and Josh had said, and it all made sense! I believe it now!"

"That's great news!" Claire exclaimed. She was almost in tears. "Did you tell your grandmother?"

Kyle's voice changed from excitement to hostility. "No! Of course not! She would judge me for taking so long, and I would never hear the end of it!"

Claire tried to stay positive. "I think you're wrong about

her. She wouldn't do that to you."

"I have yet to be proven wrong on anything about that woman," Kyle asserted. Kyle could tell that Claire did not want to continue the conversation in its current form. He also felt a prick from the Holy Spirit. Kyle brushed the compunction aside; he was too prideful to apologize.

Kyle changed the subject. "Is there anything that I should know about Christianity now that I'm a Christian?"

"Well," Claire began, "first, you should know that God still holds us against His standards of right and wrong. When we do wrong, it hurts our relationship with Him. We need to ask His forgiveness…and we need to ask forgiveness from others."

Kyle was disappointed. *Claire said that on purpose!* Kyle felt another sting for what he had spoken against his grandmother. Kyle knew that Claire was probably right. "Sorry," Kyle apologized. "I guess I shouldn't have said that stuff about her."

"I don't need your apology. You should apologize to your grandmother."

"What!" Kyle cried. Claire was serious. *I don't think I'm ready for that yet…or ever,* Kyle thought. *I also don't think Joan deserves an apology.* Again, the Holy Spirit pricked him for the untrue thought.

Kyle's soul reminded him of its previous warning that Christianity would change him.

"Fine," Kyle relented, without any actual intention to apologize to his grandmother. "When do I become perfect and not have to ask for forgiveness?"

Claire laughed. "I wish we became perfect! Unfortunately, sanctification is a slow process, and none of us actually get there in this lifetime."

"How come?" Kyle asked, obviously disappointed.

Claire considered. "I don't know. Maybe it's so that people that aren't Christians don't think they have to be perfect to get into heaven."

"Is there a time when you become mostly perfect?" Kyle asked. He could not remember a time when Claire had done anything wrong.

"It's a long process. I've been a Christian for several years, and I still struggle with a lot of the same sins. But sometimes, it's easier to resist the temptation to do wrong and choose to do good. And that is proof that God is working in me."

"And God will still forgive you even when you make the same mistake over and over again?" Kyle clarified.

"Yes. But we constantly need to check ourselves and decide not to do wrong again. When we ask for forgiveness, what we're really saying is 'I'm sorry I acted this way; I don't want to do this again' or 'I know You don't like this, help me not do it again.'"

"That doesn't sound easy," Kyle moaned.

"Some days are definitely easier than others," Claire admitted. She produced a book that Kyle had not seen her bring with her. It was a Bible. "I want you to have this, especially now that you're a Christian. I recommend starting with the gospels."

"The gospels! But that's, like, four books!"

"They're short books. You'll finish them in a few hours. It's not like you have anyplace else to be right now," Claire reminded him.

Kyle did not say anything. *This Christianity thing is getting to be a whole lot of work,* Kyle thought. He would have preferred to do whatever he wanted. But the evidence and logic left no other choice, much to his soul's disappointment.

Kyle absentmindedly flipped through the Bible and found the gospels. *Claire is right; it won't take too long to read through all of them, especially after hearing what the doctor said.*

"What do you think is going to happen to Josh," Claire finally said, her sentence more of a statement than a question.

Kyle sighed. He was actually surprised the topic had not occurred sooner. "I have absolutely no idea. Josh said that this was never the life he wanted, and now he's forced to live it for the rest of his life."

"You mean until he's killed or caught and thrown in jail," Claire finished. Kyle nodded.

"What are the police doing about it?" Kyle asked.

"I don't think anything yet. I'm not even sure his mother has reported him missing."

Kyle almost swore and remembered that Claire was in the room. He was not sure if he could still swear silently or not. He would need to read the Bible and find out for certain. Then, if needed, he would ask for forgiveness.

"Can you tell the police anything about where Josh is?" Claire continued.

"I'm actually surprised that the police haven't come to ask me anything yet. But no, I can't tell them anything. The New World knocked me unconscious when I was at the warehouse, and they took me to their hideout, and they did the same thing when they dumped me back at the warehouse when Josh saved me."

"That's not a lot to go on."

"No, it's not," Kyle agreed.

"So what are we going to do next?" Claire asked.

"*We?*" Kyle clarified.

"Josh is my friend too."

That's right! Kyle thought. *I'm no longer alone. I have someone else to help me rescue Josh!*

"Great!" Kyle said aloud. "The first thing we should do is go back to the warehouse and look around for any hidden entrances or exits. Then, I guess we should…" Kyle's voice trailed off. He stopped planning. He knew what he really should do.

For too long, he had relied on just himself. For as long as he could remember, he, armed with the power of his mind, spirit, soul, and body, was capable of overcoming any trial in his life.

But Kyle was no longer just his mind, spirit, soul, and body.

Kyle was no longer alone. He had Someone else to help him rescue Josh—Someone much greater than Claire or the police or the FBI or anyone else.

Jesus was with them, and more importantly, He was with Josh.

The first thing that Kyle needed to do was recognize that God was in control of the whole situation.

"Actually," Kyle began again, "the first thing we should do is pray."

CHAPTER 18

The police arrived later that day to talk to Kyle. They wanted to know everything that had happened to him, starting with Kyle's last conversation with the federal agents.

Kyle skipped the part about receiving the mat from the rogue cops, despite feeling compunction to tell the truth. Kyle rationalized his sin: *I don't know who I can trust, and I also have no idea how this will affect my future with the Air Force.* Still, the guilt remained.

Kyle began with him receiving another text about meeting at the warehouse. He told the police about his father—Kyle still could not think those words without revulsion—about his father being the leader of The New World and the involvement of Josh's father but did not mention Delilah. Kyle glazed over The New World's tortures while he was a captive; the memories were still too painful to relive. Finally, Kyle relayed that Josh was now a prisoner of The New World. The police were amazed at Josh's sacrifice and skeptical that The New World simply released Kyle. Kyle reminded the officers that both Augustus and Onyx were leaders of

The New World and could do whatever they wanted. Kyle finished with his being returned to the warehouse without any knowledge of where he had been. The police promised to look around the warehouse.

Kyle knew they would not find anything.

The days dragged past. Kyle received no follow-up.

****

The day after the police left, Kyle received an unexpected visitor: David from the prayer group.

"Hi Kyle, how are you feeling?" David asked.

"Better than yesterday," Kyle replied. He was running out of unique ways to describe his lousy condition.

"Your grandmother texted a few of us from the prayer group. She said that we should come and visit you."

Kyle almost cursed out loud. *Was this revenge?* Kyle thought. He received a prick from the Holy Spirit; Kyle knew his thought was a lie. Joan was trying to be helpful.

David sat in the visitor's chair. He looked like he did not know what to say. Neither did Kyle. David and Kyle sat in silence for almost a minute.

"So," David began. "I heard they have Josh now."

"Yeah," Kyle sighed and then thought, *I don't want to talk about Josh. I just want to be left alone and sleep.*

"How are you holding up?" David asked.

"Fine," Kyle said, though he was certainly not "fine."

"That's good... I...know how difficult it is to lose someone to The New World."

That's right! Kyle thought. *I'd forgotten David's prayer request so long ago! David had been a part of The New World in some capacity.*

Then, Kyle remembered that he still owed David an apology.

Kyle hesitated. *I don't want to apologize to David!* Kyle argued to himself. *I don't want to admit that I was wrong! I don't want to remind David of that incident; it was almost two months ago!* Kyle could sense himself being prompted to apologize. His being knew it was the right thing to do, despite resisting the thought. Kyle took a deep breath.

"David, I owe you an apology."

David looked at Kyle. "For what?"

"For your prayer request at the prayer group a while back. You mentioned that you had been a part of The New World, and I made a big deal out of it." David's eyes filled with recollection. Kyle continued, "I never should have reacted that way, and I should have apologized long before now. Do you forgive me?"

"Sure, Kyle. I forgive you." Kyle felt an invisible weight, which he had not known was there, lift from his soul.

Neither spoke for several seconds.

David took a sharp breath. "God saved me from The New World, and He saved you. I know He'll save Josh."

Kyle did not necessarily believe that. "But how? When?"

"I don't know..." David admitted. "God works in His timing. I know from my experience that if God had rescued me from The New World before He did, I *still* would have rejected Him." Kyle could relate. David continued, "I don't know how or if God will save Josh physically. God gave me a second chance in this life. I hope He will do the same for Josh."

"Yeah, me too," Kyle agreed.

****

The doctors were astounded at the contributions Kyle's physical prowess provided toward his rapid recovery. Within two weeks, Kyle was discharged from the hospital. Most of Kyle's wounds had healed. Even his ankle had healed enough for the doctor to remove the cast, with the caution that Kyle should not do any strenuous activity. But the doctor insisted that Kyle continue to wear the casts for his collarbones, ribs, and shoulder "for at least a few more weeks and until we tell you otherwise." Besides that, the doctors said Kyle was able to leave the hospital. Kyle was just glad to be out of the hospital *bed*.

During his hospital stay, Kyle had collected a wall full of cards from the prayer group, college friends, and his grandmother's church. Kyle even received a card without a note or name; Kyle chose not to theorize who might have sent that letter.

Claire had visited him nearly every day. Almost the entire prayer group had come at one time or another. Even Joan, after an afternoon's break, returned and spent nearly all the daylight hours with Kyle, much to his chagrin. Their relationship was still not that great, even with the extended time together.

Kyle was eager to leave the hospital. He wanted to visit Eglin before he was officially stationed there. He needed to pack the rest of his belongings. He needed to formally quit his job at Finneman's Market. He needed to start looking for apartments near the base. Above all, he needed to rescue Josh.

That case seemed hopeless. Whenever Kyle thought of Josh, he wanted to scream in frustration! He felt so powerless! Then, Kyle would remember that he was not alone anymore and would pray, *God, I know You exist now. Help us rescue Josh!*

Kyle knew that he himself needed to go to the warehouse and look for—Kyle did not know what he hoped to find—a secret passage, despite knowing he would not find anything. Still, Kyle prioritized that as his first task outside the hospital.

****

Joan, having retrieved Kyle from the hospital, pulled into her driveway. She led the way into the house, opening the doors for Kyle. Kyle followed, carrying the box filled with his cards and the Bible Claire had given him.

"Do you think you'll be okay here by yourself?" Joan asked him when they were both inside the house. "I promised my friend Irene that I would visit her today."

"Yeah, that's fine," Kyle assured her.

"You have your new cell phone if you need to call me?"

Kyle patted his pants pocket. "Yep."

"Do you need me to get anything for you before I go?"

"I'm all set. I think I might actually go for a walk while you're gone."

"...with a sprained ankle?" Joan asked.

"The doctor said it was healed."

"The doctor said not to do anything strenuous."

"It's not far," Kyle assured her.

"How far?"

"Just a few miles away." As soon as he said it, Kyle knew that he should have lied. "I'll be fine," he added quickly.

"A few miles! Kyle, if you want me to drop you off somewhere—"

"No, that's fine."

"Let me call Claire. I'm sure she could drive you."

"No! Don't do that!" Kyle shouted. *She is the* last *person I want going to the warehouse with me!* Kyle thought. *How many times has she offered to go on her own and I've told her no? It's been at least once a day.*

Kyle's grandmother started to dial her phone. "You know what? You talked me out of it," Kyle lied. "It was a dumb idea. I'm not physically up for that yet. I'll just stay here... and lie on the couch." *Or maybe not...* Kyle added silently.

His grandmother stopped dialing. "If you say so," Joan said. "I don't want you doing anything dangerous. Rest like the doctor ordered." Kyle nodded, hobbled toward the couch, and lay down.

Five minutes later, his grandmother said goodbye and left the house. Kyle sprang from the couch as fast as his injuries would allow and watched from the window. Joan climbed into her car but remained in the driveway for a couple of minutes before driving down the street. As soon as she was out of sight, Kyle sprinted to the door and jumped down the porch steps. He had not reached the end of the driveway before another vehicle appeared at his grandmother's house. It was Claire.

Kyle swore under his breath and cursed his grandmother. *Joan tricked me!*

Claire rolled down her window. "Headed somewhere?" she asked, grinning.

Kyle stared at Claire, incredulous. "She called you, didn't she?"

"Yeah, Joan said you might be trying to go someplace."

"I was just going for a walk."

"You were going to the warehouse, weren't you?"

"No...! Yes, but you can't come. It's too dangerous."

"I just came from there, actually."

"What!" Kyle roared.

"I've been there every day for the last two weeks."

"You shouldn't have gone! I asked you not to!" Kyle shouted.

"Why not!" Claire shouted back.

"Because I've lost count of how many times I've nearly died there!" At that, Claire was silent. Kyle continued, "It's been at least three times. I get hurt every time I go there. I don't want anything to happen to you, Claire."

Claire nodded slowly. She understood. "I'll be fine."

Kyle turned away and walked down the street. "I used to think that too," Kyle called over his shoulder.

Even now, Kyle's being was hesitant to go anywhere near the warehouse, but Josh needed his help. Josh deserved his help. Kyle and his being knew he needed to rescue Josh.

"Can I at least give you a ride?" Claire called after him.

Kyle did not immediately respond. *I probably shouldn't walk all the way to the warehouse,* Kyle thought, but he kept walking at the same pace. He could hear Claire back her car out of the driveway and drive slowly down the road after him.

"Kyle, I appreciate your concern for me," Claire called out her window. "But Josh is my friend too. Trust me; I'll be fine."

Kyle stopped walking and considered. He turned to Claire, who had parked beside him.

"Can you unlock the door for me?" he asked.

****

Claire parked near Josh's old apartment. Kyle recalled the "last request" from Josh's letter and knew that he should visit Josh's mom while he and Claire were here. *That's one of the last things I want to do,* Kyle thought. *This whole afternoon is filled with tasks that I never want to do!*

Kyle sighed and spoke to Claire, "Before we leave, I'll need to go up and visit Josh's mom. He asked me to do that in his letter." Both exited the vehicle.

"Do you know what she looks like?" Claire asked. "I

don't think I've ever met her."

"I haven't met her either. I don't even know her name. You can come with me if you want."

"Did you want to do that now or later?" Claire asked.

Kyle considered. *The police didn't find anything at the warehouse. Claire and I probably won't find anything either. I might not be in the mood to visit Josh's mother after searching the warehouse, and now that I'm here, I want to avoid the warehouse for as long as possible.* Kyle shrugged at Claire's question. "Sure, we can go now."

The apartment building had no elevator, only an open, central staircase, much to Kyle's dismay. He had forgotten. Kyle, with great difficulty, and Claire mounted the stairs. When they reached the apartment, there was no answer at the front door. They knocked many times and waited for several minutes. Still, there was no answer. Neither had any way to leave a note.

"We'll try again after we search the warehouse," Kyle resigned. Kyle knew he had to visit if only to fulfill Josh's last request.

Kyle hated the warehouse. As much as he wanted to rescue Josh, Kyle hated the possibility of finding his way back into the headquarters of The New World, where he had finally escaped. His whole being was terrified of what he would find, or not find, in the warehouse. Yet, his mind, spirit, soul, and body urged him forward. Kyle tried to remember that God was with him and that he should not be afraid; the fact did not dispel his fear like Kyle had hoped.

Kyle and Claire strode resolutely for the door in the back alley. The ugly memories flooded Kyle's mind stronger than he had anticipated. Kyle felt sick to his stomach. He almost threw up in the same place where he had when The New World had pummeled him so long ago. Kyle tried to calm himself. He was beginning to panic. *Oh, God, help!* Kyle prayed. *What am I even doing back here? Searching for Josh—I need to remind myself of that.*

Claire opened the door. The warehouse was just as dark as the many other times that Kyle had visited. Kyle stared into the black opening. *Have Josh be all right,* Kyle prayed again and traipsed through the opening. Claire followed close behind him.

"We're not splitting up," Kyle stated as soon as they were in the warehouse.

Claire objected, "We can cover more ground if we—"

"*We are not splitting up!*" Kyle shouted. His words echoed throughout the warehouse. "We are staying together," Kyle said in a hushed voice. "We are both getting out of this warehouse. We are not leaving anyone behind."

Then Kyle thought, *I can't afford to lose both Josh and Claire.*

"We'll be fine," Claire reassured Kyle, matching his volume. Kyle wished he had Claire's assurance.

"So how do you want to start?" Kyle asked. He had no idea where to begin.

"I've checked practically every inch of this place, and I couldn't find anything," Claire admitted. "I guess we should start looking under stuff." Kyle sighed and looked around the immediate room. There was a lot of junk to move. *The police never found anything. Why would we?* Kyle thought. *God, have us find Josh!*

Claire moved what machinery she could. She was not strong enough to move the heavier objects, and Kyle was little help with his injuries. So far, they had not found any secret passageways. Kyle and Claire moved quickly from one area to the next without moving most of the equipment.

Aside from the two of them talking, the warehouse was completely quiet, almost too quiet. Kyle fought a nagging feeling that someone was watching him. Even in the darkness, Kyle would look for the invisible spy. Every so often, Kyle would catch an odd shadow; when Kyle looked again, the shadow had either disappeared as a trick from his eyes or remained in place as an explainable phenomenon. Even so, Kyle felt that he was being watched. Kyle kept his premonitions to himself and was relieved that Claire was with him.

Before long, Claire and Kyle reached the sink where Kyle had been nearly drowned. *Have I told Claire about that?* Kyle wondered. *I can't remember. I hope that Claire doesn't know. And I want to keep it that way.* Kyle stared at the sink; the same water that had almost drowned him still filled the sink. He glanced at the floor and noticed the duct tape and zip ties still lying where he had thrown them.

"Was this where they tried to drown you?" Claire asked.

"Who told you about that?" Kyle interrogated.

"You did. You mentioned it that first night in the hospital. You were telling me what The New World had done to you. I only remember because you never told me about them trying to drown you."

"They didn't *try*," Kyle stressed. "They *nearly* drowned me. They purposefully left me alive—probably because Augustus wanted it."

A third voice erupted from the darkness. "And like your father predicted, you have returned to us!"

Claire screamed at the new voice. Every hair on Kyle's body stood on end. His mind raced wildly. *We* are *being watched! The New World has come for us! I won't be able to defend myself or Claire! The New World will take us and force us to join The New World as they have done with Josh!* Kyle despaired at the prospect.

Kyle's despair only worsened. The speaker of the third voice appeared close to Kyle and Claire, close enough for them to see that the face belonged to Bull. Every moment of Kyle's suffering with Bull flooded Kyle's mind. Kyle's fear and depression worsened. *There's nothing either of us can do to stop Bull from destroying us—just as Bull has done to Josh...and me!*

Kyle hated Bull! Despite his fear, Kyle wanted to kill Bull for everything that he had done to Kyle, Josh, and everyone else.

Bull stood grinning at Kyle. "Your father knew you'd come back. Everyone we torture always does." Bull turned to Claire. "I knew you'd come back too, Huntress."

What!? Kyle thought. *I can't believe what I'm hearing! Have I been deceived by another girlfriend?* The knot in his stomach tightened. Kyle almost vomited.

"That's not my name anymore, Jake," Claire spat back.

Jake!? Claire knows this guy!? Kyle did not know what to think.

"Don't call me that! That's not my name!" Bull screamed.

"Then I guess we understand each other!" Claire quickly assessed Bull. "What happened to you?"

"I stayed with my new family. You abandoned it. It's that simple."

"They were never a good family!" Claire screamed.

"You never stayed long enough to find out!" Bull lectured. "They protected me! They helped me! They turned me into who I am!"

"A thug and a murderer," Claire spat.

Bull growled. "I do what I have to protect my family, including nearly killing your boyfriend here." Bull grinned at Kyle.

"He's not my boyfriend," Claire retorted.

Bull glanced back at Claire. "Then you won't mind when he defects over to us?" He turned back to Kyle. "Everyone we torture always does." Bull poked the left side of Kyle's chest. "Still have a bandage on there, huh? I bet you haven't even looked at it. I dare you, take off the bandage. You belong to The New World now." Bull turned to leave. "You're wasting your time. You won't find anything here." With that, Bull disappeared into the shadows, without a sound.

Kyle did not know what to do. Kyle did not want to spend a second longer in the warehouse, knowing that Bull was lurking in the shadows. Kyle almost bolted for the exit; his fear of what Bull might do to him alone prevented him from moving. *But can I trust Claire?* Kyle was unsure. *I certainly trust her more than Bull.*

"I think we should go," Kyle said. Claire agreed.

Neither wasted any time weaving their way to the exit and the safety of daylight.

"Did you want a ride home now?" Claire asked when they stepped outside.

At the moment, Kyle did not feel like he wanted to reclimb the stairs to visit Josh's mom. Kyle was blind with rage. *I hate him! I hate Bull so much!* Kyle thought. Kyle knew that Bull had appeared only to taunt them in their search and dredge up whatever memories Kyle had from his captivity. That made Kyle even angrier. He was in no condition to talk with Josh's mom. "Let's just go," he finally said. They climbed into the car and started driving.

After a few moments of silence, Claire finally said, "I want to apologize for all that."

Kyle was too furious to think straight but asked the first question that came to his mind, "Were you really a part of The New World?"

Claire nodded sadly. "It's more complicated than that, though." Claire did not elaborate.

Kyle waited a few more seconds before asking another question. "So…how do you know him? Were you 'together' in The New World?"

Claire released a heavy sigh. "He's my brother."

"Your brother!"

"Yeah…" Claire drove in silence for a few minutes. "That's the hardest part about Christianity," Claire finally said. "We're told to forgive. We have to forgive—because God forgave us so much more than we would ever have to forgive anyone else."

Kyle was not sure if it was possible for him to forgive Bull. Kyle was incensed enough to kill Bull—and Bull deserved that. "I don't think I could forgive Bull for what he did to me," Kyle responded.

"I don't think I can either. Every time I think I've forgiven him, I learn that he's done something else horrible or he just pops up like that, and I realize that I'm even more angry at him than the last time. But the Bible instructs us to forgive; it even says to love our enemies. I keep praying for God to help me forgive Jake… God's still working with me on that."

"I don't think I'll ever be able to forgive Bull or Augustus for what they've done," Kyle repeated.

"No one said it was easy," Claire reminded him.

Kyle did not respond. *I can never forgive Augustus or Bull for forcing me to live through hell,* Kyle thought to himself. *They don't deserve forgiveness. The next time I have the chance, I will kill them—even if one is Claire's brother and the other used to be my own father! They forfeited their relations to us. They deserve to die! I'll prepare and plan.*

I want vengeance. I need *vengeance. And I need to avoid being caught. Above all, I need to be ready for whenever the opportunity presents itself. I know I can never share this with Claire; I can never share these feelings with anyone.*

The car drove the remainder of the return journey in silence. Claire pulled into the driveway and parked.

"Thanks for the ride," Kyle managed.

Claire nodded. "What about Josh's mom? Do you want to meet again tomorrow?" she asked.

"That's fine. See you tomorrow," Kyle agreed. Neither wanted to talk about returning to search the warehouse. Kyle knew they would probably do that tomorrow as well.

Claire pulled out of the driveway, and Kyle returned to the couch.

He had definitely overdone himself today. *That's what happens after two weeks of atrophying in the hospital,* Kyle thought. He could feel every muscle in his body and every injury. Even his burn irritated him from where Bull had poked it.

Kyle thought of Bull's challenge from the warehouse. Kyle had no desire to see the brand from his captivity. Kyle had even closed his eyes when Josh had been branded. Still, Kyle had no idea what it looked like. He slowly rose from the couch and crept to the bathroom. Kyle moved his shirt out of the way as far as he could and gently peeled back the bandage.

The skin surrounding the burn was still red. A strange design where the flesh had been burned black lay in the center of the bandage. The charred flesh looked like a circle with lines through it. Immediately, Kyle recognized the design as a globe. "The New World," Kyle muttered to himself. Kyle screamed and pounded the bathroom sink in frustration, almost breaking it. Kyle swore at Augustus, at Bull, and at The New World as a whole. Kyle swore that, whenever the chance presented itself, he would kill them all.

****

The next morning, Kyle was prepared to return to the warehouse. He had been busy most of the night. Kyle had scoured his grandmother's house for a suitable weapon to use against Augustus and Bull. His grandmother did not own a gun; so, Kyle became creative. Kyle found an old pair of scissors. Instead of getting rest, Kyle sharpened one blade of the scissors until it almost cut under its own weight; he deformed the other blade until it was serrated and would hurt to pull from a wound. He joined both blades together to form a shiv. Kyle was pleased with his work. As long as he had the element of surprise, Kyle knew that, even in his current condition, he would still be able to kill his targets. Kyle was ready to return to the warehouse.

When Kyle awoke, a text message from Claire was waiting on his phone.

"I just realized that I can't go with you this morning, but I'm free this afternoon. I can still give you a ride this morning if you want."

This is great! thought Kyle. *With Claire gone, I can go to the warehouse and use my shiv with impunity!*

Kyle texted back that he would appreciate the ride.

Claire shuttled Kyle to the warehouse. Kyle asked Claire to drop him off at Josh's apartment first.

"I'll be back as soon as I can to help," Claire assured him.

"Don't hurry back," Kyle replied. Claire figured that Kyle wanted to delay searching the warehouse for as long as possible.

Kyle waited for Claire to drive away. Then, Kyle climbed the stairs to Josh's apartment as fast as he could. Kyle would attempt to see Josh's mom before returning to the warehouse. If she was not there, Kyle could spend more time alone, waiting for his enemies in the warehouse.

When Kyle arrived at the apartment, he knocked and immediately knocked again. Kyle was about to turn away when the door suddenly cracked open.

A short, fierce woman peered from underneath the chain lock on the door. "What do you want?" she shot through the narrow opening in the door.

Kyle had not prepared for his knocks to be answered. "Uh...hi. Are you Josh's mom?" The woman said nothing; motionless, she continued to glare at Kyle. Kyle continued uncertainly, "Josh wanted me to stop by. I'm Kyle."

As soon as Kyle mentioned who he was, the woman's face completely changed. She slammed the door shut—Kyle heard her fumble with the chain lock—and she opened the door as fast as she had closed it.

"So you're Kyle! I thought you looked familiar. I just wasn't sure from where. You can never be too careful in this neighborhood."

"I completely agree," Kyle responded.

The woman stepped aside. "Do you want to come in?" Kyle walked into the apartment. The apartment was the same as it had been the last two times Kyle had seen it. This time, the apartment felt somehow empty to him. The woman closed the door and replaced the chain. "When was the last time that you heard from Josh?" the woman asked. Kyle felt sick to his stomach. *Does she not know what happened to Josh? I have to tell her.*

Kyle took a deep breath and forced himself to speak, "I last saw Josh a few weeks ago. We...we were both prisoners...of The New World." The woman's face fell.

Kyle wrestled with what to say next. *Do I dare tell her that I escaped at Josh's expense? I don't want to!* Kyle felt the Holy Spirit's prompting. *But I know that I should. As much as I and the rest of my being hate to do so, I know I should tell her the truth. She deserves the truth.*

Kyle began again. "I should tell you, Josh...didn't get captured. *I* was captured. When Josh found out, he surrendered himself to The New World to save me! They let me go...and they took him instead." A dark pain spread across the woman's face. Tears filled her eyes. Kyle knew what she must be thinking. She was now alone; the rest of her family had become a part of The New World.

"I am so sorry..." Kyle continued. "Josh never should

have offered himself for me."

The two figures waited in silence for a while. Josh's mother continued to weep silently. Kyle did not know what else to say.

Finally, Josh's mother dried her eyes and spoke, "That's Josh for you. Over the last several years, he has given more and more of himself for others. Sacrificing his time and money, changing his friends, breaking his bad habits—he has changed so much over the last few years." She chuckled to herself and wiped the last few tears from her eyes. "Maybe he was right about Jesus and the rest of that church stuff." She looked back at Kyle. "I know that Josh did what he thought was right. Josh wouldn't have wanted you to regret his decision. Ever since he first met you, he told me that he wanted to help you however he could; he said that so many times. He really cared about your friendship. I'm sure he was glad to give himself to save you."

Kyle was amazed! He had no idea how to respond.

"Oh, and Josh wanted me to give you this if you stopped by." The woman reached for a folded piece of paper on the kitchen table with the name "Kyle" scrawled on the front.

Another letter? Kyle thought. *How many more letters are there?*

Inside the letter, there was a crude drawing of a strange contraption on a desk with a large arrow pointing at an oversized light switch. Kyle read the letter.

Kyle,

I think I have a way to destroy The New World

for good. Call the police and have them come to the apartment. Then, and <u>ONLY</u> then, turn on the switch. It activates a tracking device that I have implanted into myself. Hopefully, they can follow it to The New World.

I'm not sure how many entrances there are to the headquarters. The only one I know of is in the basement of the abandoned apartment building behind Finneman's Market.

Josh

PS: Whatever happens, please look after my mom.

Kyle showed Josh's mom the picture of the device. "Do you know where this machine is?"

She thought for a moment. "I think it's in Josh's room." She pointed to a door on the other end of the apartment. Kyle opened the door. The room was a disaster, but the desk was even worse. The desk was completely covered with electronic circuit boards, wires, metal plates, antennas, and everything else an electrical engineer could want. In one corner of the desk, there stood a device similar to what Josh had drawn. Kyle glanced back at the drawing in Josh's letter and found the light switch.

This is it! Kyle thought to himself. *This is my chance to destroy The New World for good!*

Why did Josh wait? Why didn't he tell me in the first letter Claire gave me in the hospital room? Josh suffered for weeks *longer than he needed, waiting for me to heal and finally visit his mom.* Kyle wanted to curse Josh at his stupidity!

Then, Kyle's eyes were opened. Josh knew exactly what he was doing. Josh's primary concern had always been his mother. With the rest of her family being a part of The New World, Josh wanted to help his mother however he could. Since graduation, Josh had even paid most of their bills. But Josh, now a captive member of The New World, did not know if he could still help his mother as he had in the past. So in case he could not or in case he ended up dead or in prison, he had asked Kyle to help in his place. But Josh also knew that Kyle might ignore Josh's pleas for his mother. *That* was why Josh did not tell Kyle in his first letter! Kyle had to come to the apartment and *prove* that he would care for Josh's mom *before* Kyle would receive the information about the device. Otherwise, Josh risked alerting the police and potentially being imprisoned or killed without someone to look after his mom. Josh had orchestrated this to ensure his mother would be helped, even at his expense! That was another example of Josh's willingness to sacrifice himself for others!

Kyle marveled at Josh! *I wonder if I ever would have willingly done that for someone else. Josh's strength to do that could only have come from God!*

Kyle reread Josh's letter. *I need to call the police! This is the way for me to rescue Josh and enact revenge on Augustus simultaneously!*

Josh's mom had followed Kyle into Josh's room. Kyle

turned to face her.

"Have you read this letter?" Kyle asked, thrusting it toward her. When she glanced up from the letter, Kyle continued, "We have to call the police."

****

When Kyle finally convinced the authorities that he had a way to destroy The New World, they sent a technician to investigate the device. The technician studied the contraption and concluded that it was possible for it to be a tracking device of some kind that would allow itself to be easily located at a common frequency.

The police and FBI wasted no time. They practically moved into Josh's apartment, transforming it into a command center. The technicians pored over the device to learn everything about how the machine worked and how to repair it if it failed. They procured sensors of their own and calibrated them to track the signal.

Amid the flurry of activity, Kyle knew that a strike force was gathering to raid the abandoned building behind Finneman's Market. Kyle knew that, at any moment, they would break into a hideout of The New World.

He hoped that The New World had not discovered Josh's tracker.

He hoped that the tracker still worked.

He hoped that none of the police that knew about Josh's device were working with The New World.

He hoped that the police would finally catch The New

World and destroy them.

But Kyle hoped they would not catch either Augustus or Bull; Kyle had something special in mind for them.

Kyle was finally asked to sit in a distant corner of the apartment. The raid was probably about to begin, and they did not want Kyle in the way. Kyle nodded dutifully and sat in the chair closest to the apartment door.

The FBI turned Josh's machine on. Pandemonium erupted. At first, the tracker was not returning any signal. Then, the police were shouting that the tracker was appearing on the other side of Jacksonville. The mobile headquarters scrambled to move a secondary force to the new area of interest; the primary force was still to hit the secret entrance in the basement behind Finneman's Market.

Kyle knew that now was the time for him to escape. He had a hunch, and he needed to test it, or else he would lose his chance for revenge! Kyle gripped his shiv hidden in his pocket and sneaked out the apartment, down the stairs, across the alleyway, and into the abandoned warehouse. *The New World has used the warehouse too many times for it to be a coincidence.* Kyle reasoned. *I'm willing to bet that there still is a secret entrance somewhere in the warehouse. And if anyone comes out of it, I'll be ready to spring my ambush.*

Kyle's mind, spirit, soul, and body reveled at the thought of revenge!

Kyle silently picked his way from the warehouse entrance in the back alley to the spot where he had been nearly drowned. This was the same spot that Bull had surprised him and Claire yesterday. Kyle knew that this spot was as good as any other in the warehouse. If any escapees were going to come through a hidden entrance, it would be close to there.

Kyle waited in the darkness, his shiv in his hand. Kyle waited a long time. His eyes had adjusted to the darkness. All he could hear was a seldom drip in the nearby sink. Kyle tried to count the minutes. He had probably been there for an hour.

Have I missed them? Kyle wondered. *Not likely. I came from the apartment as soon as the raid had begun.*

Had I been wrong with my hunch? I'm starting to think that I was wrong. Either that or one of the moles in the police station alerted The New World. I'll wait just a few more minutes, then—

Kyle heard an unnatural creak from someplace close to him. Kyle felt his almost audible heartbeat quicken. Kyle held his breath. He heard the creak again. Kyle was not imagining it. It had come from less than ten feet away, seemingly from underneath the old sink. Kyle watched. A small drain in the floor underneath the sink slightly rose from the surrounding concrete with another quiet creak. A hand appeared underneath the raised metal drain.

So that's how they get into the warehouse! Kyle silently exclaimed. *There are underground pipes all over the city! That's the ideal way to travel without being detected! That's how The New World is able to suddenly appear in the warehouse! As long as someone isn't in the immediate room or isn't listening for the sound, they can come and go as they please!*

Kyle marveled that anyone could squeeze through the drain opening—especially Bull or Augustus. Kyle, still undetected, watched as the figure silently slid the drain cover aside, lifted both arms out the hole, and pulled themselves up.

Kyle immediately recognized who the figure was—Augustus. He appeared to be alone.

Now's my chance! Kyle gripped his shiv, ready to kill the man who had been the source of his troubles!

Kyle stood frozen. Now that he was ready to commit murder, the "Voice"—or the Holy Spirit, as Josh had called it—spoke above his being, entreating him to stop.

Kyle argued with the Holy Spirit. *I can't stop! I have come too far! I can't let Augustus get away!*

Kyle quenched the "Voice" and unsheathed his shiv. Augustus was bending over and repositioning the drain cover. *So he is alone!* His back was to Kyle. *This is a better opportunity than before!* Kyle released a battle cry and charged at Augustus! Startled, Augustus whipped around and pulled out a gun. The gun was too slow. Kyle redirected his aim and slashed the hand with the gun. Augustus gasped in pain. The gun fired, shattering the darkness and reverberating throughout the warehouse. Kyle slashed with the shiv again, this time, at the arm. Augustus released another gasp and gripped his arm with the other hand. Kyle's momentum carried him into his nemesis. They slammed into the sink. Kyle had knocked the wind out of Augustus, but the gun was still in Augustus' hand! Kyle had to get it away from him! Kyle dug the shiv into Augustus' side; the enemy screamed! Again, the gun exploded! Kyle released the shiv and, with both hands, struggled to possess the gun! Kyle fought with every ounce of his strength! There! He had it!

As soon as Kyle held the gun, Augustus kicked Kyle's legs out from under him. Kyle fell to the ground! The gun clattered to the floor! Kyle could not see it! Kyle quickly rolled onto his back. Augustus was now holding the shiv, and Kyle was defenseless! Kyle kicked Augustus' shin as hard as he could. Kyle felt something in the enemy's leg give. Augustus screamed again! He dropped the shiv. It bounced once and slipped through the drain cover under the sink. Now, neither of them had a weapon! Kyle needed to find the gun! Kyle wildly searched for the only weapon left! There! He found it! With one fluid motion, Kyle rolled to the gun, picked it up, stood, spun toward Augustus, and pointed the weapon at him. Augustus was where Kyle had left him, holding his shin and applying pressure to as many of his hemorrhaging wounds as possible.

In that instant, Augustus recognized Kyle. Neither said anything.

Kyle kept the weapon aimed at his enemy. *This is the moment!* Kyle thought. *I have been waiting for this moment for seven long, painful months! Vengeance is mine! At long last, I can finally avenge myself and destroy the one who had destroyed me!*

Kyle prepared to pull the trigger. Then Kyle realized that

he could not; his being, rallied by the Holy Spirit, would not let him.

That's absurd! Kyle thought. *The only thing my being has ever wanted is for me to avenge myself and kill Augustus and everyone else in The New World! That still has to be true!*

Yet Kyle's being now raged against him pulling the trigger.

Kyle's mind knew that this was murder! His mind would not allow him to kill! Kyle had chosen to give himself to God, and God demanded that Kyle love others, including his enemies. Murder and hate were directly opposed to the life that Kyle had chosen to live. Despite enduring all the psychological torture, his mind knew that Kyle should not murder anyone, including Augustus.

Kyle's spirit urged Kyle not to kill Augustus. Kyle reasoned with his spirit, *I have sworn many oaths that I would get revenge on The New World and kill the man who had become Augustus!* Kyle's spirit reminded Kyle that those vows had been replaced by a more important promise: to obey God. His spirit was inflexible; it would allow Kyle to ignore his oaths of vengeance but refused to ignore his promise of obedience.

Even Kyle's soul, which had been initially opposed to following Jesus, agreed that Kyle could no longer kill Augustus—regardless of how much he had tormented Kyle. Kyle had been determined to follow God and His standards, despite his soul's objections of how that may change his life.

The decision had already been made. His soul knew that Kyle must obey God above his own desires.

Kyle's body, too, screamed for Kyle to stop. Despite remembering every single affliction given by The New World and, specifically, Augustus, Kyle's body knew Kyle should not repay that evil with more evil. Killing Augustus would only cause more pain, even if Kyle did enjoy some momentary satisfaction. Kyle argued with his body, *Augustus does not deserve mercy!* His body admitted that even Kyle did not deserve mercy, and he had received infinite mercy from God. God endured the punishment He did not deserve to save Kyle from the punishment he did deserve. His body urged Kyle to show mercy.

Kyle was desperate! A part of himself did not want to let Augustus live! It wanted—*needed* Kyle to pull the trigger!

Frantically, Kyle surveyed his being again, hoping for a different answer. None was given.

That was it then.

But that rogue part, that dark part of Kyle's being, did not want to let go! It required vengeance! Kyle hesitated a moment more. The dark part of Kyle's being demanded that it be *restored* to its original position of power and control over Kyle!

Restored?

Kyle began to understand; the dark part of his being had been dethroned when Kyle had become a Christian. Even now, it was still struggling with the Holy Spirit for control over Kyle! Kyle was afraid to surrender and afraid to resist.

He did not know what to do!

Then, Kyle was given the strength he needed. Kyle felt God give him the strength to overcome the dark part of Kyle's being. Grudgingly, Kyle lowered the weapon. That was the hardest action that Kyle would ever do. But once he did, Kyle felt a piece of the dark part of himself die; Kyle felt inexplicably relieved that it had begun to disappear.

"Go on! Get out of here!" Kyle screamed at Augustus. Augustus scrambled to his feet and limped noiselessly into the darkness. Kyle was, once again, alone.

Kyle dropped the gun and collapsed to his knees. He had not noticed the pain of his half-healed injuries until now. The scuffle had reopened several of his deeper physical wounds. Yet somehow, Kyle thought that his unseen psychological wounds had begun to heal.

Kyle wept. His quest for revenge was over! Kyle had not realized how much those thoughts had consumed his life! He realized that revenge had been his constant obsession for the last seven months. Kyle was not yet ready to forgive Augustus, Bull, or the rest of The New World, but he was making progress. And for that, Kyle was glad.

Kyle left the gun and exited the warehouse. The alley between the apartment buildings and the warehouse was swarming with police. As soon as they saw Kyle, they rushed to him, weapons drawn, until they realized that he was the one who had called them about Josh's device and had made the sting possible. They holstered their weapons.

Kyle hardly noticed. He was looking beyond the officers.

Augustus, handcuffed, was being pushed into the back of a police vehicle. They locked eyes for a moment. The expression on Augustus' face displayed confusion above anything else. The door closed, and he was hidden from view. God had provided justice after all—without Kyle exacting vengeance. Kyle sighed in relief. That portion of Kyle's journey was finally over.

CHAPTER 19

Kyle walked through the all too familiar halls of the hospital. At least he was walking *into* the hospital this time, and his visit would not be long. Kyle found the desired hospital room and knocked softly.

"Come in," a voice moaned. Kyle opened the door slowly. Josh lay in the bed. His face immediately brightened when he saw Kyle. Kyle smiled back. Josh looked tired, which was considerably better than the last time Kyle had seen him. "Kyle!" Josh said. "Good to see you!"

"It's good to see *you*!" Kyle replied. "I wasn't sure when I'd see you next."

"I wasn't sure either… You seem to be doing all right," Josh said.

"After I spent two weeks in the hospital!" Kyle chuckled. "I'm still healing."

Josh lowered his voice before speaking. "Were, uh, the doctors able to do anything about your brand?"

Kyle shook his head. "No—"

Josh swore. "Sorry," he said. "I shouldn't have said that."

Kyle ignored him. "Not yet. I'm not sure what the doctors will be able to do. It's pretty deep."

"So much for going to the beach," Josh quipped. He and Kyle laughed.

"Were you still that wounded that you were brought here?" asked Kyle.

"No, I got shot during the attack. It wasn't that bad, but they wanted to check out some of my other wounds. You should have visited me yesterday; they almost sent me to the prison hospital."

"Whoa!"

"Fortunately, my mom vouched for me, and so did a few people from the prayer group. I guess I'm not going to be prosecuted for anything."

"That's great news!" Kyle said.

Josh shrugged. "A pretty low bar, but I'll take it. What have I missed?"

Kyle did not know where to begin. "Well, for starters, I'm a Christian now!"

"Really!" Josh asked. He was overjoyed!

Kyle nodded. "Yeah, while I was in the hospital, I thought about how you had sacrificed yourself for me. And everything that you and Claire had said about Jesus doing the same thing for me just clicked."

"That's amazing!" Josh shouted. He wept tears of joy.

Kyle continued, "With everything that has occurred since the end of winter break—and so much has happened—my life has been changed forever, and I don't think I'll ever be the same—mentally, emotionally, or physically." Josh nodded in agreement. "But I also know that this *had* to happen to me. Without these struggles, I never would have looked beyond myself. I now know that I never would have realized my need for God if He hadn't allowed Augustus—I mean, my father, to turn my life upside down. Jesus was worth all that pain; I see that now, at least better than I did before now. God allowed everything for a reason—including your sacrifice in my place. I…I can't thank you enough for that."

"Well, I couldn't leave you there alone," Josh chuckled half-heartedly. "I'm glad that God used me to save you— physically and spiritually." Josh paused. "And thank you for rescuing *me*."

"You actually saved yourself. Your tracking device and the letter you left were a big help. How did you sneak the tracker into their hideout?"

Josh shrugged. "It wasn't easy. I knew they might find a conventional tracker. So I built one that was linked specifically to my device and only sent signals when it received a certain frequency and only that frequency. That's why I wanted you to wait until everyone was ready to turn on the device."

"That's great!" Kyle exclaimed.

"You know," Josh said, "when the police started raiding the place, I had one thought: I sure hope that Kyle isn't with them. I was glad that you weren't; you always seem to be wherever the action is!" Kyle felt a knot grow in his stomach. He must have grimaced. "Kyle? Are you all right?"

Kyle took a deep breath. "Actually, I *was* in the middle of the action, just not with the police. Too much had happened at the warehouse. I figured that The New World might have an entrance there—and I was right." Josh stared, wide-eyed. Kyle continued, "I waited there as soon as the raid began. My father crawled out of a hole and…"

Kyle took another shaky breath.

Josh did not breathe.

What will Josh think of me? Kyle thought. Kyle took another deep breath and continued.

"…and…I was going to kill him. I had him at gunpoint. I wanted to kill him so badly! But Something—Someone—prevented me from killing him." Josh slowly nodded. "I knew that it was wrong, and I knew that God didn't want me to kill him. God stopped me before it was too late. Dropping the gun was the hardest thing that I've ever done…and I mean that."

Josh did not say anything for a while. He had dropped his gaze to the floor at the far end of the small hospital room. Finally, he looked Kyle in the eyes and spoke, "And now, you have something even harder to do: choose to forgive him."

"I don't think I could ever do that," Kyle admitted.

"After what I've just been through, I agree. Fortunately, God is the One that teaches us and helps us to forgive."

"Yeah, Claire said it takes a long time."

"A lifetime," Josh sighed. "Every day was a struggle for me to forgive my father; now, it will be even worse." Both silently pondered the grim and hopeful prospect. "What happened to your father?" Josh asked.

"I saw the police arrest him," Kyle said. He was afraid to ask about Josh's father but cared enough to ask anyway. "What about yours? And your brother and sister?"

"I don't know." Josh sounded pained and concerned. "I wasn't with them. None of them would ever give up without a fight, even if they were surrounded. I…I fear the worst." Silently, Kyle said a quick prayer, asking that they be all right—for Josh's sake, and Josh's sake only.

Josh spoke again, "Will you visit your father while he's in prison?"

Kyle almost answered with an expletive. He checked himself in time. Then, he checked his answer. "I know the answer is supposed to be yes," Kyle grumbled.

Josh laughed. "It doesn't have to be. I was just asking."

"But the answer should be yes, right?" Kyle pressed.

"What's the Holy Spirit telling you?" Josh asked.

Kyle did not want to think about that right now. He knew what the answer would probably be. "Would you visit your father if he ended up in prison?" Kyle returned.

Josh shrugged. "I don't know."

"Why would you?" Kyle asked.

"I don't know," Josh shrugged again. "I guess to let him know that I care about him. Or at least that God loves him and offers him forgiveness."

"Even him?" Kyle asked.

Josh shot Kyle a disapproving look. "Yes, Kyle. God

saved *us*, after all."

"We weren't that bad," Kyle objected. Josh's expression deepened. "Okay, fine. We *all* were that bad, according to God. I know *that*."

"That's something we all need to *remember* more," Josh stressed.

"Yeah, yeah..." Kyle did not want to continue the discussion. Undoubtedly, he would be prompted to think more about this topic in the future. "Before I forget, I'm going to be leaving in a few weeks. I'm going to be stationed at Eglin Air Force Base for the next few years, out near Pensacola."

"Oh..." Josh said, sad again. "You'll come and visit us, right?"

"Absolutely! It's only a few hours away." Kyle smiled mischievously, "Besides, Claire will still be in the area." They both laughed. "Do you think I have a shot?" Kyle asked.

"I think so. I think she likes you already, and if she asks me, I'll nudge her in your direction."

Kyle laughed. "You're a good friend, Josh. I'm glad to have had you with me through all this. I'm excited to see what God has in store for the future!"

Josh smiled and nodded. "I'm sure the best is yet to come."

The End

CPSIA information can be obtained
at www.ICGtesting.com
Printed in the USA
LVHW081804190322
713875LV00015B/1384

9 781685 561338